Turning Point

A Mark Landry Novel

By Randall H. Miller

Table of Contents

Dedication

This book is dedicated to John S. Irving,
April 13, 1971—November 19, 2018
This one is for you, John. I know you would have loved it.

—Randall H. Miller
January 15, 2019
North Andover, Massachusetts

Acknowledgments

I am deeply grateful to John S. Irving (R.I.P.), Steven D. Branca, Todd Bennett, Eric Curtis, Colonel Donald L. Paquin (U.S. Army, Ret.), Lieutenant Colonel Michael McCarthy (U.S. Army and Captain, California Highway Patrol), Lieutenant "Hog" Hennessey (A Troop Commander, New Hampshire State Police), Lieutenant Colonel John Palo (U.S. Army, Ret.), Trooper Haden Wilber and his Belgian Malinois K-9 Gauge (New Hampshire State Police), Steve Tarani, my editor Bruce Bannon, the Sig Sauer Academy, David Ortiz, Paul Bernsten, Rob Pincus, Christopher Halleron, Dr. and Mrs. Stephen Autry, Dick and Susan Miller, Steve Perkins, my loving wife Maggy, our incredible son Michael, our faithful German Shepherd Floki, and all the badass men and women who protect us while we sleep.

"The antidote for fifty enemies is one friend."
—*Aristotle*

Prologue

Time was running out for Mark Landry.

He glanced down at his watch. Less than an hour to find and isolate the target. Still six more floors to go. Innocent lives on the line. He cursed what had to be the slowest elevator in the world.

This is when most people—even experienced operators—would start to feel the walls closing in. Breathing becomes shallow. Pulse rises. Despair and panic bubble to the surface. Some would abort mission and accept failure. But Mark Landry was built for these moments. He was a world-class operator at the top of his game. At times like these, he shined like Michael Jordan at the buzzer. Always taking—and making—the winning shot. Trying not to think about the inevitable day when he'd miss.

"Guten abend," Mark said with a nod and a smile. The elderly couple smiled back. He extended his arm to keep the door from closing on them as they exited the elevator. They moved slowly. The woman mumbled something about what a nice young man he was. Her husband looked the stranger up and down, then shrugged. Mark waved goodbye to her as the doors slowly closed.

Lady, if you had any idea what I'm about to do when I find this guy, you would have taken the stairs.

He looked up and watched the floors slowly tick by. Three. Two. One. Basement. Ding.

Focus. Get ready to click. Get ready to click.

"Clicking" was how Mark described initial recognition of potential threats. If his hotel room looked the slightest bit different from how he had left it—click. Someone in the crowd doesn't look like they belong—click. The car behind him is following too closely—click. A person of interest narrows their eyes, inhales sharply or suddenly move their hands toward their beltline—click, click, click. Clicking was the spark that got the ball rolling. It was a visual and mental snapshot, like the first frame of a movie. Once Mark clicked, he could rapidly assess the threat and choose the best course of action to neutralize it.

"Clicking is an esoteric skill that improves with each high-risk experience," one of Mark's black-ops instructors had taught him many years earlier. "You get better and better the more you are forced to perform under pressure. Your brain creates more memory files with each experience. On subsequent missions, your brain will automatically access those files when considering solutions. Unless, of course, you die. Then it won't. Just remember, he who clicks first usually wins. Action beats reaction. Especially when you're up close and personal."

Mark, a former U.S. Army Ranger and special operations veteran, was deadly with a rifle. But he didn't thrive behind the scope as he did in close quarters battle (CQB). Basic sniping is simply a math challenge. You apply quantitative skills to solve a problem. In contrast, CQB scenarios are much more opaque and unpredictable. Often, there are multiple possible solutions. It is more art than science. And if choosing the right action at the right time is an art form, Landry was the Leonardo da Vinci of his organization. He was a sight to behold when the shit hit the fan.

His instructor was right. The more experience Mark gained, the better he got and the more he was able to compress into those critical first seconds—more data processing, more and faster consideration of options. Now, in the prime of his career, whenever Mark Landry clicked, events would seem to unfold in slow motion.

The elevator doors crept open.

A lone young man in his mid-twenties with closely cropped hair stood inches away. He cautiously looked Mark in the eyes. Then he made the mistake of subtly turning his head ninety degrees to the side before snapping his gaze back to Mark.

Click.

That was sloppy. What or who are you looking at, my friend? Maybe a quick "witness check" before trying to get cute with me? Or maybe you're not alone and were letting your partner know it's show time. And was that a neck tattoo peeking out from under your collar when you turned your head? The guys I'm looking for are sporting plenty of those. That's enough for me. You're about to have a bad day.

Before the man's eyes could refocus, Mark grabbed him by the shoulders and delivered a crushing head-butt to the bridge of his nose. He then yanked the threat into the elevator and greeted him with an explosive knee-strike to the solar plexus. Holding the bent-over thug by the back of his belt with both hands, he pulled hard and launched the threat head-first into the mirrored elevator wall. Blood splattered. The unconscious body crumpled to the floor.

Mark leapt to the side, pushed his back up against the inside control panel, and drew the Sig Sauer P226 9mm from his waistband. He held a razor-sharp curved-blade karambit above his head with his free hand. The first guy had been either unarmed or too slow to deploy any weapons he might have had. The next guy—if there was one—might be better prepared. And the crashing noise of the first guy's head colliding with the elevator wall would have tipped him off that trouble had just arrived.

Wait for it. Wait for it.

Approaching footsteps tapped on the concrete floor in the long basement hallway. They slowed as they came closer. Mark heard anxious breathing. The tip of a long hunting knife broke the plane of the elevator door first, followed by a black glove and an exposed wrist. Mark dropped his center of gravity and brought the karambit down with everything he had. The razor-sharp blade passed through its mark as if moving through air, instantly relieving the threat of the hunting knife along with the tips of several fingers. The broad blade and bits of flesh wrapped in black leather seemed to float in the air for an instant before falling to the floor. The man stumbled forward. A thin stream of blood sprayed against the far wall. Mark could feel his CQB instructor's presence as he executed his next move. "The only way to fight is with everything you have—no holding back," the instructor had always stressed. "Hit first. Hit hard. Send shock waves through the nervous system. Get his brain to shut down before he even knows he's in a fight."

Mark charged the disarmed man and hip-checked him with all his weight. Then he stood in place and cocked his arm. The thug bounced off the wall and stumbled face-first into a devastating elbow strike to the side of the head. Lights out. He joined his friend on the elevator floor. Mark looked down at the bleeding man and then refocused his attention on the basement hallway. He heard rapid footsteps getting quieter. Someone was running away. He reached down and used a piece of the broken mirror to peer into the hallway without exposing himself. A figure wearing a red jacket scurried down the hall.

Red jacket. That's him.

The figure stopped at the end of the hall and paused. He looked confused and unprepared, as if he had no idea what to do. *Good,* Mark thought to himself. The target finally entered the last room on the right. That was the boiler room, according to Mark's recollection of the floor plans—assuming they were accurate.

No other way out. He's stuck. And stupid. Get control of him quickly while he's still in shock and can't think straight.

Mark stood off to the side and swung open the unlocked door. He raised his 9mm and peered over the sights to scan the parts of the boiler room he could see.

Clear.

He sidestepped enough to expand his field of vision and stopped to scan again.

Still clear.

He continued scanning the boiler room in small slices, hoping to get his eyes on the threat from the hallway. He would cross the threshold and enter the room blind if he had to. But doorways are called "fatal funnels" for good reason—the unseen guy on the inside has the advantage. Had the figure in the red coat understood that, he would have hidden and tried to draw Mark into the room. That would have been his best chance, especially if he had a weapon. Instead, he picked an awful spot and stayed there until he was almost looking down the barrel of Mark's gun.

The target must have been unarmed and figured his best shot was to fight his way out. He screamed and charged at Mark with a mop tightly gripped in both hands, swinging it wildly. Mark stepped back and let the threshold absorb the blow. The mop handle snapped, and half of it skipped down the hallway along the concrete floor.

Mark stepped forward and kicked the man in the side of the knee with all his might. The thick heel of his hiking boot connected with an audible crack. The knee joint broke clean and the leg folded sideways. The lower half dangled as if skin was the only thing left connecting it to the rest of the body. The threat went down and screamed in agony. Mark stepped over him and quickly cleared the boiler room. Then he shut the door, holstered his gun, and dragged the target to the center of the room by his good leg.

The young man continued to scream in German while Mark bound his hands behind his back with a long extension cord that he found coiled up in the corner.

"Wer bist du?! Was wilst du?!" *Who are you? What do you want?*

Mark ignored him and wrapped the remaining extension cord slack several times around his head and open mouth as a gag. It would not silence him, but it did bring the volume down considerably. Mark needed to think. He had work to do.

The captive switched to English and repeated the same questions. Maybe he mistook Mark's silence for not understanding German. "Please! Who are you? What do you want? I swear I'll do anything—just tell me what you want!" he pleaded.

Mark pulled out his phone and started a secure video connection with a number he knew from memory. He moved to a dusty work bench in the corner and rifled through the top drawer. "Yeah, I got him. Tell me when he's watching," Mark said calmly into the phone as he found a hatchet in the bottom drawer. He looked closely at its edge. Sharp enough. Mark approached the prisoner. He held the cellphone up so he could hear and looked at the hatchet as he waited for the green light.

"He's watching," said the voice on the other end.

Mark focused the cellphone camera on the prisoner's distraught face until he could hear muffled screams coming from the phone's speakers. Then he panned out to a wide shot and strapped the phone to his forehead. The rest of the broadcast would be his POV.

"Who are you?!" he begged one last time. "Sprechen! Say something! Please!"

Why bother?

Mark Landry looked down and slowly raised the hatchet above his head.

CHAPTER ONE

Blue Mass

Detective Sergeant Luci Landry poked her husband in the rib cage with her elbow. When Mark turned his head, she motioned toward the pulpit with her chin. He paused before slowly raising two fingers to cross himself. She nodded once in approval and winked at him out of the corner of her eye.

Mark Landry had discreetly removed the phone from his pocket and glanced down to check for messages from Billy, his longtime special operations partner and right-hand man. Their primary mission was to find and eliminate Oleg Borodin, a career Russian intelligence operative who had had a run-in with several of Mark's operators in Boston two months earlier. The unexpected collision—why Borodin had been in Boston remained a mystery—had turned deadly and put the Russian spymaster under the very microscope he had spent his long career trying to avoid. The National Security Advisor and President wanted Oleg dead. Mark and his team were now trying to make that happen.

They were also tasked to clean up a string of traitors. Billy was in Silicon Valley, about to roll up a private defense contractor who had been selling secrets, known as ECI (exceptionally controlled information) in the cyber world, to a foreign intelligence service. The insider threat (or, as Billy called him, the "cyber dipshit") had been under close FBI surveillance and it was now time to make him disappear. That meant that the already overworked federal agents would be pulled from the case and quickly reassigned to another one. Mark Landry's team would take things from there. The fewer witnesses, the better.

Luci nudged Mark before he could finish checking his messages. The screen was blurry anyway, and he hated wearing the glasses he increasingly needed. Work would have to wait.

Mark leaned forward and turned his head sideways so he could see the twins sitting on the other side of his wife. Five-year-old Carlos and Amanda were originally uninterested in attending the Blue Mass with their parents. Luci tried to entice them with a chance to meet the Cardinal—a man who personally knew the Pope! No interest. How about the Governor? He could be President one day. Nothing. She didn't bother mentioning that the mayor of Boston would be there too. The only mayor they cared about was Andy, the mayor of their own town and a close friend of their parents. But he was more of an uncle to them than a mayor. Mark sat them both down the day before the service, when Luci was not around.

"Guys, your mother is retiring very soon. That means this is her last Blue Mass. So you are both going. It will mean a lot to her to have the whole family there."

"Can Murphy go?" asked Amanda, referring to the family's German Shepherd.

"If it were up to me, yes. But you know Murphy is away for training and won't be back until next week."

"Then how can you say it's the whole family?" Amanda asked with a proud smile.

"Did I mention there's going to be bagpipes? If we get there early, you can choose our seats. I'd suggest an aisle right in the middle of the church where they have to march right past you." The kids' eyes and mouths popped open. "So why don't you go pick out your clothes for tomorrow evening? Or do you want me to do that?"

Mark had zero sense of style or occasion when dressing the kids. He just grabbed whatever fit and matched—or didn't match—and told them to throw it on. Carlos never seemed to notice, but the threat of having Daddy pick her outfit was enough for Amanda. She grabbed Carlos by the hand and whisked him away without another word.

The Cardinal was standing in front of the altar. He clasped his hands and rested them on his round potbelly. It seemed as if he had a basketball under his scarlet cassock. He smiled warmly and looked out over the sea of blue covering every inch of the pews in the cathedral. A sucker for regalia, he paused to admire the golden embroidery, medals, bars, and stars that adorned the first responders' dress uniforms. He did his best to look happy and send the crowd on its way inspired. But despite his best efforts, there was a touch of melancholy about him as he prepared to make his final remarks.

"I am in awe," he began. "No matter how many Blue Masses I am blessed to deliver, I am always in awe. But it's not for the reasons you may be thinking. It is not because of the pomp and pageantry—although God knows I love those things." He gestured toward the three-peaked biretta sitting atop his bald head, nodding thanks in response to the polite laughter. The police, fire, and emergency medical personnel—along with many of their family members—listened closely, hungry for encouragement during a time of low morale. "I am in awe because of what you do for our communities every day—serving your fellow citizens at great risk to yourselves, in the face of some of the most grotesque threats imaginable."

Additional detail wasn't necessary. Everyone knew he was talking about the horrific video released the previous day by the Trinitarios—a predominantly Dominican gang of narco-terrorists. With production value reminiscent of the so-called Islamic State, the video opened with a captured Massachusetts State Trooper strapped to a chair in the center of a room. The walls, ceiling, and floor were all painted bright white. The camera panned out to reveal two figures dressed in blue jumpsuits and clown masks with bright red hair—each holding a Louisville Slugger baseball bat. *Insane in the Brain*—a well-known rap song by Cypress Hill—started to play in the background as the clowns commenced their "batting practice."

Mark had zoned out through most of the Cardinal's homily. It had been some comparison between first responders and Saint Michael—the archangel who leads God's armies against Satan in the book of Revelation. Saint Michael was also the patron saint of paratroopers. Now the Cardinal was mentioning him again. Mark perked up at the reference this time. Jumping out of airplanes at Fort Benning, Georgia was how his career had begun twenty-five years earlier. He briefly paid attention before retreating back into his own thoughts.

Fort Benning, Georgia. Airborne school. Lawson Army Airfield. All chuted up. Ready to waddle across the tarmac, board a C-141 Starlifter and make his first jump. Hurry up and wait. Two nice old ladies who might have been nuns wandered among the troops, smiling and handing out what looked like little square pieces of silver. One of them held out her hand and asked Mark if he would like one. He reflexively placed his hand under hers to accept the gift.

It was a small silver medallion. Engraved on one side were the words "Saint Michael, Protect Us." On the other was the archangel's image with a sword in one hand, a shield in the other, and his foot on Satan's windpipe. Mark remembered how the Georgia sun glittered off the sword and shield as he stared into the palm of his hand.

Although raised by a nun and a priest after his mother gave him up for adoption at birth, Mark had never been a religious man. But he remembered glancing back and forth between his hand and the U.S. Air Force plane he was about to jump out of and wanting all the good luck he could get. He remembered quickly running one end of his dog tags through the small loop on top of the medallion and wearing it like a good-luck charm around his neck. He could hear it jingle as he adjusted his equipment one last time. He recalled the adrenaline spike at the moment of truth when he hooked his static line to the interior of the aircraft and shuffled out the open cargo door at fifteen hundred feet above Fryar Drop Zone.

One thousand. Two thousand. Three thousand. Check canopy!

Fear gave way to elation when he found himself on the ground with all his equipment and body parts intact. Afterwards he taped the Saint

Michael medallion to one of his dog tags so it wouldn't make noise, and it remained there for his next twelve years of service in the U.S. Army's 75th Ranger Regiment. Then he met a man named Dunbar and was offered the opportunity to join a clandestine unit known as the Family. He accepted and removed his uniform—and lucky dog tags—forever, as a snake sheds its skin. What followed was eight years of global special operations missions, most of which would remain classified for quite some time—perhaps forever.

Mark looked at Luci. He adored her smooth, coffee-brown skin. She was gorgeous, intelligent, kind, and passionate. She was a fantastic mother and wife. But she was a horrible singer. She nudged him in the ribs again—this time much harder—when she heard him chuckle at her singing.

He thought about how much his life had changed when he had retired at the twenty-year mark. He and Luci had been off-and-on sweethearts since their teenage years. When he retired and returned home, they rekindled their love and got married. The twins came immediately thereafter. His personal life had changed drastically, his professional life not so much.

Mark started working for Dunbar again at Imperium, a private security company where he ended up doing many of the same things he had done for the Family. The money at Imperium was spectacular and the operational tempo much slower at first. That all changed when Dunbar retired—after which he seemingly disappeared from the face of the earth—and tapped Mark to take command of the organization. He accepted the baton and ran with it. When the opportunity came to ditch all private contracts and dedicate Imperium to working directly—secretly— for the National Security Advisor and President of the United States on "special projects," Mark jumped in with both feet. Who wouldn't?

All he had to do to keep things happy at home was promise Luci that he wouldn't travel too much and that his role would be managerial— no door-kicking. Those days were gone. His job was to lead the organization and he promised not to put himself in harm's way unnecessarily. Not when they had two kids to raise and the rest of their lives to spend together. He was doing his best to honor those promises, but it was not always easy. He did what he felt he had to do to get the job done. Sometimes that meant bending the rules or completely throwing them out.

The Cardinal, Governor, and Mayor led the procession down the aisle through a thin cloud of incense. Luci locked arms with Mark and rested her head on his shoulder for a moment. He kissed the top of her head. They both smiled at the twins' glee as the Boston Police Gaelic Column of Pipes and Drums marched past them and out the front doors of the cathedral. The crowd soon spilled outside where police cruisers and unmarked sedans lined the streets.

"I'm going to ask the Cardinal to bless the kids," said Luci.

"Okay. I'll be down there," Mark replied, pointing to a spot on the sidewalk below. He reached for his phone as he weaved through the crowd and descended the front steps. Billy picked up on the first ring.

"Forgive me, Father, for I have sinned."

"Did you take out the trash yet?" asked Mark.

"Did you go to confession yet?" quipped Billy sarcastically. They had worked in the dark underworld of black ops for over fifteen years together. Billy was the closest thing Mark had to a brother. They could say anything to each other.

"Confession? I don't think so."

"Not enough time or not enough guilt?"

"Both. Give me a quick update. I don't know how long I have."

Billy briefed Mark on his current op. The "cyber dipshit" would be leaving his job any minute with a USB full of classified information. If history was any guide, he would run several surveillance detection routes (SDRs) and do errands to kill time. Then he would enter the shopping mall's public bathroom to make final preparations before heading for the designated dead drop where he would leave the USB. The team was in place. Billy was looking forward to wrapping things up and heading back to Boston. When he finished talking, Mark was silent for a moment.

Should I ask him? Yeah. Just throw it out there and see what he says. Maybe he wants to talk about it—maybe not. That's up to him, but I gotta at least ask.

"Are you going to stop off at home on the way back? You have some time before London." Mark's words hung in the air as the phone went silent for several seconds.

"No. No, that's not going to be necessary."

Billy had been married to his high-school sweetheart for as long as Mark had known him. They had always seemed madly in love, but things had changed once Billy retired from the Family shortly after Mark. The painful separation of deployments was gone, but so were the emotional exuberant homecomings that always seemed to add fuel to their long-burning romance. She left him immediately after their only daughter graduated from college. There would be no counseling. There was nothing to work on. It was over. Mark left it at that. Billy would talk when and if he wanted to. He pivoted back to the mission.

"Let me know when this guy is wrapped up so I can brief the boss," Mark said, referring to the National Security Advisor, a former Senator named Johnson. "Then I'll see you back here at the office before we go to London."

"We? You're gonna go on this one?"

"Hell, yeah. Why should you get to do all the fun stuff?"

Mark slipped the phone into his pocket and quickly scanned the area out of habit. Much of the multitude had followed the pipers down the street. The crowd outside the cathedral was thinning. Luci appeared at the top of the steps with Carlos and Amanda on either side, each holding a white-gloved hand tightly. When she saw Mark looking up at them from the sidewalk, she gave him a wide smile. He smiled back and they started their descent down the long marble steps. Mark took a deep breath of the South Boston air and held it in for a moment. Someone nearby was baking fresh bread.

Mark followed them down the stairs with his eyes and counted his blessings, just as Agnes (his adoptive mother) and Father Peck, the only father figure he had growing up, had always reminded him to do when he was stressed.

One, two, three blessings coming my way right now. The three most important things in my life.

13

Mark felt for Billy. He couldn't relate to the relationship difficulties that seemed to plague so many couples. He and Luci had their disagreements and maybe a few small things they'd change about each other if they could. But they were still madly in love and trusted each other. They were the lucky few. Mark had never questioned Luci's love, loyalty, or honesty. And he doubted that he ever would. She was the one person in the world he could trust with all of his heart.

But that was about to change.

CHAPTER TWO

Trash Day

Scotty Bukowski reached down to remove the USB drive from his desktop and dropped it into the rolled-up cuff of his jeans. Not the ideal place for valuable national security information, but it was only a temporary storage location. Then he laced his fingers behind his head and leaned back in his leather chair. He darted his eyes back and forth a few times and casually glanced over his shoulder to confirm that nobody had been watching. After a few deep breaths, he tapped his wristwatch.

"Well, looks like quitting time," he said to no one in particular. Scotty powered down his system. Then he tidied a few things on his desktop and scribbled a few notes on the to-do list in his cubicle.

Drying his hands, he looked at himself one last time in the mirror before exiting the rest room. He practiced a smile and tried to ignore the boiling lava in his stomach. It was not very convincing. He reminded himself that this was not the first time. Just take deep breaths and walk out the door.

Walking across the main lobby of CMS Cyber Solutions, Scotty pretended to whistle. He waved to a coworker and turned toward the exit. There were three employees in front of him. The security guard charged with returning their personal items—cell phones, backpacks, purses—was taking his time. He spent his nights trying to make it as a stand-up comedian and often used the captive audience at the exit to test out new material. Scotty stood in line patiently with his hands on his hips. Ahead of him there was some mumbling followed by polite chuckling.

Scotty held up his employee badge, not for the guard as much as for the security cameras. The guard knew who he was, but if the company didn't record ID checks on all employees entering or exiting the building, the oversight could jeopardize lucrative U.S. government contracts.

The guard held up Scotty's backpack and cellphone. "These look familiar?"

"Yeah."

"All right, then. Here you go," the guard said, handing them over. "Next time try not to look so guilty."

Scotty froze. "What do you mean?"

"You know what I mean. Two weeks off when the rest of us got to work." The guard smiled broadly. "You going anywhere special?"

"Oh, that. No, not really. I'm just going to try and get some stuff done around the house and relax. You know how it is." He slung the backpack over one shoulder and slipped the cell phone into his front pocket.

"Actually, I don't. The only two weeks I ever had off was for rehab. But I hope you have a great vacation anyway," offered the guard with a thumbs-up sign.

Scotty managed a polite chuckle and mumbled his thanks on the way out the door. He headed for his car in the far corner of the secure lot. He tried not to walk too fast as it might attract attention. Halfway there, he felt that he was walking too slowly so he picked up the pace. Inside the car he gasped for air as he fastened the seatbelt.

The exterior guard raised the gate. Scotty exited, turned right, and melted into the current of mid-afternoon traffic. The clock on the dashboard read 3:35 p.m. He had two hours to kill before he needed to make the drop. He would fill the time with errands just in case he was being surveilled.

Scotty spent forty-five minutes browsing in the Apple store at the mall. Then he passed half an hour walking around the ground floor before heading toward the food court and restrooms on the second floor. The door to the men's room was surrounded by construction scaffolding and two workers appeared to be preparing for a project. Scotty froze and one of the workers spoke to him as he zipped up his overalls.

"Go ahead if you got to. We haven't started yet. Plenty of time. We're paid by the hour anyway," he said, opening the door for Scotty to enter.

Scotty said thanks and nodded. As he passed through the scaffolding, a full body scan confirmed that he was unarmed and free of surveillance devices. The only items on him besides his wallet were the key to his car, his cell phone, and the USB he had smuggled out of the office. The only other person inside was a custodian wearing light blue overalls and a ball cap, whistling as he mopped the floor in front of a line of urinals. Scotty ignored him and headed straight for the stall farthest from the entrance.

He peered through the gap on the hinged side of the stall door. It had appeared that the custodian was about to finish when Scotty walked in, but now he was changing the water in his mop bucket and cleaning a different part of the floor. Scotty decided to wait a few minutes to see if he would leave. But when the custodian finished mopping, he kept whistling and moved on to wiping down the sinks. Scotty looked at his watch and felt beads of perspiration developing on his forehead. He wiped them off with the sleeve of his dress shirt and took a deep breath. The custodian didn't hear the subsequent groan coming from the stall.

"I'm gonna be about another ten minutes in here if you boys wanna go get a cup of coffee or something, okay?" the custodian called out to the construction workers after pushing the door open a few inches. Then he started wiping down the hand drying machines mounted on the wall next to the sinks. Scotty flushed the toilet and peeked through the crack again as he fastened his belt.

After pumping the remaining few drops of soap from the dispenser, he reached for the faucet. The custodian abruptly stopped whistling and did the same at the adjacent sink. He smiled at Scotty in the mirror. "How you doing today, Sir?"

"Fine, thanks."

"Can I ask you another question?" he asked, adjusting his Oklahoma ball cap.

"Sure," Scotty answered cautiously, without looking at the other man.

"I already know the who, when, and what. But I want to know why."

Scotty nervously dried his hands on the front of his pants and tried to smile. "Why what? What are you talking about?"

"Treason. I'm wondering why? I've been around long enough to know that there's lots of reasons. MICE, right? Isn't that the acronym? Money, ideology, coercion, and extortion. Or is the E for ego? I always forget that part. Anyway, what's your excuse? Why did you sell out your country?"

Before Scotty could answer, Billy grabbed him by the throat and slammed him backwards into the wall, taking care to stun the "cyber dipshit" but not hurt him. Billy still needed him for now.

"Actually, don't bother answering that because I really don't give a shit. You did it. For whatever reason, you sold out your country. And now, if you want any chance of living, you're going to do exactly what I tell you to do. Understand?"

Nothing. The traitor was in shock. A deer in the headlights.

Billy reached over and turned on the faucet with his free hand. He splashed the traitor's face with cold water and slapped his colorless cheeks a few times. "Wake up and stay up. Wake up and stay up. It ain't over for you yet. You got a chance, but you gotta do exactly what I say, okay? If you do, you'll be okay. Trust me," he lied.

Billy released his grip from Scotty's throat, reached into the front pocket of his overalls and removed a small USB drive. He placed it on the sink. "You can start by swapping this out."

Scotty grasped the edge of the sink and tried to steady himself. "Swap what out? I don't know what you're talking about."

The crack of Billy's open-handed slap across the face echoed throughout the empty restroom. "Do not fuck with me! You know damn well what I am talking about. Now, let's try this again. Take that," he said pointing to the USB he had placed on the sink. "And swap it out with the one you just pulled out of your ass."

Scotty's jaw dropped and his eyes opened wide like those of a Looney Tunes cartoon character.

"Then you're going to make your dead drop like normal. After that we can talk about what to do with you. But believe you me, any chance of you ever having any semblance of a life will disappear like a fart in the wind if you mess this up. Got it?" Billy put his hands on Scotty's shoulders and pulled him close. "Do you understand me?"

Scotty's eyelids slammed shut and he exhaled slowly. As he did, the wet spot on the front of his pants grew. Urine ran down his leg and a puddle started to form on the restroom floor. Billy stepped back and looked at Scotty with a mixture of disgust and contempt.

"I just mopped that, asshole."

· · ·

An hour later, Billy was on his way to the airport. Mark was at home and had just put the kids to bed when his phone rang. "Tell me something good."

"We can scratch another traitor off the list. That's good, right?"

Mark kept his voice down as he walked into his kitchen. "Sounds good to me. How did it go?"

"Good. He made the drop without a hitch. Since you're such a busy man, I'll spare you any further details. Suffice it to say nobody will ever see or hear from him again."

Mark had known Billy long enough to know he was smiling as those words came out of his mouth. "Okay. Sounds good to me."

"That means in his current state, the chances of recidivism are zero," Billy added.

"Yeah. I got that part. Are you on your way to Boston?"

"Yup."

"I'll see you when you get here."

Mark grabbed a frosted mug from the freezer. He poured himself a beer and joined Luci on the couch. She was fast asleep. He turned off the television, took a long sip of his beer, and thought about the traitor

Billy had just disposed of. National Security Advisor Johnson had made himself crystal clear. Black Hat Hackers, leakers, and enemy cyber warriors around the world needed to receive the clear message that the U.S. intelligence and special-operations communities will find them wherever they are and treat them like the enemy combatants and terrorists that they are.

According to the American interpretation of international laws of war, digital attacks constitute direct participation. And direct participation makes one a combatant. Thus, the gloves were off. Cyber operators used to stay up at night worrying about federal agents in windbreakers, FISA (Foreign Intelligence Surveillance Act) warrants, criminal indictments, frozen accounts, and restricted travel. Soon they would add grave bodily injury, public humiliation, and all the horrifying ways they could be killed by intelligence operators to their list of worries.

Things were better this way anyway. Maybe not for Scotty Bukowski himself, but at least those who shared his name wouldn't have to live with the stigma of having a traitor in the family. Billy had spared them the unrelenting media coverage and social harassment that would have accompanied a trial. The threat was eliminated. Done. End of story. Next slide, please.

Mark considered his next two major near-term missions. He'd been tasked by National Security Advisor Johnson to take care of a notorious Greek hacker who had been holed up in the Venezuelan embassy in London for the past year. Johnson explicitly told him to send a message to all hackers and leakers, one they would never forget. Exactly how he did that was left up to Mark. His team had a solid plan. No worries on the London mission.

After that he would travel to Berlin to collaborate with German intelligence and continue the hunt for Oleg Borodin, a powerful yet murky figure in Russian foreign intelligence operations. Mark was having trouble sizing Borodin up because so little was known about him. He needed help. That meant spending time with Heike, a top-notch German spy and assassin with whom he shared a personal and professional history. He was uneasy about working with her again but couldn't quite put his finger on why.

Mark and Heike had worked and played intimately together, but that was a long time ago—before Mark married Luci and became a father. He had seen her briefly in Boston recently, but the interaction had left him confounded. Something had seemed off. She had seemed frustrated, even a little angry. Perhaps she was jealous that although they did similar work, Mark had managed to marry and had a normal life on the side while she was still single. Or maybe he was overthinking it. Whatever it was, he was sure he could handle it.

He shifted his thoughts to the woman whom nobody else knew to be his birth mother, Senator McDermott of Connecticut. To further his own interests, he had manipulated her to cross the aisle and cast the sixtieth vote to confirm Judge Midas, a controversial man to say the least, for the Supreme Court. Mark knew the fallout would be bad, but he had no idea it would be this bad. The last time they spoke, she had been holed up in her Washington apartment for weeks, avoiding the cameras and the public as much as possible. She had been barely responsive on the phone. Mark worried that she'd been through so much in her life that maybe she lacked the strength to get through this nightmare and snap out of it. Could her emotional tank finally be out of gas? No, she just needs more time. She's still got plenty of sand left in her hourglass, he told himself. Plenty of time for her to heal. Plenty of time to one day honor her wish and publicly acknowledge their secret family ties.

He was wrong.

CHAPTER THREE

At Home with Oleg

Oleg Borodin pried open his wallet and peered inside it over the top of his glasses. The taxi driver tapped his hand on the stick shift impatiently. Oleg took his time peeling off just enough money to cover the fare—no tip. He pretended to count cash while quickly scanning the taxi's side and rear-view mirrors for threats. He secured his things before handing the money to the driver.

"*Děkuji*," he said softly.

The taxi sped away, leaving Oleg on the sidewalk. He cut a thoroughly sympathetic figure: thin, slightly hunched over, wearing slip-on canvas shoes, a Jonesy hat, and black, round-framed glasses.

Oleg joined the stream of pedestrians and walked north for several blocks. Pausing at the crosswalk, he looked at the three-story building on the other side of the street. Nothing appeared out of the ordinary. He stepped forward and continued to scan the area as he slowly made his way across the street. Traffic stopped. He nodded thanks to a female driver. The young lady smiled and waved back at the elderly man. His awkward appearance and slow shuffle reminded her of Woody Allen. The door opened from the inside as Oleg approached. He entered the building. The door locked tightly behind him.

Oleg nodded to the chubby man awaiting him inside and handed over his suitcase before kicking off his shoes and slipping into an expensive pair of Italian loafers. He could smell a strong lemon scent. The winding marble staircase must have just been polished in anticipation of his arrival. He started to climb the stairs. On the way up, he removed his glasses and slipped them into his front pocket. He stretched his arms high above his head to straighten out his back and pulled off the subtle hairpiece. At the top of the stairs, he turned left and entered the bathroom.

After relieving himself, Oleg washed his hands, removed his sweater, and splashed cold water on his face. Then he scratched the skin at the bottom of his nose until it started to break free from his face. He pulled harder. The prosthetic feature stretched like a rubber band before breaking and snapping into the palm of his hand. He threw it in the toilet and cleaned the remaining debris from his face with a towel before applying a thick lather of shaving cream with a brush. "Pew. Pew. Pusillanimous," he said to himself in the mirror as he shaved with an old-fashioned straight razor. "Pusillanimous."

Oleg slapped aftershave on his cheeks with both hands. He then changed into a plain white T-shirt and tucked it into the pants of a gray track suit that he found in the closet. He leaned in close to peer at his own reflection, his face just inches from the mirror. "Pusillanimous," he said one last time, happy with his perfect pronunciation. With wet, slicked-back hair and a clean-shaven face, he was an entirely different figure as he made his way down the long hallway to the office. Woody Allen was gone. Hannibal Lecter had arrived.

The man who had let Oleg in and taken his suitcase was waiting for him outside the closed door of the office. He was unbathed, unshaven, and uninterested in bathing or shaving. A gun was tucked into the back of his close-fitting waistband. An enormous layer of fat kept it in place. Oleg picked up his scent—a toxic combination of booze, cigarettes, and body odor—as he approached.

"He's inside," said the man.

"Come inside, Fabio," answered Oleg. He pushed open the French doors and inhaled deeply through his nostrils. Fabio's unpleasant aroma had competition. The familiar smell of impending death hovered in the office. Oleg welcomed it and motioned for Fabio to pour him a drink. He took a sip. "Bring him closer."

A high-backed leather chair sat in the corner, facing the wall. Fabio turned the chair around and rolled it into the middle of the large room. He looked down to make sure that it was centered on the thick plastic he had rolled out earlier to protect Oleg's Persian rug. An unconscious man's naked body was tied stringently to the chair by its hands and feet with thin electrical wiring. The man's head was taped to the back of the chair with a thick band of duct tape—a bloody and thoroughly beaten head distracted from his swollen, purple limbs. His face was barely recognizable to Oleg.

"Nico, Nico, Nico. Is that you? Look what you have done to yourself. I wish I could say I feel sympathy for you. But you have brought this on yourself by taking what is mine, even after all I have done for you and your family. Do you have anything to say for your crimes?"

No response. Oleg looked at Fabio. "Is he dead already?"

Fabio reached a hand into the bloody mess to check for a pulse. "Still ticking."

"I see. Well, I'll give him a minute then. And the wife?"

Fabio smiled naughtily, like a little boy hearing his first dirty joke. "Yes, we found her at one of his apartments. The men just finished."

Oleg finished his drink and placed it softly on a mahogany table. "Tell me, Fabio. Why didn't you have the men bring her here and make him watch? Otherwise it's a pointless exercise."

Fabio held up his cell phone and smiled proudly. The screen was blank. Oleg looked back at him impatiently until he realized his folly. Fabio quickly punched some buttons with his thick fingers and held up the phone again. High-pitched shrieks of terror—interspersed with laughter and grunting—came from the phone's speakers. "I made him watch until he passed out. Then I figured I'd let him rest until you got here to finish him off."

Oleg watched for a few moments, then smiled widely and clapped a hand on his most trusted lieutenant's barrel-of-a-belly. "Good, Fabio. Very good." He looked down at the beaten man and shook his head. "And you, Nico. Bad. Very bad." Oleg nodded to Fabio that it was time.

Fabio retrieved the small stepladder used to reach books and other items from the shelved walls. He placed it behind Nico's leather chair and rummaged through the drawer next to the wet bar. "Here it is, Boss. Brand new. Never been used." He removed an ice pick from its original packaging and paced across the room. The damp soles of his shoes squeaked against the plastic-covered floor.

Oleg took the ice pick in his open palm and tightly closed his fingers around the sharp instrument. Then he ascended the stepladder until he was looking straight down at the top of Nico's head. He probed for a soft spot, then he clasped the ice pick with both hands and raised it high above his head. Fabio held his breath in anticipation.

Chirping from the encrypted satellite phone on a nearby table broke the silence. Oleg exhaled, lowered the ice pick, and climbed down the ladder. The phone chirped again. Fabio knew to leave the room.

Oleg grabbed the phone and answered it on the way to his desk. "Yes. Speak." After a brief pause, the other party spoke in a reverberating electronic voice—obviously the product of a voice masking system.

"Hello, Oleg."

Oleg sat back, put his feet up on the desk, and pulled out a nail file. "Yes. Hello. Speak." He did not like to engage in small talk with his people. "I have only two or three minutes for you. What do you have for me?"

He listened for a few minutes, nodding his head and rolling his eyes. "Okay. Got it. You have mentioned this man before. This … Landry person. This information is useless. Yes, yes … I do not care about his skills or experience. Men have been after me for years who would make this little American wet his pants. Now, please tell me you have something more valuable to offer me. I pay you a great deal of money for information. So tell me something I didn't already know."

"Europol will raid your location in two days," offered the emotionless voice.

Oleg put his feet on the floor and sat up in his chair. "Which location are you talking about?"

"Your current location. Prague."

"What makes you think I am in Prague?"

Oleg ignored the answer, muted the phone, and called Fabio back into the office. "We are leaving immediately. We won't be back. You know what to do."

"Scorch the earth?" Fabio asked excitedly.

"Yes, start immediately. We are moving locations." Oleg did not inform him where they were going. Being the most trusted lieutenant simply meant Fabio was trusted more than the others—a low bar to clear since Oleg didn't fully trust anybody. For Oleg, the world contained two groups of people—those who have betrayed you and those who haven't yet. He told Fabio what he needed to know, but not until he needed to know.

Oleg listened to the rest of the call silently before hanging up. He had been hoping for a few days' respite in Prague before changing locations again. But the heat was on and he was determined to stay at least one step ahead of his many pursuers.

Oleg made his way back to the barely breathing Nico. "Sorry to keep you waiting, Nico. Let's finish our business together. Don't worry about your wife. She has probably cried herself to sleep by now. She will heal over time. Physically, at least." Fabio was lingering by the door, hoping to catch a glimpse of Nico's final moment. Oleg let him remain. Fabio grinned like a child watching a special episode of his favorite TV show. Oleg raised the ice pick for the second time. Fabio crossed his fingers, hoping that he would hit Nico in just the right spot—the one that would send his dying body into a spasmodic seizure, like a vibrator sputtering the last drops of energy from its batteries before going limp.

Oleg paused. The caller had had two pieces of information for him: a covert team of American assassins led by a man named Mark Landry could be added to the list of people who wanted to find and kill him, and Europol would soon raid his Prague safe house. On its face, the latter item seemed much more pressing. And yet the caller had mentioned the American first. Oleg wondered why. Maybe the informant had simply delivered the information in random order and he was overthinking things. Or had the informant prioritized the threats and presented them accordingly? And if so, why? Oleg's ability to quickly assess emerging threats—and stay one step ahead of them—had kept him alive for decades in the most dangerous circles of Russian intelligence and organized crime. He made a mental note to find out what was so special about Mark Landry. Then he returned to the task before him.

The sharp tip of the ice pick popped through Nico's skull and penetrated several inches into his brain. Oleg let go when it wouldn't penetrate any further and left the thick wooden handle sticking out the top of his head. Nico didn't move. No spasms. No vibrator effects. Oleg grabbed the handle and pumped the ice pick up and down several times at different angles, looking for the sweet spot. Nothing. He turned to his disappointed lieutenant.

"Maybe next time, Fabio. Maybe next time."

CHAPTER FOUR

Justice Delayed

"One second," McDermott called out on her way to the front door of her apartment.

She paused in front of the full-length mirror and tightened the bathrobe around her rail-thin body. Then she pulled a knit cap over her head and made sure that all her hair was tucked underneath. Maybe she couldn't stop the thinning, but she could still hide it.

She had cast the deciding ballot to confirm Judge James Midas to the U.S. Supreme Court. A lifetime appointment. Not because she approved of him, but in exchange for giving fifty thousand refugee children a chance at life. Mark had secretly coached and encouraged her to confirm President Calhoun's controversial nominee. She didn't regret the decision or the experience of sharing with Mark. It was one of the few times she had felt emotionally connected with her son. She wanted more of it.

At age sixteen, McDermott gave Mark Landry up for adoption at birth—a decision she had questioned ever since. As an adult, she lost her husband Jack in the Twin Towers. She also lost one of her daughters in a Connecticut school shooting. Then Mark mysteriously walked back into her life as a grown man, and she had been struggling to connect with and truly know him ever since. But nothing—not even the perpetual hardships of her life—could have prepared her for the inescapable 24/7 onslaught that began the moment Midas was confirmed.

It started with the major cable news networks. "Breaking news" alerts with snarky headlines exploded across the digital landscape. McDermott was labeled a sellout. A traitor. An indecisive and irresponsible woman. Easily influenced. Many questioned her mental state; others wondered aloud what she got in exchange for casting the poisonous ballot. A torturous week went by before the Patriot Child Refugee Act was publicly announced and they got their answer. She thought it would make things better, even if only marginally. Instead, they got worse.

Now McDermott was accused of selling out America's children to help someone else's—a dereliction of her duty to her own constituents. A growing wave of Connecticut voters was calling for her resignation. Reporters were camped out everywhere she went. Death threats piled up. She would lay awake at night asking herself: what hurt worse? The pure hatred from those who once embraced her, or the newfound affection and accolades from her historical foes like the pro–Second Amendment and pro-life movements? The hostility took its toll quickly—both mentally and physically. When it started to show, the story shifted to her debilitation. People made bets on how long she could take it before quitting. Others gleefully predicted suicide.

Midas's post-confirmation conduct wasn't helping. He was not approaching his elevated position with the traditional solemnity and decorum of a new justice. Typically, newly confirmed members of the Supreme Court treaded lightly and showed respect for the norms and traditions of the institution. Midas felt no such compulsions. He gave exclusive access and interviews to mostly fringe media outlets that fawned over him while virtually ignoring the mainstream media. He appeared on the cover of *Field and Stream* magazine in hunting lodge apparel, holding up a twelve-gauge shotgun. "From his cold dead fingers!" read the caption. The controversial picture was apparently taken in his second-floor office at the Supreme Court before he was even sworn in.

Midas was late for his first Friday court conference run by the Chief Justice. His peers bristled when he flouted well-known tradition and respect for seniority by speaking out of turn. In the Supreme Court gymnasium, he was overheard commenting, "I didn't think I'd see you down here. Isn't the basketball court on the top floor?" to one of the court's two African American justices. When the *Washington Post* reported the incident, his publicist—Midas was the first justice ever to have one—said the justice was referring to his colleague's record-breaking college basketball career at Villanova, and that anyone who inferred racism from the comment should examine their own conscience.

Midas attended the Washington Nationals game on opening day wearing a seersucker suit and a skimmer hat with a red, white, and blue band around it, plus a thin black, unlit cigarillo clenched in his teeth. He raised eyebrows by speaking to special-interest groups at closed-door dinners and events, and he sparked outrage by accepting fees. None of this was illegal, but it was wholly out of step with traditional Supreme Court norms. Midas's detractors started to think it couldn't get any worse.

Then he started tweeting.

His first snipe was directed at the National Organization of Women in response to its #believewomen campaign. Unjustified stigma, shame, fear of retaliation, and potential loss of social status were all strong disincentives for women to hurl false accusations of sexual misconduct. The justice apparently disagreed. He tweeted a recent cover of *Time* magazine celebrating a dozen women whose cases of abuse had been widely reported in the mainstream media. "Does this look like a loss of social status? Or perhaps an elevation?" he asked.

"Look, the justice's tweet speaks for itself and needs no explanation," the publicist explained to the cameras an hour later. "Justice Midas is one of the top legal minds in the country. He obviously has opinions on the significant current events that impact American society. And he has a constitutional right to share those opinions."

One of the first cases on the high court's docket was an intellectual property case involving a Silicon Valley technology company. Midas's pre-confirmation financial disclosures indicated that he owned a significant amount of stock in the company. He was expected to recuse himself but stunned his colleagues and court reporters when he showed up for work that day. "Listen," said his publicist. "Simply owning stock does not make someone biased, and Justice Midas is a professional jurist. If he thought he needed to recuse himself, he wouldn't hesitate to do so. Besides, anyone who has money in mutual funds or index funds—which I'm sure includes the other justices—probably owns some of the same stock. Yet nobody seems to be worried about anyone else being able to do their job. This criticism is politically motivated. No further questions. Thanks, guys."

The avalanche of digital hatred focused on McDermott got even worse after that. Off came the gloves and out came the knives. People who had previously held her up as a paragon of virtue and strength now completely turned their backs and hurled the ugliest of personal insults. Late-night comedians, celebrated journalists, most of Hollywood. CNN legal analyst Jeffrey Toobin was the worst. His endless updates on Justice Midas's shocking behavior were the knife in the Senator's side that never stopped twisting, reliably fanning the flames.

The Office of Protective Intelligence and the Judicial Security Division of the U.S. Marshals Service were overwhelmed by the unprecedented stream of death threats against Midas. They had to borrow people and resources from the Capitol Police and FBI. The result was an imperial presence wherever Midas went. Most new justices needed time to adjust to the traditional trappings of the office; Midas was intoxicated by it all—and fully insulated from political threats since he had a lifetime appointment.

Rapid knocking again—this time much louder. Senator McDermott opened the door and mustered a smile. "Hey, Peg. You look pissed off. What a surprise."

"And you look even more haggard than before," answered Peggy wryly.

"Come on in. Can I make you a coffee or something?"

McDermott was standing in the middle of the doorway. Peggy squeezed by without answering and made her way to the kitchen table. She pulled a brown paper sack from her shoulder bag and tossed it onto the center of the table as she took a seat. The familiar rattle of refilled prescriptions put a smile on McDermott's face.

"This is the last time I'm doing this," said Peggy, folding her arms and trying to make it look as if she was serious this time.

"No, it's not," said McDermott, already peering into the bag. "Remember, you can break curfew. You can break laws too. You can even break regular promises." She held up her pinky without taking her eyes off the bag. "But you can never break one of these promises, Peg."

"I only have a few minutes, so forgive me for jumping to the big stuff. Have you told him yet?"

"Who?"

"Don't play with me. I'm really not in the mood. Have you told him about his father?"

"No."

McDermott looked down at the table to avoid eye contact. Peggy continued, "I'm going to say it yet again for the record—tell him. Tell him who his father is. He has a right to know."

"I know he does," McDermott said in a low voice.

"Then just tell him."

"I will."

"When?"

"Soon. Right now is not a good time, but things will get better soon. I'll be better soon."

Peggy wondered how McDermott could possibly think that. "And if you aren't? What then? And what about him? Anything new going on with him?"

McDermott ignored the question. Peggy knew not to push it. She had asked some tough questions about Mark during Judge Midas's confirmation fiasco. Wasn't it strange that all of a sudden, after several years of distance, he suddenly wanted to have lunch and coffee and talk about the Supreme Court? Maybe he had a dog in the fight, she offered. McDermott would hear nothing of it. When Peggy persisted, McDermott became defensive at the suggestion that her son was covertly lobbying her. Mark Landry is a good and decent man, she declared. "How the hell can you be so sure?" Peggy asked. After that, they didn't speak for several weeks.

Peggy had learned to bite her tongue and hold back. Mark Twain supposedly said it's easier to fool someone than to convince someone they've been fooled. Trying to do so is also a good way to lose a friend. And McDermott needed her now more than ever.

"What about Megan? When is she coming home?"

"Any day now."

"You need to tell her about Mark. Just do it. Rip the Band-Aid off. The longer you wait, the harder it's going to be on both of you. And she's a handful to begin with, right?"

McDermott ignored the question again. "Do you know how lucky I am to have a lifelong friend like you? Through thick and thin you've always been there. You are very special to me, Peg."

Peggy nodded and walked toward the door. "I gotta run."

"Hey, Peg," McDermott called out, holding up her pinky. "Thank you."

Peggy paused in the doorway and reluctantly returned the gesture before leaving.

Regardless of their lifelong friendship, McDermott knew she was testing the relationship. But she just needed more time to make things right. She walked onto her third-floor balcony and reached up to touch her favorite wind chimes with the tips of her fingers. They needed to be cleaned. A tiny green light below the balcony's security camera indicated that it was functioning. She leaned against the railing and peered over the edge, watching Peggy exit the building and nervously scurry down the street. McDermott felt a tinge of guilt. *I'll make it up to you next time we talk,* she thought, unaware that there would be no next time.

CHAPTER FIVE

London Calling

The Venezuelan ambassador to Great Britain cursed the day he had opened the London embassy's gates to a notorious Greek hacker seeking asylum. Initially, the ambassador had jumped at the chance to offer safe haven to SocraTeez, who was high on the Americans' list of most wanted cyber criminals. Taking him in was like displaying a middle finger to Washington, D.C. The ambassador expected that the move would greatly please his superiors in Caracas—and it did. Venezuela's president praised him publicly for offering support to a fellow revolutionary in the struggle against American hegemony.

But within just a few months, it became painfully clear that the ambassador had not thoroughly considered the implications of his action, and now, approaching the one-year mark, he was still in a pickle.

The U.S. and its allies were putting collective pressure on Venezuela to respect international law and release the hacker into their custody. Clearly, the Venezuelans could not do that without losing much of the only currency they had that still carried much value—credibility with fellow leftists. But keeping SocraTeez was proving economically costly. The flow of money from states aligned with the U.S. slowed to a trickle. Venezuelan political leaders and oligarchs had their international accounts frozen. And talks with the World Bank and International

Monetary Fund on crucial debt restructuring were placed on administrative hold, with no formal explanation.

In short, Venezuela was being squeezed from every direction because of the ambassador's shortsighted decision. To make matters worse, SocraTeez had proved himself to be a colossal pain in the ass. The Venezuelan president was growing frustrated. Something had to be done quickly, but every option they discussed ran the risk of making things worse. They could not have known that Mark Landry was about to resolve the problem for them.

. . .

National Security Advisor Johnson had already made up his mind by the time Mark finished pitching him on the specifics of the SocraTeez snatch mission. He looked down at the materials Mark had laid on the conference table in the Presidential Emergency Operations Center (PEOC), located far below the White House on level ZP, the most secure area of the building.

"Operation Hemlock," he read aloud. "Cute name. What's the lead time again?" he asked.

"Seventy-two hours from your order. Sooner if you need it. I'm building in some extra time for the Brits. They are on board with the idea, but their guys are on especially short leashes right now so we have to keep our footprint as small as possible. If we had to cut the Brits out and go it alone, we could still pull it off, but not without significant costs. There's no easy way to get this done. And since embassies are supposed to be sacred, we'll have to get it done as quietly as possible. That obviously makes things harder."

Johnson poured the rest of his drink down his throat and felt the warmth go all the way to his toes. He never drank in the PEOC when others were around. But since he had to meet with Landry late in the evening and they were alone in the conference room, he made an exception. "Sacred—everything is sacred until it isn't. Diplomatic laws were written for a different world, back when you had to actually show up for a fight. Now any asshole with the money can threaten an embassy from Bumfuck, Egypt as long as he has wifi. Stick to the plan. Treat these digital guys the same as we would any other terrorists. Take care of this SocraTeez guy and we alleviate future problems by taking embassies off the list of safe havens. Let the Vienna Convention be damned. Our enemies—and perhaps more important, our potential enemies—need to know that there's nowhere to hide. No safe spaces. Period. What does your gut say on the potential downsides of the mission, Mark?"

"It's tough under any circumstances. The domestic political hostility and distrust of MI-5 and 6 among the British public make it worse. Thankfully we don't take the same kind of heat on our side of the pond."

"Give it time," Johnson snickered. "Congressional oversight committees are on the same path. They have threated to subpoena the entire national security apparatus whenever I don't answer a question to their liking. They're a thorn in my ass and getting worse."

"Regardless, my guess is we'll only have to do this once and embassies will quickly fall of the list of places to hide. And I'd rather do it in a place like the U.K. because it's unexpected. Nobody would be surprised to see a guy like SocraTeez get snatched from an embassy in Nigeria or some other backwater. The U.K. is a different story. London has enough government surveillance to make the Chinese jealous. Like I said, it won't be easy, but our plan takes all of this into consideration and the Brits will help to the extent they can."

"Yeah. Well, I always prefer a nice clean 'warhead to the forehead' but we gotta play the cards we're dealt. What else?"

"I think the timing is right. We got lucky early on with the cleaning lady, Milagros, who planted the devices for us. But I think she has had enough, so we need to pull her too. We have obtained a treasure trove of information so far but SocraTeez is too dangerous to leave out there any longer. We need to snatch him now."

Johnson told Mark to get it done at his earliest discretion. Mark touched base with the closest thing he had to a counterpart in London that same evening and set Operation Hemlock in motion.

. . .

SocraTeez was high on his own press after taking up residence in the Venezuelan embassy almost a year earlier. His face was plastered throughout the international press, and requests for interviews from prestigious media outlets were abundant. On the deep web, the mention of his name sparked digital holy wars between factions of hackers and cyber criminals, but in the much more civilized and closely managed real world he was simply the talk of the town.

SocraTeez basked in the glory. And he never forgot to publicly praise the Venezuelan government's wisdom whenever he had a captive audience. Both parties seemed happy with the arrangement.

The U.S. and its allies would need a miracle to get their hands on SocraTeez. They couldn't touch him. Conversely, SocraTeez thought his infamy gave him license to touch whomever he wanted.

Enter Milagros, the embassy's night shift cleaning lady.

Milagros had been a dyed-in-the-wool supporter of the Socialist Revolution. The twenty-five-year-old Caracas native was a tireless campaigner, demonstrator, and anything else the administration needed. After the most recent election, she had been singled out and honored for her loyalty and dedication. She would no longer have to clean floors in Caracas; instead, she would clean floors in Venezuela's embassy in London.

The supposed prestige of her new job was not exactly what Milagros had in mind. She had bigger goals in life and would have rather been offered a scholarship to pursue further education. But "if cleaning floors is what the cause requires, then hand me a mop," she told herself.

Her first few months on the job in London had been uneventful. She was assigned the night shift, which left her days open to sightsee and discover the exciting new city in which she found herself. She was disappointed, however, when the embassy's personnel manager—a man with a distractingly thick black mustache—casually denied her request to take English classes. She pushed back against his knee-jerk dismissal of what she thought was a perfectly reasonable and logical request, considering that they were in England. In response, he switched tactics and questioned her commitment. "Are you here to serve the Socialist

Revolution or perhaps for more selfish reasons?" he wanted to know. She thought his answer and justification were bullshit, but she never brought up English classes again. Besides, the embassy was quiet at night. Milagros would instead buy headphones and learn English from tapes as she worked.

Then SocraTeez showed up and threw her new life into turmoil.

The graveyard shift was a skeleton crew to begin with. Now, in addition to cleaning, Milagros had to spend her time waiting on the obnoxious night owl who arrogantly strutted around in various states of undress. As an attractive young Latin woman, Milagros was not unaccustomed to how men often looked at her. Growing up in the barrios of Caracas, it came with the territory. So SocraTeez's constant leering and occasional comment or whistle insulted her, but she took them in stride. Even when he started going out of his way to touch her unnecessarily—putting a hand on her shoulder as she served him his tea or brushing up against her when there was plenty of room to get by—she thought it easier to just deal with it rather than complain to the ignorant, oversized mustache she reported to.

But SocraTeez took silence as consent and upped the ante by steadily lowering his touches. He moved from the shoulder to the center of her back, where he would make small circles with his hand until she couldn't take it anymore and broke contact. "You're warming up to me. I can feel it," he would chide in broken Spanish. Then one night, as she placed the tea tray on the table next to his laptop, he reached down and cupped her rear. Running his hand back and forth just above her tailbone, he stated, "Nice thong. I always wondered what kind of underwear you wore. Mystery solved."

That was it. Milagros stayed after her shift ended in the morning and was waiting for the mustache in his office when he arrived for work, hung over and reeking of booze from the night before. Since she was visibly upset and his head was pounding, he listened to her while holding an icepack to his forehead.

Milagros recounted her experiences with SocraTeez from the very beginning. Tears welled in her eyes a few times, but she fought them off

38

and managed to finish explaining what she had been going through. He was harassing her with impunity, she explained, and she did not feel safe at work. Then she sat stunned as the embassy personnel manager turned it all back around on her. If their important guest had been harassing her since his arrival, why didn't she do something about it before now? Had she told him to stop? Why not? Wasn't she encouraging SocraTeez with her silence? If things were so bad, why did she say nothing until now? The manager said he would add another cleaning woman to the night shift so that she wasn't alone. Then he asked, "Don't you put on makeup and do your hair up nice before coming to work?"

The question rendered her speechless. It was true that Milagros wore makeup and tried to look good at work. So what? That was not an invitation for a stranger with the emotional maturity of a child to fondle her, and she resented the implication that it did. But she resisted the urge to unleash her pent-up fury on the mustache. It wouldn't accomplish anything. It might even get her a one-way ticket back to Caracas—which, ironically, was the last place on earth where many of the Venezuelan president's supporters working in the London embassy wanted to live. Conditions and the overall quality of life between London and Caracas were at opposite ends of the spectrum. She wouldn't press her complaint. She had a better idea.

Twice a week, Milagros was tasked with picking up the deputy ambassador's three children from their expensive private school, since his wife was too busy shopping and traveling around Europe on the Venezuelan people's dime. Each time, the two bodyguards assigned to the children would remain in the car when she went into the building to round up the kids and their things. On those days she often saw a young American woman with a U.S. embassy badge attached to her belt picking up her own children. The American would always smile and nod hello.

A week after her harassment complaint fell on deaf ears, Milagros went to pick up the deputy ambassador's children. She took her time and waited for the American woman to show up. When the other woman knelt down to help one of her kids with his backpack, Milagros knelt beside her and held out a folded piece of paper. "You drop something," she said quietly in broken English.

"Excuse me?"

"You drop this," Milagros repeated.

"I don't think—"

Milagros cut her off. "Read. Read it." The American woman saw the seriousness in Milagros's eyes and unfolded the piece of paper with four words written on it: *I help get SocraTeez.* Then she looked back at Milagros and smiled. "You're right. I did drop this. Thank you very much. I'm Jennifer," she said extending her hand.

"Milagros." She handed Jennifer another piece of paper with her contact information and then exited the building, a suitably blank expression on her face.

A different American woman made contact the next day and set up a meeting with another man. Milagros assumed they were CIA. They listened to her experiences with SocraTeez and spent several hours carefully vetting her. They had to make sure she was who she claimed to be and not simply dangling a false opportunity designed to embarrass the United States or to determine which embassy employees were actually CIA working under official cover. Milagros passed with flying colors.

When they made the pitch for her to plant surveillance devices, she didn't blink. They stressed how careful she would need to be and the gravity of the consequences if she failed. She said that she fully understood and had already considered all that before deciding to approach Jennifer. "I am no worried," she offered, explaining that most of the men in charge of the embassy were arrogant and ignorant. "But they think I am stupid. Is good, right?"

She had been right. A week later, Milagros planted the first device without incident. Over the following months she placed a dozen more, giving the CIA unfettered surveillance of the inner workings of the Venezuelan embassy as well as SocraTeez's activities—including anything he did on his laptop. But she was growing tired of babysitting him and having to be on constant guard. She was elated when she learned it would all be over soon.

...

Mark and his team met with Milagros on the day of Operation Hemlock to go over the plan one last time. They handed her a small vial and instructed her to put the entire contents into Socrateez's tea. The embassy medical staff did not work at night. The chemicals would cause intense abdominal pain, severe enough that SocraTeez would think he was dying and would panic. The chances of him waiting hours for the embassy's physician to be tracked down and summoned were absolutely zero. He would demand an ambulance. The thinly staffed night security staff was on strict orders not to let him leave the compound under any circumstances whatsoever, so they would have to be dealt with. Once the pain started, Milagros would need to quickly get SocraTeez out of the residential area, down six flights of stairs, and across the staff parking lot to the private rear entrance of the embassy. Just get him to the gate. Mark's team would do the rest.

"Then you get to disappear and start your new life," Mark said in Spanish.

Milagros had noted his masterful grasp of the language during the briefing and his barely detectable accent. "Usted habla español excelente," she remarked.

"Gracias," Mark replied, somewhat struck by the awkward timing of the compliment.

"Usted tiene una mujer latina." *You have a Latin woman,* she declared confidently.

Mark smiled for the first time during the meeting. "Maybe I do."

Milagros started to laugh and then restrained herself. The quick flash of her beautiful smile made him want to call Luci and see how she and the kids were doing. But right now he was fully focused on the mission. Calling home would have to wait.

...

Milagros took several deep breaths and reviewed the plan as she walked the last few blocks to work. Approaching the rear gate of the embassy, she inserted her ID badge into the designated slot and entered the guard shack at 11:45 p.m. The two men on duty looked away from the television just long enough to see who it was. The other two guards were probably asleep already in their break room on the opposite side of the embassy.

Milagros reached into her bag and placed a bottle of Venezuelan rum—Diplomático Exclusiva Reserva—on the table next to the television. "Para ustedes." The men's eyes opened wide and they thanked her for the gesture. Milagros passed through the guard shack and entered the embassy grounds.

Dulce sueños, chicos. Sweet dreams, boys.

. . .

Mark settled into a chair next to Kenny and his cyber team with a cup of coffee in the tactical operations center he had established just two blocks from the embassy. Next to them were two British operators representing MI-5, the United Kingdom's domestic security service, and General Communications Headquarters (GCHQ), the British counterpart to the Americans' National Security Agency. Mark's team appeared cool-minded and focused, ready for the mission. The two Brits looked anxious, as if they had drawn the short straws and had no choice but to be there. Mark understood their angst. But he also had his marching orders and would finish the mission come hell or high water.

Real-time video of the embassy interior populated Kenny's multi-screen work station. It was getting late and most of the staff had left for the night. SocraTeez sat in the chair in front of his computer, finishing a live interview with an Australian news outlet. He was wearing a blue oxford cloth button-down shirt and boxer shorts. SocraTeez rolled his eyes and chuckled as the female journalist listed some of the many crimes he stood accused of, including the hacking of the U.S. Joint Special Operations Command (JSOC) and subsequent publishing of soldiers' identities, dependents, and home addresses.

"Are you saying that knowing what you know now—that your actions have undeniably caused loss of human life and you are basically living in a kind of prison—you still have no regrets?" pressed the journalist. "No second thoughts at all? I find that hard to believe. No remorse?"

"None. Because I've done nothing wrong. I simply shine light where there is darkness. I expose corruption, hypocrisy, abuse of power. People make choices. Those people chose their professions and have to deal with the consequences. But what about you? Why are you silent when countries like the U.S. and its allies including Australia intentionally bomb entire families in the most poverty-stricken places on earth? You've seen the footage and photos. Why is that okay with you?"

"Intentionally? No, that's inaccurate. Accidents do happen, yes. But it's inaccurate to say that those tragedies are intentional. Yet you published the personal information of thousands of service members and their families, knowing full well that it would become a feeding frenzy for violent extremists and belligerent state actors. Isn't that true? Weren't you hoping for the subsequent targeted attacks in North Carolina, Georgia, and Texas, just to name a few?"

"You want the truth? The truth is I don't care either way. How's that? I haven't lost a wink. I sleep like a baby," he said through clenched teeth. "And you know what else? Can I tell you something about this so-called prison you say I live in?"

"Go ahead. I'll give you the last word," the interviewer replied professionally.

SocraTeez leaned in close to the camera on his computer and whispered creepily, "I'll still get laid tonight. Will you?" The journalist immediately ended the call. The screen went dead and he was immediately on his feet. His shirt came off and he began ranting out loud in Greek while admiring himself in the mirror on the far side of the room.

Mark and Kenny both shook their heads and looked at each other. There was nothing to say. SocraTeez was about to pay the piper anyway. *Almost time for your hemlock, asshole.*

Mark looked at his watch. *Shit.* He had wanted to say good night to his kids and now it was too late. But at least he could still touch base with Luci. He pulled out his phone and dialed the number.

CHAPTER SIX

Elicitation

Luci looked down at her phone and saw that she had three missed calls and a text from Mark.

Mark: You ok?
Luci: Yes, working. Training new detective. Talk later.

He responded almost immediately, telling her that he missed and loved her and would be home soon. She read the message, put her phone on "do not disturb," and placed it on the desk without replying.

Christian Goodwin, aka "Goodie", a former hockey player turned cop, was sitting next to her. Luci had never heard of him, but it seemed that every other cop in Massachusetts had. He was a two-time All-American forward at Boston College and played two seasons for the Boston Bruins before blowing out his knee. Goodie had his eyes fixed on the interrogation video they were reviewing together. But he was fully aware that she was mostly watching his reaction to the questioning as it unfolded on the screen in front of them.

The subject had been arrested for armed robbery. He had knocked over a 24-hour convenient store with a butcher knife. There were no images or footage of the crime because the security camera had previously been damaged and never fixed. The cops on duty had to go by the description that the clerk gave to the 911 operator. They found the perpetrator a few blocks away, but he had already ditched the weapon and money. Neither was recovered. He adamantly denied knowing anything about the robbery to the two policemen questioning him. Luci paused the tape.

"What do we have so far, Goodie?"

"Nothing we didn't know already. He's guilty as hell but not giving them anything."

"Why not?"

"Because bad guys don't like to confess?"

"Sure they do. Deep down, they all do because they want to be understood. They just need a little nudge. What about these two guys playing bad cop and worse cop?"

"A lot of yelling and table banging. High pressure. Intimidation. Lots of threats about doing hard time."

"Correct. Now keep watching and make a note if you see anything you and I have already talked about. I gave the guy fifteen to twenty minutes to cool off before giving it a shot." She pressed *play*. The two original questioners left the interrogation room. Then the tape cut to Luci entering alone with a plate of food and a legal pad. Goodie immediately smiled, nodded his head, and started scribbling notes. A short time later, Luci stopped the tape.

"What did you see?"

Goodie ran the fingers of both hands through his thick blond hair and took a few breaths. "Ah, yeah. I just saw a master in action. You got a confession—in writing—in about twenty minutes."

"Seventeen, actually. But how did I get it? What did I do?"

"Okay. Well, you were amazing right from the start. The first two guys were way over the top. No attempt to build rapport. All ego. But you checked yours at the door and got everything you wanted."

"Keep in mind, I think the guy is just as much of a dirtbag as the first two cops did. But you have to contain those feelings—even if you're sitting across from a murderer, child abuser, rapist, whatever. The point is to get information, preferably a confession, and not project your own feelings on the subject. Now, what specific techniques did you see me employ?" Luci continued.

Goodie read from his notes. "You started building rapport before you even spoke ... looked him in the eye, gave a quick eyebrow raise like two people greeting each other on the street, head slightly tilted, simulated smile ... greeted him professionally ... you gave him food when you didn't have to, which encourages reciprocity ... it also puts people at ease ... and I think you mentioned before that something like seventy percent of information exchanged between humans is done over food." Luci nodded. "You asked him a few easy questions while he ate. You downplayed the alleged crime by pointing out that nobody actually got hurt. You showed empathy and offered a few reasons why normally good people sometimes resort to extreme actions, like needing the money for medical bills. Then you left the room and returned with a cup of coffee, like a reward. You kept him from thinking about long-term consequences like jail and got him to concentrate on appeasing you instead. You kept saying, 'It's not the end of the world' and 'This isn't as bad as it sounds.' Whenever it sounded like he was about to deny doing it, you interrupted him, because once people verbalize a position they tend to dig in and not reverse themselves. Basically, you were right—he wanted to confess but needed a nudge and not a sledgehammer. I think you had him the minute you walked in the door."

"Very good. Two more things about the coffee. First, it's warm. People feel comfortable when they have a warm drink in their hands. Second, after he took the first sip, did you notice where he put the cup down? It sounds insignificant, but believe me, it's psychologically huge. If he places it on the table between us, he's using it as a protective barrier. That would have meant I hadn't built any rapport or trust with him. Instead, he placed it exactly where I wanted him to—off to the side—leaving nothing between us. That's when I knew his ass was mine."

"Seriously, I'm impressed. And lucky to get to train with you. I mean that."

Luci nodded at the compliment.

"This should be required viewing at the academy."

"Well, it's not. And I'd prefer to keep it that way."

"Why? It's useful and you look like a hero in it."

Luci shut down the computer and started gathering her things. "And what about the first two cops? How did they come off?"

"Not great," he answered.

"Exactly. So there's no need to share it. Listen, there's no shortage of people itching for the chance to criticize cops and throw us all under the bus. They don't need any help from the inside. Know what I mean?"

"Absolutely. And you're one hundred percent right. Team player. I was just so impressed with you, I never thought about that. This is why you're the mentor, right?"

"That. Plus, nobody else really wanted to work with you. They were all too worried they'd have to listen to you babble nonstop about hockey," she said, flashing her signature thousand-watt smile to make sure he knew she was kidding. They walked out of the station and into the parking lot. It was late in the evening but they chatted for a few more minutes.

"I meant what I said before. I feel lucky to get to train with someone like you. That was a stellar performance. You got everything you needed from that scumbag after those two bozos got nothing. I guess it doesn't hurt that you're ..." he cut himself off and didn't finish the sentence.

"That I'm what? A woman?"

"No. Hell no! I wasn't going to say that. What kind of sexist do you think I am? Actually, I was going to say it doesn't hurt that you're so ... easy on the eyes."

Goodie smiled and looked down at the pavement like an embarrassed schoolboy. Luci was caught off guard. They didn't know each other very well yet. He was pushing it. But she had to admit to herself that the compliment felt good—a much-needed boost to the ego—so she let it go.

"Good night, Goodie. It's quitting time. Homeward bound."

"Yeah, I know. But I'm not really in a rush. The only thing waiting for me is my cat."

"Well, I have two kids and a nanny waiting for me. Usually a German shepherd too, but he is currently on vacation."

"Does your husband work nights or something?"

"He's traveling. Again. Good night."

Goodie stood by as Luci got into her car and threw her bag into the passenger seat. As she backed out, he waved. She drove away shaking her head. She had been a cop for decades, and the men she had worked with over the years usually guarded their words and actions around her. Not because they were afraid of retribution, but because they respected her. If a colleague started to get out of line, she would simply give him a look and he would immediately feel as if he had just told a dirty joke and his mother overheard. Goodie's comment about her looks was flirty and his question about Mark a bit nosy, but in the grand scheme of things, neither was a big deal. He was ten or fifteen years younger and less experienced. It was all just harmless chitchat. Besides, she still had plenty of time to mold him.

CHAPTER SEVEN

Tea Time

Milagros opened her small locker in the employee break area and gazed at the thick silver bracelet on her wrist, engraved with the stations of the cross, for several seconds. It was a goodbye present from her grandmother when she accepted the job at the London Embassy. Her grandmother died several months later; word did not reach Milagros until the day after the funeral. The bracelet was the only possession she had taken with her when she left her small apartment for the last time earlier in the evening. After tonight, she would be starting life under a new identity. This would be her only connection to the past.

Milagros grabbed her faded red sweater from the locker and hung the bracelet in its place. Then she pinned up her long black hair and checked the time. SocraTeez would be ready for tea soon.

In the residential area she called out for Juanita, the other cleaning lady. There was no answer, and the door to SocraTeez's bedroom was closed. Milagros went to the basement of the building to check on the laundry. When she returned fifteen minutes later, the door was still closed. She called out for Juanita and again got no answer. Milagros started dusting. She stopped when the bedroom door opened and music spilled out into the common area.

Juanita emerged first. She adjusted her apron, gently touched the back of her bunned hair a few times, and tried to look innocent.

SocraTeez came out next. He was bare-chested and smoking an e-cigarette. He stopped when he saw Milagros.

"Jealous?" he asked, exhaling.

Milagros ignored the question. "Would you like your tea?" He nodded and sat down in front of his laptop. Milagros asked Juanita to finish the laundry, figuring that would keep her away long enough to do what needed to be done. Juanita sheepishly scurried away.

"I'll prepare it for you," Milagros said. She took a deep breath to calm her nerves. Then she glanced quickly in the direction of a video surveillance device she had placed months earlier and silently prayed to God that she had made the right decision.

. . .

In an underground garage three blocks east of the Venezuelan Embassy, Billy was sitting in the passenger seat of an ambulance. He could see silent video of the embassy interior on a small monitor. He had the sound off so he could talk smack to Quincy, a new guy and former U.S. Navy SEAL platoon medic who was organizing his equipment in the back of the ambulance. Once they got their hands on SocraTeez, Quincy would reverse the effects of the poison and sedate him. Both men were wearing EMT uniforms.

As Mark's right-hand man, Billy was in charge. The two had worked together for years and trusted one another with their lives. Both were world-class operators, but they had very different personalities. Mark was generally laid back—until he was forced not to be—and typically got along with operators of all stripes and backgrounds. Billy was generally more intense and instantly jelled with other operators—as long as they were current or former Delta operators. He viewed anyone else with a healthy competitiveness and skepticism until he got to know them. Until then, he kept the small talk to a minimum unless he was breaking someone's balls. And when he did break balls, they were usually attached to a SEAL.

"I forget, which stage of SEAL training is it where they teach you to write a book about being a SEAL?"

"It comes right after ... what was it ... trying to remember ... oh yeah, fuck you." Quincy was finishing a final check of his medical kit and his personal weapon, a suppressed Sig Sauer P226 9mm. "Actually, that's the short version. It's officially called 'Fuck you, Billy.' At least that's what it was called when I went through," he added with a smile.

"Don't take it so personally, man. I'm just saying that there seem to be quite a few books written by SEALs—I figured it was a requirement or something. Has the Navy considered giving sabbaticals so y'all don't have to wait until you retire or get fired to publish your shit?"

"You Delta boys have written plenty of books," Quincy pointed out matter-of-factly.

"Not nearly as many. And that's different. Those fuckers get declared PNG, and their pictures get ripped off the wall in the compound," said Billy, referring to Delta Force's headquarters at Fort Bragg, North Carolina. "But it's been nonstop books from SEALs going back to Marcinko, so I just assumed you guys were all kosher with it."

"Beckwith wrote a book."

"So what? What's your point?" Billy asked defensively.

"The founder of Delta Force wrote a book about Delta Force. Did you rip his portrait off the wall?"

"Totally different," answered Billy, waving off the comment like he was shooing a fly.

"How's that?"

"Because Beckwith gets a bye."

"Why does Beckwith get a bye?" Quincy asked incredulously.

"Because he does."

Quincy softly tapped Billy on the shoulder several times. "And I'm sure that makes perfect sense to you," he said in a tone that landed on Billy exactly as he intended—somewhere between sarcasm and condescension.

Billy inhaled and was about to reply when Sadie, sitting in the driver's seat, cut him off. She was Mark's top female operator. Besides Billy, she was the only other operator who had served covertly alongside

Mark in the Family. And although Mark had tremendous respect for all his operators, the three of them had a special bond.

"How about you both shut up for a while?" Sadie was paying close attention to the happenings inside the embassy and monitoring communications from Mark and Kenny in the command center. Her short blonde hair was tied behind her head in a stubby ponytail. Her seatbelt was fastened. A Glock 43 9mm was strapped to the inside of her left ankle. Whenever Mark gave the word, she would exit the underground garage and drive to the Venezuelan Embassy's staff entrance three blocks away. The Brits had the route blocked off from traffic and promised to blind neighborhood CCTV cameras along the way and jam digital communications until the ambulance had exited the area. "Seriously, you guys sound like two little boys," Sadie added.

"What?" Billy said pointing to the back of the ambulance. "He started it."

Sadie shook her head. "Thanks for proving my point," she said under her breath. "Now shut up for a second. I want to be able to hear." She reached down to the secure tactical communications device attached to her belt and depressed the talk button. "Kenny, are there any other camera angles or am I getting everything we have available?"

. . .

"You have everything we have. The main areas we need are covered, but there's definitely a lot of blind space. Sorry," answered Kenny from the tactical operations center.

Mark was standing behind Kenny's chair with his arms folded across his chest. He tapped a few fingers against the ultra-thin body armor under his shirt. In one hand he held clear tactical glasses that featured a heads-up video display. The 3D printed shades were perfectly customized according to Mark's precise measurements. Once the action started, he would be able to see live video feeds from Billy, Sadie, and Quincy's perspectives. He gripped his custom-molded tactical earbuds in the other hand. If things got loud, the earbuds functioned as hearing protection. But they could also be used to filter and manipulate audio in real time, allowing him to amplify the things he wanted to hear while suppressing everything else. They were a particularly useful tool for eavesdropping on specific targets in noisy venues. All you needed was a digital audio sample of the target's voice. Then you could simply amplify the voice or voices you wanted to hear and suppress the rest of the crowd. Once inserted, the buds were barely noticeable.

The two Brits looked nervous. Mark gave them a nod and a quick flash of a smile. "Appreciate your help, guys. We'll be out of your hair—and SocraTeez will be out of everyone's hair—within the hour." Both nodded back politely, but Mark could tell they were dying to get this episode over with. He looked back at the screen. SocraTeez was typing away on his laptop when Milagros appeared in the doorway, carrying a tea platter.

"Showtime," Kenny announced.

Over the preceding months, Milagros had learned how to avoid SocraTeez's wandering hands. She stopped several feet from the table, extended her arms, and placed the tray next to SocraTeez's laptop. He seized the cup and brought it to his lips without taking his eyes off the screen. Just a few sips would be enough. Milagros felt her whole body tense up. She looked directly into the surveillance camera again as she exited the room, appearing mortified.

"Hang in there, Milagros. Just get him to the gate when it's time," Kenny said aloud, even though he knew she could not hear his words of encouragement.

Mark took a step closer to Kenny. "Is everyone in position?"

"Check."

The Brits were watching the video and talking into their phones. Mark placed a hand on Kenny's shoulder and lowered his voice so they wouldn't hear. "That means everyone, right?"

Kenny turned his head ninety degrees and nodded. "He's there."

...

Milagros hummed to herself as she dusted the windows in the main hallway outside the residence. She kept checking the time. Her mind was racing. She had hoped the humming would calm her nerves, but instead it was making things worse because she kept forgetting the tune.

Her eyes scanned up and down the hall anxiously and she wondered if Mark's team could tell that she was hanging on by a thread. She felt a panic attack creeping up on her and kept it at bay with deep breaths as Mark had taught her. *Breathe deep. Hold it. Let it out slowly. Repeat.* She was still petrified, but it helped to take the edge off.

Within just seven minutes, she could hear moans coming from the residence. They started slowly, like someone reacting to a rough hit in an American football game.

"Ohhhhh."

She looked up and down the hall and moved closer to the door. The moaning grew louder and sharper. Milagros leaned sideways so she could peer inside the residence.

"Fuck!"

SocraTeez was bent over, resting his head on the keyboard. Both arms were wrapped around his midsection. He wondered what the hell was happening. He had felt fine all day; now he felt as if he had just swallowed a razor blade. His breathing became labored and he started to panic. This was not normal. And it was not going to pass. He tried to stand up, but he couldn't take his hands off his midsection. SocraTeez's legs buckled and he collapsed into a ball on the floor. He looked up. Milagros was standing over him.

"Doctor," he said as loud as he could—which ended up being only a whisper.

She stared down at him, frozen. The blood drained from her face. SocraTeez gasped for more air. "Doc … tor … get me a fucking doctor!"

Mark and the rest of the team were silently on the edge of their seats for the next few seconds. You never really know how people will react in a high-stress tactical situation, regardless of their training. And this was a cleaning lady with no experience, at the center of an audacious mission. Would she succumb to the freeze and botch the mission? Or would she dig deep and muster the steel to pull this off? Milagros inhaled deeply through her nose until she thought her lungs would burst and broke the freeze.

"Sí!" she replied and ran out of the room. SocraTeez rolled back and forth in a ball on the floor until she returned and knelt next to him. She put a hand on his back. "The embassy physician is traveling. The nurse on call will be here in twenty to thirty minutes," she said convincingly.

"No! No! Can't wait … call an ambulance! I can't wait that long! Call 911!" he pleaded.

"I can't. We have orders. You are not allowed to leave without permission from the Ambassador himself. I'll get in trouble and lose my job. I told the nurse to hurry. She will be here as quick as she can."

SocraTeez lay silent for several seconds until the pain worsened. He started to sweat profusely. "Call! Make the call! Fuck your job—I'm gonna die before she gets here! Do it now … please … please!" he begged.

She looked him in the eyes as he writhed on the floor. Feeling a moment of sympathy for him, she quickly reminded herself that he was an international criminal and a pig. "Okay. I'll call but they can't enter the embassy grounds. You will have to get to the back gate. I will help."

Milagros left the room for a brief moment—just long enough that he would think she had made the call to 911. Then she helped him get to his feet. With SocraTeez doubled over in intense pain, they slowly shuffled out the door. He fell several times while moving down the hall. At the top of the stairs, they paused briefly. All she had to do was get him to the bottom of the stairs, exit the building, and cross the parking lot to the gate where the ambulance would be waiting. Milagros took a deep breath.

"Let's go. Keep moving. We are almost there."

. . .

Billy, Sadie, and Quincy were on their way in the ambulance with the lights and siren off. Mark and Kenny watched the monitors. The coast was clear all the way to the gate. The few embassy employees on the grounds were either sleeping or otherwise distracted. As long as they kept moving, Milagros and SocraTeez should be able to walk out the door and right into the ambulance. Within the hour, everyone involved would be on a plane bound for the United States.

The pain intensified even more and SocraTeez fell to the ground at the bottom of the steps. For a moment Mark worried that the pain had become too crippling for him to move. But Milagros quickly stepped up. She grabbed SocraTeez by the leg and dragged him toward the exit. When he screamed out, she reached down, grabbed him by the hair, and told him to shut up if he wanted to live.

"Damn," remarked Kenny. "She's even tougher than I thought."

At the exit, Milagros struggled to get SocraTeez to his feet. She pushed open the door and welcomed the cool air as the two made their way across the moonlit parking lot. They were moving much too slowly for anybody's liking. But at least they were moving.

"Ready for pickup," said Sadie as she brought the ambulance to a stop outside the gate. Billy exited from the passenger side and quickly moved to the rear of the vehicle. Quincy exited from the rear. They approached the guard shack. Both guards were out cold from the sedative-spiked rum Milagros had gifted them earlier. They could see Milagros and SocraTeez approaching through the bars of the gate.

"Keep moving. Keep moving. You're doing great. Don't stop, Milagros. Do not stop," encouraged Billy. Once inside the guard shack, she let SocraTeez fall to the floor. His head bounced off the concrete with a thud. She reached behind the reception counter, felt for the door release, and depressed the button. A brief buzzing sound was followed by a metallic click. Billy pulled the gate open. He and Quincy both entered and each grabbed SocraTeez by an arm.

"It's okay. Try to relax. We'll take care of you. Everything is going to be grand," said Billy in the best London accent his Oklahoma mouth could muster. It wasn't very convincing. Quincy suppressed his laughter.

When Billy and SocraTeez were safely inside the ambulance, Quincy turned around to assist Milagros. She was frozen in the exit. He extended his hand to encourage her.

"Come on! Come on! Let's go. One more step and you're home free!"

But Milagros didn't move. It was as if she was being held in the doorway by some invisible force. "Let's go!" he repeated in a more assertive tone. She didn't move. Then she looked down and rubbed her bare wrist in a panic.

"No. No. Wait. I forget something!" she exclaimed.

Quincy watched dumbfounded as she quickly turned around, exited the guard shack, and ran back into the compound. "Shit! Are you guys seeing this? What do you want us to do, Mark?"

. . .

Mark saw the look in Milagros's eyes when she froze and knew something was seriously wrong before she started to turn back toward the embassy.

Click.

"Leave the exterior gate unlocked. Give her sixty seconds. Then get the hell out of there," answered Mark.

"Roger," replied Quincy.

Kenny turned around and looked at Mark. His tactical glasses were fastened firmly around his head and he was inserting his ear buds. Thirty seconds passed. "What the hell is she doing? All she needs is the clothes on her back. Why would she go back inside?" asked Kenny. When he didn't get a reply, he repeated the question and turned to face Mark. But when he spun around in his chair, there was nothing behind him but empty space. Mark was already on the street in a full sprint toward the Venezuelan Embassy.

. . .

Milagros reentered the building. She was moving as fast as she could, but the adrenaline and fear were inhibiting her coordination. Grabbing the handrail tightly, she descended two flights of stairs to the basement level. She entered the employee break room, scurried to her locker, and started fumbling with the padlock. Her fine motor skills were shot. She forced herself to breathe and focus. The lock finally popped open. She opened the door and grabbed her grandmother's silver bracelet from its hook. She felt a modicum of relief as she headed for the door. Now she could walk away and never look back.

She twisted the knob, pulled open the door, and immediately recoiled. Standing between her and the life she had just earned—the life she deserved—was her boss. It was the first time she had ever seen him in the embassy at night. She could smell his booze-soaked mustache as the large man stumbled forward, pushed her back into the room, and closed the door behind him.

. . .

The ambulance was safely on its way to the extraction point when Mark arrived at the embassy gate. It was open. Both guards were still unconscious, but Mark didn't know how much longer they would stay that way. He entered the compound and sprinted across the parking lot toward the building.

"Talk to me, Kenny."

"She's in the break room on the bottom floor. The coast is clear the whole way, but she's not alone."

"Third door on the left, correct? Lockers are inside to the right?" Out of habit, Mark had memorized the embassy floor plan during the operational planning phase.

"Roger," Kenny confirmed.

"Who is she with?"

"Some big guy with a humongous mustache," answered Kenny. "We don't have any audio but it looks like he's giving her a hard time. She's trying to get away but he's backed her up against the lockers. He looks shitfaced. Doesn't appear to be armed."

"Got it."

. . .

The boss had Milagros pinned against the lockers. She squirmed but couldn't break free. He was babbling incoherently about being underappreciated by his ungrateful wife, who was threatening to leave him after all he had done for her. She almost gagged on his thick, acrid breath.

"Por favor! Por favor! Suéltame!" *Please! Please! Let me go!*

She struggled, but he ignored her pleas and pressed harder to keep her in place. When it became clear that Milagros was entirely unsympathetic to his plight and not about to acquiesce to his demands, he put his hands around her neck and started to choke her into submission. She pulled and clawed at his thick hairy arms and gasped for air. Worried that he would kill her, she banged her fists against the lockers and prayed that help would arrive before it was too late. Neither of them heard the break room door open.

Mark wrapped his left arm around the big man's neck from behind. Then he jerked backwards and squeezed as hard as he could. The drunk let go and tried to gain his balance. Milagros's hands reflexively went to her throat and she fell to the floor. Mark's arms were locked tight as a vise, with pressure focused on the carotid artery. The simple chokehold would restrict the target's ability to breathe while simultaneously restricting blood flow to the brain. The threat was out cold in less than thirty seconds. Mark took the unconscious man's ID badge and clipped it to his own belt. Milagros was catching her breath. Mark held out his hand.

"Let's go. All we have to do is walk out."

"Mark, this is Kenny. You've got company."

Mark looked at Milagros and held an index finger to his lips. "Go ahead," he replied to Kenny.

"Three guards snooping around in the hallway. They must have heard the noise. Only one of them is armed, as far as I can see. Sending you the live feed."

"Got it." Mark turned to Milagros. "Don't worry. Don't say anything. Just walk with me. That's all you have to do. Smile if you can." The two approached the door and grasped the doorknob. "Let's both take a deep breath first, okay? You're going to be fine. You can do this."

Milagros nodded. Mark opened the door and they exited into the hallway.

. . .

The three guards were at the end of the hallway when Mark and Milagros emerged from the break room, holding hands. Mark was smiling. The guard with the sidearm called out to them, asking if they had heard a ruckus. Mark ignored him. He spoke to Milagros in a low voice as they slowly made their way down the hall toward the only exit.

"Listen very closely. I don't want to shoot these guys, but I will if I have to," he said, tapping a hand on the Springfield XDS compact 9mm tucked inside his waistline in the appendix position. "For now, let's see how close we can get to the one with the gun before he notices that the guy on the ID badge with the huge mustache isn't me. Okay? Sound good?"

Milagros nodded with a blank stare on her face. The danger was palpable. She could smell it in the hallway. Mark worried about her going into shock.

Keep her moving. The more she moves, the less time she has to think about how fucked we might be. Keep. Moving.

Mark smiled and waved at the guard when he called out a second time. "What kind of noise did you say it was?" he asked cheerfully in the best Venezuelan accent he could mimic. It wasn't very good. But since Mark's demeanor was calm and he was with Milagros—a loyal patriotic employee— he hoped it was good enough to buy the few precious seconds he needed to get closer to the threat. He whispered under his breath for Milagros to keep walking. The guard started to explain the banging noise they had heard minutes before. Mark nodded as if he were listening.

When they were within just a few feet, the guard looked down and squinted at the ID badge on Mark's belt. Before he could look up, Mark released Milagros's hand, stepped forward, and delivered an explosive elbow uppercut to the chin. The blistering strike snapped the man's head backwards, overloading his central nervous system before his brain even realized he had been hit. The back of his skull hit the tile with a loud crack that echoed throughout the hallway.

With the armed guard unconscious, Mark oriented his attention to the other two. One was frozen in place. The other—the youngest of the three—was already in motion, charging directly at him. He swung at Mark's head. Mark took a step back and let the punch whiz by his head. Then he dropped to a low crouch and attempted a strike to the side of the knee—a move that would typically tear and crush the ligaments enough to immobilize the threat. But the younger man must have seen it coming. He stutter-stepped to throw off Mark's timing and pulled his leg out of the way as he passed by. Mark struck air. Both men spun around to face each other. The guard attacked again without hesitation—moving his body like he knew what he was doing.

We've got a fighter, ladies and gentlemen! Testy little bastard, aren't you?

He threw a flurry of punches at Mark's head and upper body. Mark dodged and parried as he backed up. When none of the blows landed, the guard moved in closer, as if he wanted to try to grapple his way to victory instead. Mark locked arms and moved backwards, forcing his foe to increase his forward momentum. The inexperienced guard misread the movement and, assuming that he was gaining the upper hand, pushed forward hard with his legs like a rugby player. Mark held on tight to his arms. Then he pulled back violently while simultaneously swiveling his hips and partially turning his back to his opponent. The complex move— known in Brazilian jiu jitsu as the Uchi Mata—sent the guard flying through the air in a forward roll. Knowing that experienced fighters could anticipate hard landings and adjust their bodies to mitigate the impact, Mark accelerated his opponent through the fall to disrupt the catch-fall reflex and throw off his timing. As a result, instead of the guard landing flat on his back, all his weight came crashing down on the back of his neck. He rolled onto his stomach, stunned. Before he could move, Mark came down on him forcefully with both knees—one to the back of the head and one to the kidney. Guard number two was out of commission and would piss blood for the next week.

After witnessing how quickly Mark had incapacitated his two colleagues, guard number three broke his freeze and ran for the exit.

Mark looked to Milagros. "Keep moving toward the door!" He took off down the hall after the final guard, hoping to catch up with him before he could sound the alarm. He could hear Kenny's voice in his ear along the way.

"Mark, it looks like the guy in the break room is starting to move."

"Got it."

Just as the guard reached for the door, Mark hit him from behind at a slightly upward angle with all his weight. His face hit before the rest of his body. A broken nose sent blood splattering as he bounced off the door. Mark swept both legs, sent him crashing to the tile, and landed on top of him with a stiff elbow to the side of the neck. The guard was still conscious, but sufficiently incapacitated that he wouldn't be a problem. Mark called out to Milagros and waved her forward. As she reached the exit, Mark cocked his head to scan the hallway behind her.

Shit.

Milagros's boss stumbled out of the break room. He bent over and rested his hands on his knees while he caught his breath and tried to shake out the cobwebs. He saw the downed guards and caught a glimpse of Mark and Milagros as they rushed through the exit. The door closed behind them.

"You gotta move faster, Milagros!" declared Mark. She was walking as if wearing concrete shoes. "Come on! Come on!" She picked up the pace. Mark scanned for threats and made sure that she didn't fall as they ascended the stairs. Then he spoke to someone else. "Chucky, this is Mark."

"Go ahead," replied a gravelly voice.

"We'll be out the door in about five seconds and we may have company. You got me, right?" There was urgency in Mark's voice. In his haste to neutralize the second and third guards, he hadn't had time to take the sidearm from the first. He was worried that Milagros's boss might notice and try to be a hero.

"Check. I'll have you the whole way."

Milagros froze when they reached the bottom of the stairs. There was no time for talk or encouragement. Mark wrapped a hand around her bicep and jerked her toward the exit, leaving the other hand free to access his weapon should he need it. Heavy footsteps echoed from the stairwell above as they exited into the cool air.

"Mark, this is Kenny. Your backup ride is at the gate. Two Brits. Blue car. Female driver. Male in passenger seat."

Milagros stumbled with a thousand-yard stare on her face. The stress was overwhelming. She was fading. Mark had to practically drag her across the parking lot. Finally, she collapsed. He hoisted her back to her feet and looked back at the building. Milagros's boss stumbled out the door in pursuit, a semiautomatic pistol in his hand. Mark and Milagros neared the guard shack. Their pursuer raised the pistol and pointed it at them.

Nestled between two smokestacks on a rooftop seven hundred meters away, the sniper took a deep breath. Barely five feet tall and dressed in his trademark overalls, Chucky, a twenty-year veteran and legend in Boston SWAT before joining Mark's team, slowly exhaled as he acquired his target. The custom suppressor at the end of the barrel would take most of the edge off the weapon's report, and a nearby after-hours party with live music would mask any remaining noise that could give away his position. Someone along the trajectory might hear a crack above their heads, but they were unlikely to know it was a sniper round breaking the sound barrier on the way to its target.

Chucky held his breath and smoothly pressed the trigger of the U.S. Army M24 SWS (Sniper Weapon System), sending a 7.62x51 bullet spiraling across the London skyline. The round sliced through the air, over the back gate of the Venezuelan Embassy, and hit the target exactly where Chucky had intended—smack dab in the mustache—sending a chunk of the man's skull flying when it exited the back of his head. He crumpled to the ground and dropped the gun. It skipped across the pavement.

The two British agents in the car scanned for threats as Mark pushed Milagros to the floor in the back seat and lay on top of her to shield her from danger. Nobody spoke until they were several blocks away and certain that they hadn't been followed. The male agent unfastened his seatbelt and turned around to check on his passengers.

"Everyone okay?"

"Yeah. She's scared shitless but she's not hurt," Mark answered between breaths.

"What about you, mate?"

"I'm good."

"Let's have a quick look anyway." Even experienced operators could suffer grave injuries and be completely unaware of them, especially when their focus was on someone else's safety. With a penlight clenched between his teeth, he ran his hands down over Mark's shoulders and down his back to check for injuries. Mark understood the purpose and let him do it. After a quick body scan, the Brit slapped him on the back. "You look good to me, mate."

"We're clear," declared the driver.

Mark rubbed Milagros's shoulder and ensured her that everything would be okay. It was over. They would link up with the others in just a few minutes. Advising her to stay on the floor as a precaution, Mark climbed off her, sat on the back seat, and took several deep breaths. Then he checked in with Kenny.

The rest of the team was standing by at the extraction point, ready to go as soon as Mark arrived. Milagros had done her part and was about to start life over with a brand-new identity and a pile of cash. SocraTeez was sedated and bound to a stretcher. His future would be much different. Even though the covert U.S. surveillance of him over the previous months had yielded a treasure trove of information and actionable intelligence, he would be aggressively interrogated and extensively probed for every last drop of data they could squeeze from him. It was rare to have someone like SocraTeez alive and in captivity, so intelligence community shrinks would get a crack at him too. They would try to determine what made him tick and work up a psychological profile that could be used to help identify and thwart others.

After that, his fate was anybody's guess. They could stick him in a cell far below the earth's surface where he would never see sunlight or a blade of grass ever again. Or if he was lucky, they may simply dispose of him. Only two things were sure: SocraTeez would have no say in the matter, and Mark didn't give a shit. His work was done.

The dead guy back at the Venezuelan Embassy was unfortunate collateral damage, but Kenny and his team of cyber illusionists were already on the case. They would return control of the embassy's communications to the Venezuelans as soon as possible—but with a twist. Investigators would roll back the video to piece together what happened. They would see SocraTeez walking toward the rear gate and Milagros's boss attempting to confront him. Then they would see SocraTeez turn, pull a pistol from his waistband, and casually shoot him in the face before exiting the grounds alone. To muddy the waters further, Kenny's team would push a half-dozen conspiracy theories—ranging from "SocraTeez was actually a foreign agent" (from any number of different countries) to "it's all a hoax, SocraTeez never really existed"—across the dark web. The Brits would publicly decline comment, citing the existence of an ongoing investigation, but would privately feed whichever explanation suited them best until things blew over.

Mark checked the time and then gazed out the window and thought of his family. The twins should be sleeping peacefully in their beds. He wondered if Luci was home or out on the street doing her job. She was near retirement but determined to work hard to the finish line. He hoped she was safe. Then he felt a tinge of guilt, but he quickly shrugged it off. He had promised Luci that his role these days would be strictly supervisory—no door kicking. But what was he supposed to do? Milagros had put it all on the line to help nail SocraTeez. He couldn't have left her behind, so he did what he had to do. And truth be told, he relished the adrenaline rush and craved more of it.

Mark couldn't wait to get home and hug his kids. He hoped for time to lay on the floor and play games with them before heading to Berlin to meet with Heike and her German intelligence counterparts. She had been hinting that they knew more about Oleg Borodin than anyone else, and that by working together they could take him down quicker. But first they had to find him. And right now his location was anybody's guess.

CHAPTER EIGHT

Turnover

Oleg peered out over the Dubai skyline from the thirtieth-floor window of his luxury hotel suite. He used his shoulder to keep the phone to his ear while he adjusted his black sapphire cufflinks. His white shirt was perfectly pressed; his hair was uncombed and still slightly damp from the steam bath. A thin layer of clouds blanketed the city. In the distance, a rooftop construction crane poked through the blurry haze like a ship on water. There was a firm knock at the door. Oleg ended the phone call and fastened the leather band of his vintage Omega wristwatch.

"You are early, Dmitri," he said on the way to the door. "Come inside and give me a minute." Dmitri entered the suite and closed the door. Then he stood off to the side and silently waited for directions— avoiding direct eye contact with Oleg the whole time.

Oleg disappeared into the suite to gather some of his things. He returned with a rolling suitcase and a Louis Vuitton garment bag. He removed something black from the bag and placed the item on a chair. He checked the time again and peered down the long hall of the suite that led to the bedrooms. *Now is as good a time as any*, he thought to himself.

"I have one more thing to do. Take my things to the car and wait for me there," he said, turning back to Dmitri. Then Oleg looked down at his pristine white shirt and snapped his fingers. "Give me your jacket first." Dmitri obliged and left with the bags. Oleg put Dmitri's sport coat on backwards to cover his outfit. He didn't want to chance getting blood on it.

In the room at the end of the hall, Fabio was planted in an easy chair in front of the widescreen television. He had been watching a Steven Segal movie marathon on a local United Arab Emirates cable channel. But since the audio was dubbed in Arabic and he could not read the subtitles in any of the available languages, he had fallen asleep and was snoring loudly.

Oleg walked down the hall, whistling as if he were strolling through the park. In his head he was going through a checklist of loose ends that needed to be tied up. He had sold off most of his assets and dispersed much of his wealth to accounts across the globe. Another sizable chunk would be converted into anonymous cryptocurrencies. He was less than thrilled with the volatility that would accompany the move to digital money, but the anonymity offered by cryptocurrencies made any potential losses more acceptable. Besides, it's much easier to stomach a loss when the money wasn't yours to begin with. He had stolen every penny.

Oleg approached the easy chair and looked down. Fabio was sleeping peacefully as Steven Segal unrealistically punched and clotheslined his way through multiple waves of attackers. He was a simple man and had served Oleg well, but he still had to go. It was simply good policy to tie up loose ends permanently—a lesson Oleg had learned from his historical hero Genghis Khan, who managed to forever conceal the location of his grave from his foes by arranging in advance for his entire funeral procession to be killed on site, with the final man committing suicide. He was supposedly buried somewhere in Mongolia, but nobody knew where. Oleg smiled. Even in death, Genghis Khan continued to outsmart his enemies.

He refocused on the task at hand and looked down at the top of Fabio's head. He picked out what he thought would be a good spot and turned up the TV. Oleg clasped the ice pick with both hands and raised it high above his head. He took one deep breath and brought it down with all of his strength as Steven Segal opened fire with a machine gun. Fabio's moans were drowned out by the sound of movie gunfire. Oleg let go and watched the big man's body convulse and vibrate for a few seconds. Then he removed Dmitri's sport coat and draped it over Fabio's head.

Oleg checked his shirt. Satisfied that there were no bloodstains, he casually walked back down the hall toward the front door without a second thought. Killing Fabio was simply just another thing on his long to-do list. He retrieved the black garment he had pulled from his bags. It was a large women's burqa. He dropped it over his head. With his identity and figure concealed, he left the suite and quietly made his way to the elevators.

...

"Airport," said Oleg as he settled into the back seat. "And turn up the air conditioning."

Dmitri pulled out of the underground parking garage. Oleg waited until they were on the highway before removing the burqa and tossing it aside. After checking quickly for encrypted messages on his satellite phone, he wiped the sweat from his brow and opened a cold plastic bottle of water. He removed a comb and a small compact mirror from his pocket.

"Tell me, Dmitri. Are you familiar at all with Genghis Khan?"

Dmitri looked at Oleg in the rear view mirror and furled his brow. "Sir?"

"Genghis Khan. The great Mongolian leader."

"No, sir."

Oleg finished combing his hair. He turned his head side to side to check his work in the mirror and snapped it shut. "Then it's settled. You are my new assistant. Fabio had other plans."

CHAPTER NINE

Mcmucker

"Watch how fast Max takes him down," said Kenny, pointing a finger at the monitor. He was sitting at his workstation with the newest member of his team, Kimberly, a recent MIT grad and the only cyber operator Kenny had ever chased after to recruit. Having cut her teeth at the institution's world-famous Media Lab—a global epicenter of technological research and innovation—she had no shortage of job offers when she walked across the stage, snatched her diploma from the university president's hands and squeezed him around his portly waist. The aging scholar turned red, the crowd erupted in applause, and Kenny wanted her on the team even more. He knew Mark would like her too. She was brilliant.

But straight-up tech smarts and digital chops weren't enough to impress the boss. Mark didn't want one-dimensional people. Operators—cyber or other—had to be well-rounded. He needed people who knew a lot about the world, but who were also keenly aware of how much they didn't know and had an unquenchable thirst to bridge that gap. People who, like Mark, always needed a mountain to climb. It was difficult to define, but he knew it when he saw it. They had swagger and a twinkle in their eye. Kimberly appeared to have those attributes in spades, with a splash of badass. And so far, she was a perfect fit. Kenny and Mark were both happy with the hire, and she felt like a fully accepted member of the team.

"Daaayum, that was fast! How did Max even know that guy was an assassin?" asked Kimberly after watching their operator walk down a busy sidewalk and suddenly take down a nearby pedestrian without warning. "Seriously, he just looked like some guy standing there on the corner. How did Max know?"

"I thought the same thing at first until Mark pointed it out for me. Let me go back and show you," answered Kenny. They both watched as he rewound the video in slow motion. Max's body jolted upright from the ground. Then he and the other pedestrians slowly walked backwards across the screen. Kenny froze the scene when Max was about ten feet away from the threat along the sidewalk. Max was on an executive protection detail, working the forward point of a floating security box. The protectee—a senior bureaucrat in the U.S. Treasury Department responsible for East Asia—was positioned behind Max in the center of the square, where he could be protected on all sides. As he moved, the formation would move with him and make necessary adjustments to keep him within the safety of the box at all times.

"Now watch." Kenny played the video forward at half speed.

"Which clip is this?" Mark was standing behind Kenny and Kimberly with his fingers laced behind his head. He was rotating his upper body back and forth to stretch his lower back, which had been sore since his return from London. Most likely he had strained a muscle while taking down the three guards in the hallway of the Venezuelan embassy. At age forty-seven, Mark still worked hard to maintain his physical skills. And so far, so good—he hadn't lost his step yet. But his recovery times were getting longer and he was starting to feel the physical toll from a long career in special operations. He knew the day would eventually come when his body wouldn't perform the way his mind wanted it to, so he tried not to think about it. "Is this Max's Hong Kong clip?" he asked.

"Yup. Mighty Max's Magnificent Hong Kong adventure," answered Kimberly without taking her eyes off the screen.

Kenny paused the action. "Right there. You see the guy's left hand? It's in his pocket, right? You know what he's doing?" Kenny asked

70

rhetorically before explaining.

The assassin had a handgun tucked deep into the front of his beltline without a holster. With his hand in his front pocket, he could place his index finger into the barrel and push the gun upward until the handle popped out of his waistband. Then he could grip and draw the weapon with his free hand and engage the target. It was a common tactic among Filipino organized crime thugs. This particular henchman had been sent to assassinate the American bureaucrat in retaliation for his push for economic sanctions that would strangle the organization's ability to operate.

"Bad luck for the assassin that Max recognized the tactic and clicked before he could even draw his gun."

"What do you mean, he clicked?" asked Kimberly.

Kenny explained "clicking" exactly as Mark had explained it to him when he was new to the team. It was how operators described the initial recognition of a threat. If they returned to their hotel room and things looked different from how they had left it—they would click. If someone in a crowd didn't seem to fit in—click. If the car behind them was following too closely—click. If a person of interest narrowed his or her eyes, inhaled sharply, or, as in the Hong Kong example, suddenly moved a hand near the beltline—click. Once an operator clicks, he or she can assess the threat and respond. Max had clicked when the would-be assassin put a hand in his pocket and made furtive movements. From there he sprang into action and smashed his target to the ground, rendering him unconscious before he could access his weapon. It was a textbook example of clicking at the right time.

"Got it. Cool," Kimberly responded. She and Kenny spun around to face the boss. Mark was signing off on some paperwork for another team member. When he finished, he returned the clipboard and redirected his attention to the pair in front of him.

"How are you doing, Kimberly? Still glad to be here?"

"Hell, yeah. No regrets. Not yet, at least," she answered.

"Refresh my memory. How did Kenny finally convince you to join the team?"

"I was looking for a serious job in a serious place, not a job in an office that felt like a daycare center. I'm not into laser tag and foosball tables. You offered me a career and didn't talk to me like I was a child."

"How's all that working out for you?"

"So far, so good. Although an air hockey table might be nice to have around the office," she suggested with a smile.

Mark turned to Kenny. "You're coming for a ride with me. We'll be in the car for a few hours so we can get some work done on the way. You have some updates for me, right?"

"I do."

"Good. But first—" Mark pointed to Kimberly but kept his eyes on Kenny—"bring her up to speed on all things Oleg Borodin. Maybe she can answer the million-dollar question I've been asking for months. It might be unknowable at this point. But maybe a fresh perspective will help."

"Okay. Good idea," Kenny answered, scratching the top of his head unconsciously. He wasn't entirely sure which question Mark was referring to. They still had lots of unanswered questions about the Russian.

Mark sensed his confusion and spoke directly to Kimberly. "We don't know as much about Borodin as we'd like to—yet. So we're piecing it all together as best we can. Bottom line, we still have no idea why Borodin was in Boston in the first place when Kenny and Billy had their run-in with him. See if you can find out why he was here in town. Maybe he was just passing through. Figure it out and you'll make a name for yourself quickly around here, and your quarterly bonuses will reflect that. Then you can buy as many air hockey tables as you want."

"I'm on it," she answered.

"Kimberly, I'll give you access to everything right now," said Kenny, tapping on the keyboard in front of him. "Mark, I'll meet you in your car in like ten minutes if that works for you?"

"It does." Mark turned and headed toward his office, calling back over his shoulder as he walked. "Impress me, Kimberly."

. . .

Mark and Kenny sped north on I-93 toward the middle of New

Hampshire. Kenny was working on his laptop in the passenger seat of Mark's Range Rover.

"Are you going to tell me where we're going?" asked Kenny.

"Yeah, we're going to pick up Murphy," answered Mark. "He's been up north getting a training tuneup for the past week. I need to bring him home before my kids disown me."

Kenny looked up from his laptop. "We're going to get your dog from the trainer?"

"Yup."

"And you need me for this?"

"Not really. I just figured you might want to meet him."

"Meet Murphy? We've met. The dog loves me."

"I'm wasn't talking about Murphy," Mark answered as he maneuvered into the middle lane to pass several slow cars on the far left. "I'm talking about McMucker."

"McMucker? The Irish guy you trained with? Get the hell outta here. I've been dying to meet that guy."

"And you will in about an hour," answered Mark. "In the meantime, show me what you've got going on."

Kenny briefed Mark on the status of several teams of operators they had deployed around the globe. Max's executive protection team had finished its mission in Hong Kong and would be back in Boston by the end of the day. Then they would only have a few days to unwind and do maintenance on their gear before traveling to South America ahead of a senior American intelligence official's multi-state visit. Two other surveillance teams were operating in Central and Southeast Asia. Another team had conducted a raid that morning on a safe house in the Horn of Africa, but the al-Qaeda operative they were after was gone by the time they kicked in the door.

"The team leader thinks the locals may have tipped him off that the heat was on," said Kenny.

"Shocking," Mark responded sarcastically. "See why my default setting is to not tell anyone jack shit unless they absolutely, positively need to know? You can't trust many people in this business."

Kenny nodded and then asked, "Is that why we didn't tell the Brits we had Chucky on a rooftop within sniping range of the Venezuelan Embassy? Because we don't trust them?"

"Not really. It's more that I didn't want to give them a chance to object or otherwise throw a monkey wrench into the operation. Simply applying the old adage that it's better to ask forgiveness than permission," Mark added as he exited the highway. It would be all back roads the rest of the way to McMucker's farm.

Kenny showed Mark some of the new technologies in which he and Kimberly had been immersing themselves. Both men were impressed by but also worried about the ease with which false audio and video files could be produced. Kenny played a few practice videos that he had created using the new techniques. One showed Kenny scoring the winning goal for Brazil in a World Cup match from more than a decade earlier. Another put both Kenny and Kimberly on the infamous grassy knoll in Dallas as John F. Kennedy's fated motorcade rolled past.

"Okay, last one. This one is my favorite," declared Kenny. It was the final play of game six of the 1986 World Series—something most Red Sox fans don't care to remember—when a slow ground ball rolled right through first baseman Bill Buckner's legs. But in this version, Kenny, playing first base in Buckner's place, easily gloved the ball and made the out.

"Jesus, this stuff has come a long way since Forrest Gump," said Mark.

"It's come a long way since last week. That's how fast this tech moves. On one hand, it's cool as hell. On the other, it's frightening. Once this stuff hits the mainstream, people will be able to create files that appear to support their interests and positions, no matter how crazy those interests and positions might be. And people caught red-handed doing stupid things will just claim the evidence is fake. People are going to question anything and everything they see and hear. We're heading for a major societal turning point once this shit gets unleashed. People won't know which way is up or down and it'll drive them crazy. And all you need is a few pictures, a brief voice sample, maybe a video of them taken in public to make a decent fake. It's not like you need their DNA."

Mark shook his head and tried not to think about it. Bad actors had long been using technology to deceive and blur the lines between fact and fiction. But putting these specific capabilities in the hands of the general population could dissolve those lines completely. "Wonderful. Like we're not fucked up enough as is." He turned onto a narrow gravel road. "We'll be there in about two minutes," he added.

Kenny checked a new text message and chuckled. Kimberly had already reviewed everything they had on Oleg Borodin. "She wants to know if Oleg has any hobbies that we know of," he said to Mark. "I imagine being evil and on the run take up most of his time." No, Kenny replied to Kimberly. Everything they had was in the file. They had high confidence in the information on Oleg's early career, but everything after that was suspect.

Mark's team had consolidated information from the CIA, FBI, State Department and any other American institution that may have had useful data. Then they followed up with the few individuals who had personal exposure to Oleg. Allies were tapped for information as well.

Oleg was born somewhere in Russia prior to the collapse of the Soviet Union. Archives bearing his name verified that as a young teen he had become a Son of October, an important first step for any red-blooded patriot wishing to establish his communist credentials. After that he joined the ranks of the Young Pioneers and the Komsomol, otherwise known as the Young Communist League. In his early twenties he had applied for and received full party membership. While studying civil engineering at Moscow State University, he was recruited by the Komitet Gosudarstvennoy Bezopasnosti's (KGB) elite First Chief Directorate, responsible for foreign intelligence and eventually renamed the Sluzhba Vnezhney Razvedki (SVR) after the Soviet Union's collapse. Oleg was whisked away to the prestigious Red Banner Institute, now known as the Academy of Foreign Intelligence, where he graduated near the top of his class.

As his first official duty station, he was assigned to the USSR's permanent mission to the United Nations, at East Sixty-seventh Street between Lexington and Third Avenues in New York City. There, in a secure area deep inside the mission, Oleg learned the ropes of Russian foreign intelligence operations. He worked directly for the Deputy Resident (second in charge) and alongside members of the Main Intelligence Directorate—Russian military intelligence known now as the Glavnoe Razvedyvatel'noe Upravlenie (GRU). With experienced Soviet intelligence operatives as his mentors, he developed his espionage tradecraft. Under their watchful eyes he mastered the arts of surveillance, counter-surveillance, interrogation, counter-interrogation, asset handling, use of dead-drops to exchange information, cryptography, forgery, lockpicking, safecracking, and a litany of other important skills. He also learned to steal identities from foreign visa seekers by purloining their original documents. In his New York City post Oleg learned everything he needed to know to do his job and stay alive. He was such a quick study that Oleg's boss nicknamed him *gubka* ("the sponge").

Oleg kept up on technology by befriending local agents from the KGB's Sixteenth Directorate, the Russian equivalent of the U.S. National Security Agency (NSA), now known as the Federal Agency for Government Communications and Information (FAPSI). He helped to devise a warning system that continuously scanned American law enforcement frequencies, mapped their routes, and tracked their locations in real time. If something seemed out of the ordinary or officials started to cluster in areas where his colleagues were operating, they could adjust their plans accordingly.

Although Russian intelligence services were all on the same team, they were not all created equal. The SVR, his institution, was the only outfit permitted by law to spy on anyone in the world, including members of Russia's other intelligence services. Under the law, none of them could spy back on the SVR. As a consequence, Oleg's supervisor kept a close eye on their counterparts, and during his first year of service a senior GRU operative was caught passing information to an FBI counterintelligence agent. Instead of quickly arresting the traitor, Oleg's boss cheerfully informed him that he had recommended him for the Order of Lenin and the Kremlin had just approved the request. A drunken party was thrown in his honor and then the agent was placed on a plane back to Moscow where, instead of receiving the prestigious award, he would immediately be taken into custody and executed after a lengthy and tortuous interrogation. The experience taught Oleg the first and most important lesson about working in Russian intelligence—don't trust anybody, not even your colleagues.

After the Soviet Union's collapse, Oleg's bio got murky. Instead of moving in and out of jobs with regularity like most government employees and bureaucrats, he bounced around the globe unpredictably. A year in one post, followed by just a few months or perhaps even just a few weeks in another. Then he would disappear before popping up somewhere else. At times he was highly visible, attending social events and networking among diplomats and businesspeople. At other times he seemed to actually live inside Russian government offices, rarely being seen in public.

And much of the dossier information about Oleg was contradictory. One State Department official's notes from an Embassy cocktail party conversation with Oleg in Moscow said that he was born in Leningrad and had fought against the Nazis as a young teen. But that was impossible because it would put Oleg somewhere in his late nineties, whereas most sources placed his current age in his late sixties.

Notes from an experienced CIA case officer stationed in Kiev claimed that Oleg was actually born in Moscow and described him as a tall, thin man with blue eyes. But an FBI counterintelligence officer in Washington, D.C. noted him as shorter, with a stocky build and dark brown eyes. Some mentioned that he spoke only broken English and was difficult to understand, while at least one allied intelligence officer lauded his linguistic skills. Another American military intelligence asset in Kosovo contended that Oleg was almost entirely deaf and spoke with a lisp. One of the only consistent pieces of data was that Oleg had no immediate family or close relatives to speak of. He was married to his job.

Either none of these people and institutions knew what they were doing or Oleg was a true master of deception who knew how to cover his tracks. The latter was much more likely. Mark hoped that the corroborated bits of information from the spymaster's early career would prove useful, but it was obvious that Oleg's career path had taken an unorthodox turn and the subsequent dearth of information was not an accident. Great care had been taken to make it so.

The flat gravel driveway weaved gently through thick woods for close to a mile before arriving at a metal gate. Mark unrolled his window. He reached for the small intercom on the driver's side but heard a voice before he could push the call button.

"You're late, Landry," said the strong voice with just a hint of an Irish accent.

Mark smiled into the small camera. "Just a little bit."

"Who's your friend?"

"This is Kenny," Mark answered. He leaned back to give the small camera on the intercom a clean line of sight to the passenger seat. "He's relatively harmless without his computers."

"Good enough. Come on up, my old friend. Main cabin. Murphy is right here. He misses you."

Mark smiled as he heard his dog bark through the intercom.

"On my way, Murph."

. . .

They arrived at the cabin and Mark shut down the Range Rover. The front door of the cabin opened and Murphy bolted toward his owner's vehicle. Kenny went to open his door.

"Don't get out yet," said Mark. "Trust me."

Two more German Shepherds, both pitch black, sprinted to catch up with Murphy. They silently circled the vehicle several times. The larger of the two rose on its hind legs and rested its huge paws on the passenger side window. Snarling, it peered through the glass. Kenny leaned away from the window and turned his head to see Mark smiling back. A figure appeared in the cabin doorway and whistled. All three dogs sprinted to the front porch, where they immediately sat and awaited further instructions. Mark got out of the car and clapped his hands.

"Murphy, come!"

The dog didn't move. Mark called out again.

"Murphy, come! Get over here, buddy! Come on, Murph!"

Murphy looked up at the figure in the doorway and waited, frozen in place.

"Okay, McMucker. You've made your point," said Mark.

McMucker folded his arms and waited a few more seconds before barely nodding his head at Murphy. As if released from a spell, the dog barked excitedly and sprinted to reunite with his owner, almost bowling him over in the process. Mark motioned for Kenny to get out of the car.

"Screw that," Kenny said, shaking his head nervously and cracking the window open. "What about the other two?"

Murphy was up on his hind legs, with his paws on Mark's shoulders. Mark scratched him behind the ears as the dog licked his face. "Just get out," he said, turning to Kenny. "If McMucker thinks you're a pussy, he'll mess with you the whole time we're here."

"Why didn't I stay in the office?" Kenny muttered under his breath as he unbuckled his seatbelt and cautiously stepped out of the vehicle. McMucker approached Mark and the two men greeted each other with a warm hug and pats on the back.

"How have you been?" asked Mark. He squeezed McMucker's shoulder. "Keeping in good shape for an old man, I see."

Mark didn't know his precise age. He guessed McMucker had to be somewhere in his mid- to late sixties, but he had the fit build of someone decades younger. His thick, gray hair was well-coiffed and his chiseled jawline was freshly shaven. He was wearing a pressed flannel shirt buttoned at the wrists, casual jeans, and hiking boots. But the way he carried himself made it look regal. The glimmer from a vintage gold Rolex barely poking out of his sleeve didn't hurt. Mark could smell a trace of aftershave on the veteran intelligence operator. "Watch it, Landry. I've still got plenty of petrol left in the tank," he said, lightly tapping the younger man on the ribs with a clenched fist.

Kenny came around the vehicle. "Kenny Harrington. Good to meet you, sir," he said, anxiously extending his hand. McMucker gripped it firmly and stared him in the eye.

"Ah, yes. The computer whiz I've heard so much about. Tell me, Kenny, do you like dogs?" he asked.

"As long as they like me."

"Let's find out, then." McMucker whistled. His two dogs leapt from the porch and bounded toward the three men. When they reached Kenny, they crouched low to the ground and craned their heads upward—their eyes fixed on the stranger. Kenny pinned his arms to his sides and froze in place. McMucker let him sweat for a few moments. "Congrats, it looks like they like you," he said, clapping Kenny on the back. He looked down at the dogs. "Go play." They quickly jumped to their feet and darted toward the training area on the far side of the cabin. Murphy was laying on his back and Mark was crouched down, rubbing his belly. "You too," commanded McMucker, pointing to the dog. Murphy quickly spun around, abandoned his owner's affection, and sprinted after his two friends. "Don't worry, Landry. He still loves you. He just loves me more," chided McMucker with a satisfied grin.

McMucker turned toward a giant barn about one hundred feet from the main cabin he lived in. "Bolo! Bolo! Come here, boy!" He had to call out several times. Eventually, an eight-year-old black Labrador appeared in the open sliding door on the side of the structure. A slight breeze was blowing in the barn's direction. Bolo raised his snout and sniffed a few times while slowly moving his head back and forth. "That's a good boy," McMucker said, turning to Mark. "See, he's got your scent already. A fine dog! I don't care what those know-nothings say. Come here, boy!"

The Labrador sauntered toward the men as if he had all the time in the world. Mark and Kenny looked at each other as the three men waited. After what seemed like an eternity, the dog was still only halfway to them. Mark turned to McMucker. "Is it me or is that dog moving in slow motion?" he asked in a low voice. Getting no reply, he added, "No offense."

Kenny leaned toward Mark and whispered. "Never seen anything like it, but it's not slow motion. It's more like … ." He paused to search for the right word to describe the Labrador's demeanor. "Nonchalance?" he asked quizzically.

McMucker gave both men a stern look. "You're both wrong. He's just pacing himself." When the dog finally arrived, it yawned and sat at McMucker's feet. Its thick tail made a loud thumping sound as he wagged it against the ground. McMucker reached down and patted it on the head. "Good boy, Bolo."

"Where on God's green earth did you find this guy?" asked Mark.

"U.S. Army K9 Corps," McMucker muttered. "Three times he got all the way to the end of training but didn't qualify. Poor handling, if you ask me. There's absolutely nothing wrong with this dog."

"If you say so," said Mark, scratching his head.

"Not to change the subject, but I have to go like a race horse," said Kenny. "May I use your bathroom?"

"Indeed. Follow me inside, Mr. Harrington," answered McMucker, heading toward the main cabin.

"I need to get the car ready for Murphy. I'll be there in a minute," said Mark.

The rear seat of the Range Rover was cluttered. Mark tossed various items into the back of the vehicle and covered the seats with Murphy's favorite blanket. Then he shut the door and looked up at the big barn. He glanced at his watch to make sure they had enough time to chat briefly with McMucker before heading back to Boston. They did. As he walked toward the main cabin, he paused and looked back at the two-story barn again. From the outside it looked like a regular barn, not the extraordinary training facility that Mark knew intimately. He reflected on the first time he had seen it.

How long ago was that? It's gotta be fifteen years.

. . .

Mark had been an E-6 Staff Sergeant in the U.S. Army's 75th Ranger Regiment when Dunbar recruited him into the underworld of black ops. He had heard whispers of the existence of units like Dunbar's, known then as the Family, but never in his wildest dreams could he have imagined joining them. Mark had always planned on serving the rest of his twenty years with the Rangers, where he had built a reputation as a natural leader and tremendous operator. That all changed the day he met Dunbar and was offered the unexpected opportunity to shed his uniform and operate under deep cover. And although Dunbar's pitch lasted all of five minutes and lacked any substantive details, Mark had immediately accepted. The challenge of working side by side with the best of the best was too good to pass up. He left the Rangers immediately and started Dunbar's special operator training course within days. Six months later, he was sitting in the passenger seat of Dunbar's car as it rolled to a stop in front of McMucker's barn.

"And here we are, Mark," said Dunbar. "I spoke to him yesterday so he's expecting you. You'll be here for a few weeks. What do you think?"

Mark looked out the window and then back at his boss, who had treated him like a son from day one. "What do I think about what? That?" he asked pointing out the window. "It's a barn. Honestly, not what I expected. But it's still a major step up from the kinds of places I'm used to sleeping in, so no big deal." He pointed to the surrounding landscape. "These hills will spice up my morning runs. And since it's New Hampshire, if I want to do some shooting all I have to do is open a window first."

"Live Free or Die," Dunbar remarked.

The previous six months had been spent mastering the bread and butter of deep-cover special operations, and Mark had performed remarkably well. Dunbar and the rest of his cadre were impressed and glad to have him on the team. His close-quarters fighting skills, armed or unarmed, were among the best anyone had seen. And he had demonstrated his considerable capacities by grasping new things quickly. He was a lightning-quick thinker who could distill substantial quantities of complex information and solve problems even under immense pressure. Espionage skills and tradecraft came naturally.

Overall, Mark had performed above expectations and had reached the point where most new operators were sent to join the rest of the team in the field. But Dunbar had something special in mind for him—a few weeks with McMucker. A charm school of sorts, Dunbar had called it—a final polishing of his newly acquired skills. Mark was unclear exactly which skills the final phase with McMucker would focus on polishing, but

Dunbar said that McMucker was the best in his field and the boss didn't give out praise lightly. Besides, Mark unequivocally trusted Dunbar, so he marched forward with an open mind and his signature enthusiasm for learning. The two men shook hands and Dunbar drove away.

Mark approached the barn door and gave it a pull. It was locked, so he pressed the intercom button. He turned and scanned the area as he waited. "Yes? May I help you?" The voice was somewhat weak and slow, obviously that of an elderly man. Not what he expected.

"Yes. Good afternoon. Mark Landry to see Mr. McMucker. He's expecting me."

"Yes, he is. I'll buzz you in. Come on up to the second floor, please."

Mark heard a buzzing sound and the lock popped open. He pulled open the door, expecting to see stalls and mostly open space as in most barns. Instead it opened to reveal a small, dimly lit room with bare walls. There was another door on the far side and a narrow staircase to the left. Mark closed the door behind him and made his way up the steep stairs to the second floor. At the top of the staircase, a single hallway cut diagonally across the length of the barn. There were several rooms on each side of the hall. All the doors were closed. Mark was standing in place for a moment, wondering where to go, when the old man appeared at the end of the hallway, leaning heavily on a cane.

"Hello, Mr. Landry. Sorry for not greeting you at the door," he said. "But at my age and in my condition, getting up and down those stairs isn't easy." He was slowly making his way down the hall toward Mark. "If you can call them stairs at all. Way too steep. More like a God-damn ladder if you ask me." He paused for a moment to rest before continuing. "Excuse my language, son. I'm usually not this grumpy."

Mark turned and looked behind him at the staircase. "They are steep. I can't argue with you about that." The old man took a deep breath and transferred the cane into his left hand so he could offer his right. It was thin and felt frail, so Mark gripped it much more gently than he usually would and smiled. "Good to meet you, Mr. McMucker."

"I'm not McMucker," the old man replied, taking a deep breath and exhaling slowly. "He sends his apologies. Got called away on some urgent business just a few hours ago. At least that's what he said. Between you and me, he's probably sipping Irish whiskey with one of his mistresses. But he said he'd be back early tomorrow morning, and I believe that part at least. I'm Nathaniel Hockenberry. Please call me Nate. My family's been in this town for generations. I broke off a piece of our land and sold it to McMucker a few years ago. I swore I never would, but he sure was persuasive. Anyhow, that's not your problem."

"No worries. Good to meet you, Nate," Mark replied cheerfully. But inside he was wondering what the hell he was going to do between now and then. McMucker's farm was in the middle of nowhere and he didn't have a car. Mark smiled and waited silently for Nate to say something.

"He asked me to look after you until he gets back. It's nice to have someone to talk to. How about we go down the hall to his office and get to know each other? Sound good, Mr. Landry?"

"Sounds good to me, Nate."

It's not like I have anything else to do.

Mark spent that entire first night talking with Nate. At first, they mostly chatted about Mark's military background, travel experiences, and language skills. Nate was old but still sharp. Although Mark enjoyed talking with him, the dialogue reminded him of the extensive oral psychological exams he had to complete when he joined Dunbar's team. Nate was methodically covering a lot of the same bases, but at least he was doing it in a conversational way.

Mark was starting to get tired when he noticed the subtle United States Marine Corps emblem on the old man's cane. When he learned that Nate was a Korean War veteran who had fought at the Battle of the Chosin Reservoir with the 1st Marine Regiment, he perked up and the conversation went on for another two hours as the two sipped Kentucky bourbon. Nate's memory of the battle was impressive, but Mark thought it odd that he could not recall the name of the 1st Marine Regiment's commanding officer. He chalked it up to old age, booze, and the late hour.

Nate was impressed with Mark's knowledge of military history and asked him how someone with only a high-school diploma could know so much. He was clearly commending the younger man, but Mark had a bit of a complex about his lack of formal education. He knew full well that he had read more and could converse more freely on many topics, history included, than most men of letters. But they had fancy diplomas hanging on their walls and he didn't. It must have shown on his face momentarily. Nate cut him off before he could answer. "That was a compliment, Mark. It just came out wrong. I meant no offense," he offered sincerely.

"No, no. Not at all," Mark replied, feeling like a baby for wearing his feelings on his sleeve. "You're absolutely right. I never went to college. You were just stating a fact, not insulting me. I didn't take it like that at all," he said unconvincingly. Then he credited his knowledge to the intense training he had received as an adolescent in the church basement, also known as the Dungeon, with Father Peck. "He taught me a lot more than just how to fight. Between the punches and kicks, we read more books and discussed more topics than I could have possibly absorbed. Father Peck owed me nothing but gave me everything he had," said Mark, looking down at his last sip of bourbon and then raising his glass. "Here's to Father Peck. I never even came close to repaying him."

Nate raised his glass in tribute and finished his drink. Then he leaned forward and placed the empty glass on the table. "I think you just did, Mr. Landry." Both men were tired and ready for bed. "The guest room in the main cabin is already prepared for you. You're welcome to any food in the kitchen. McMucker wants you back here in the barn ready to go at zero seven hundred."

Mark still had no idea what he was there for.

The next morning, he ran five miles through the New Hampshire hills with the album *Appetite for Destruction* by Guns N' Roses blaring is his ears. He got back to the cabin with just enough time to shower and eat a quick breakfast. Nobody else was around. At zero seven hundred, he pulled on the barn door. It was locked, so he buzzed the intercom, waited, and buzzed again. Still no answer, so he paced around the building's perimeter to see if there were other entrances. There were, but they were all locked too, so he returned to the only door with an intercom and buzzed again.

Next to the barn was a picnic table. Mark sat on it and waited. At roughly zero seven thirty, he heard a vehicle approaching and hopped off the table. A black Ford F-150 pickup truck rolled to a stop in front of the barn. "You Landry?" asked the man through the open driver's side window.

"I am. Are you McMucker?"

"Indeed I am," he replied, getting out of the truck and slinging a backpack over his shoulder. Mark guessed that he was in his early fifties. He looked fit and confident as he strutted toward Mark with his hand out. "Apologies for my late arrival. It was unavoidable," he declared, gripping Mark's hand firmly. "Did Nate take good care of you last night?"

"He did."

"Good. Bet he talked your ear off as well."

"He did. But I did my share of talking too. Good guy."

"Great guy. Took forever to talk him into selling me some land, though," McMucker commented as he unlocked and pulled open the barn door. "I have to grab some things from my office upstairs. I'll meet you in the big room. Straight through there," he added, pointing to the interior door Mark had seen the previous day.

Mark sat at a circular table in the middle of the room and looked around. A pile of different-colored dry markers sat in the middle of the table; a large whiteboard hung on the wall. Sections of the room were partitioned off by black curtains. Wardrobe racks filled with clothing lined one of the walls. Piles of various hats, gloves, watches, rings, and other accessories sat on shelves. A scaffolding with attached multicolored lights was suspended from the ceiling by steel cables. Large white lightbulbs populated the perimeter of a rectangular mirror that sat atop a small makeup desk in the far corner. Mark felt as if backstage at a theater.

What the hell am I doing here?

McMucker returned with a thermos, two styrofoam coffee cups, and a thick folder. "This is hot as hell, so give it a minute. Hope you like it black," he said, pouring them each a cup of steaming hot coffee.

"I do. Thanks."

"Impressive bio," said McMucker, nodding toward the folder on the table. "You've had quite a career so far." Mark nodded and gently blew on his coffee to cool if off. McMucker motioned to the vast room. "It's just us. I wouldn't think you immodest if you agreed, Mark. May I call you Mark?"

"Please do. And yes, it's been an interesting ride so far. Which I look forward to continuing as soon as possible."

"I'm not surprised," said McMucker, taking a small sip of his coffee and grinning. "You've spent the last six months or so training and preparing. I'd be chomping at the bit too. So I'll cut to the chase and let you know why you're here, in case you haven't figured it out yet." Mark put down his cup and leaned forward attentively. "This," said McMucker, tapping his hand on Mark's file, "is impressive. You've got world-class technical and tactical skills. Dunbar and all your instructors agree on that. You're very good at kicking in doors and sneaking through windows. But," he added, picking up the file and waving it back and forth, "wouldn't it be easier to just walk in the front door after getting yourself invited inside?"

Mark didn't answer, assuming that the question was rhetorical. He sipped his coffee and waited for his new instructor to continue. He had learned the basics of undercover work, like memorizing the personal history, or backstop, of an alias. But judging by the wardrobe and props that surrounded them, he figured he was there for some kind of acting class—a prospect that did not excite him. McMucker seemed nice enough, but Mark had no desire to channel his inner Robert De Niro and play make-believe while the rest of the unit worked on real-world missions. He felt sidelined.

No wonder Dunbar dropped me off without a word. He was probably worried I'd run for the hills.

"I know what you're thinking, but don't worry. You're not here to learn how to act. I'm going to teach you how to lie. How to deceive, manipulate, obfuscate, misdirect attention, steal, and use human nature to your advantage. How to create conditions so people do what you want them to do and think it's their idea. And you'll be able to detect when someone else is doing the same to you. When you leave my barn for good, you'll look at the world much differently. But you're going to have to pay closer attention to detail than you ever have. Can you do that?"

Mark smiled. This sounded much more interesting than acting. Things were looking up. "Absolutely. Sounds good to me. You have my full attention."

"Good!" said McMucker, slapping his hand on the table in celebration. "It's going to be a lot of work, but I think you and I will get along splendidly. Let's finish these coffees and then we'll get started. What time have you got?"

Mark pulled back the sleeve of his sweatshirt. Glancing at his bare wrist, he sat up and started patting down his pockets. "Not sure where my watch is. I could have sworn I was wearing it. I thought I checked the time while I was waiting outside, but I must have left it on the nightstand in the guest room," he said, perplexed.

"I'll keep an eye out for it. What kind of watch is it?"

"Just a cheap G-shock. I've had it forever."

McMucker pulled back his sleeve. "Does it look anything like this one?"

Mark squinted and looked across the table at McMucker's wrist. "Yes, exactly like that."

"That's because it's yours, Mark." He unfastened the watch and tossed it across the table.

Mark caught it and strapped it back onto his wrist. "Nice trick. How'd you do that?"

"Step one is getting the target to trust you. After that you can do pretty much whatever you want. Remember that little lesson. Now let's get started."

The first few days were focused entirely on manipulating the facial muscles. McMucker would toss out random emotions and Mark needed to respond with the appropriate expression. When they finished, he sent Mark to practice them in front of the mirror so he could see how inaccurate most of his attempts were. McMucker explained that what you think is a smile may not actually look like one, and what you believe to be a neutral expression may in fact be provocative. And these differences could get you killed. He taught Mark how to manipulate his facial muscles, primarily the zygomaticus major and the orbicularis oculi, to emulate the required emotion and fool anyone.

When Mark had made sufficient progress and was starting to build confidence in his deceptive capabilities, McMucker threw a monkey wrench into the training program. He had Mark turn his back and wrote out very simple math problems on the whiteboard—nothing fancy, just basic addition, subtraction, multiplication and division. "Now I want you to demonstrate the emotions I call out while simultaneously solving the problems. Let me tell you in advance why we're doing this so you don't think this is some Mr. Miyagi wax-on, wax-off lesson where you have no idea why you're doing it until much later. In the future, you will very likely find yourself in situations where you need to convince others that you are harmless while simultaneously and quickly determining the most efficient way to kill them. Juggling competing thoughts and emotions takes deliberate practice. This exercise will help you develop those mental muscles."

They moved on to body language and the art and science of isopraxism, or mirroring. He taught Mark how to detect deception in even the most experienced liars by noting small physiological changes and micro-expressions that most people completely miss, like a subtle increase in a person's blinking rate. "Again, the challenge is to notice all this while convincingly playing a character and carrying on a conversation like a normal human being. Before you leave me, I expect you to be able to juggle more than most people think is humanly possible. Not everyone can do it. But so far I have no reason to think you unable."

Mark's undercover skill set prior to his arrival had been restricted to basic pretexting—like how to bullshit his way into places where he had no business. McMucker forced him to take much deeper dives into alias identities and memorize obscure details of their pasts. If he was supposed to have grown up in Chicago, for example, he needed to know the address, which school he attended, his teachers, and other tacitly acquired cultural information that real people knew about themselves. The technical side of the unit was responsible for creating the historical and digital legacy to backstop the identity—for example, a believable Facebook or Twitter profile with years of posts or tweets. But success would always come down to Mark's ability to deliver a believable performance. Mark spent many evenings reading about history's greatest spies and con men and memorizing identities that he would be expected to represent convincingly the next day.

Throughout his stay at McMucker's farm, Mark was asked to complete menial tasks with his left hand. "I know you can punch and shoot and handle a knife with either hand, but have you ever tried to brush your teeth lefty?"

"No, can't say that I have."

"That right there might be enough to blow your cover if the alias you've adopted or the identity you've stolen is reported to be left-handed. Remember, anybody can do the big things, but the little things keep you alive."

On some nights, as they hung out together in the main cabin before bedtime, McMucker would retrieve a large wooden box filled with dozens of valuable watches from his bedroom closet. Some looked brand new; others were vintage. All of them were much more valuable than the G-Shock on Mark's wrist. As both sipped bourbon, McMucker would hold a jeweler's loupe up to one eye and examine the inner workings of the older watches. He told stories as he tinkered. Mark never knew which tales were true.

When they explored the art of seduction, McMucker's humor and wit came through most strongly. "The younger the target, the harder she'll make you work. You need to get inside her head, read her thoughts, embrace her interests, and identify her turn-ons, fears, and motivations. But the older they are, the easier it gets. Would you like to know the one foolproof, never-fail secret to seducing a woman over forty-five?"

"Of course."

"Just smile and give her a little attention. Make her laugh. She'll do the rest of the work for you."

They broke down the involuntary body language and demeanor

that broadcasts whether a person has been in a particular place previously. "You need to be able to walk into a room you've seen a hundred times and make it look like the first. And you need to be able to walk into a room you've never been in and make it look like you've been there one hundred times." Then they practiced both scenarios.

Mark started every day with a morning run through the hills to clear his mind, listening to the same album—*Appetite for Destruction* by Guns N' Roses. At the end of the third week he was becoming impatient. After his run, he cooled down and sat at the breakfast table. McMucker was reading the newspaper and sipping his morning coffee.

"It's been three weeks," said Mark.

"Uh-huh," acknowledged McMucker from behind the newspaper.

"How close am I to finishing?"

"Pretty close."

"Would you mind elaborating? What else is there to learn?"

"Nothing, really. I'm just waiting for you to impress me."

"Impress you? How do you want me to impress you?" asked Mark, slightly annoyed but trying not to sound disrespectful.

McMucker lowered the newspaper. "I don't know. That's up to you. Just impress me."

Mark decided not to push it. Obviously he wasn't going to get a straight answer. Instead he showered, shaved, and then meditated for ten minutes before heading over to the barn, where McMucker had him practice speaking in different accents all day. They barely spoke during dinner, and Mark went to bed frustrated. How was he supposed to impress McMucker? What he was missing? He thought back to his arrival at the farm and reviewed all he had learned. Then he went back and reviewed it again. And then it hit him.

You are a sneaky little bastard, aren't you, McMucker?

Mark put on his clothes, grabbed a small screwdriver sitting next to McMucker's box of watches on the kitchen table, and quietly slipped out of the cabin. The barn door was locked. Since there were no windows on the first floor, he scaled a large drainage pipe that ran down a corner of the building. When he reached the top, he reached over and used the small screwdriver to pry open the latch of a window. Once inside, he made his way down the stairs into the main training area. In the corner he rifled through the huge container of props until he found what he was looking for. Then he returned to the main cabin.

McMucker sensed movement in his bedroom. He sat up quickly and gasped at the figure standing at the foot of his bed. "Jesus, Mary, and Joseph, Mark! You scared the shit out of me. What the hell are you doing?"

"Just hanging out." Mark was smiling and tossing a long object back and forth from hand to hand.

McMucker turned on his bedside lamp and rubbed his eyes. "Well, it's a good way to get your ass shot."

"Not really," replied Mark, pulling a semiautomatic Ruger handgun from the small of his back and tossing it onto the bed. "I left the magazine in the nightstand." McMucker pulled the drawer open to verify Mark's claim. "Don't worry. I didn't touch anything else. Although that's a pretty stupid place to keep your passport and safe-deposit box key, McMucker. Or should I just call you Nate?"

McMucker cleared his throat and took a sip of water from the cup on his nightstand. Then he climbed out of bed, wearing only his boxer shorts. Mark was twirling the cane with the USMC emblem in one hand like a baton. He looked McMucker up and down. "You keep in pretty good shape for a Korean War vet. What's your secret, Nate?" he asked cheerfully, obviously pleased to have discovered that Nate, the gentleman who had greeted him the first night at the farm, had actually been McMucker in full disguise.

McMucker clapped his hands slowly in mock applause. "It took you long enough. And you could have waited until morning. But I suppose congratulations are in order." He yawned and grabbed the cane as he walked past Mark toward the bedroom door. "Have a seat at the kitchen table after you wipe that giddy smile off your face."

McMucker removed the top from the wooden box that housed his watches. He took a gold Rolex with a circle of encrusted rubies where the Roman numerals usually are and fastened it around his wrist. Then he pointed to the remaining watches. "Pick one," he said. "You've earned it."

"Seriously? I can't accept that. You've done enough for me. I appreciate the offer, but it's unnecessary. My watch works just fine. But thank you for offering," replied Mark.

McMucker pointed to the black rubber G-Shock on Mark's wrist. "That monstrosity is not a watch. You need an upgrade, and any of these fine chronometers will do. Besides, they were meant to be worn, not to sit in a box. Happy graduation. Pick one."

"I'm not picking one," Mark protested.

"Fine. I'll pick one for you," McMucker muttered under his breath. After browsing for several minutes, he settled on a stainless steel Breitling Chronomat with a blue face. "Put this on and see how it feels. I can adjust it if necessary." Mark reluctantly replaced his watch with the gift and wiggled his wrist to check the fit. It was perfect.

"Good," said McMucker. "One last thing to do." He flipped over the wooden top of the box and pointed to a white index card taped inside. It had been there so long that the card was slightly discolored, but you could still real the quotation written in elegant cursive with a black pen. He pointed to the card. "Read that, Mark."

Every man has reminiscences which he would not tell to everyone but only his friends. He has other matters in his mind which he would not reveal even to his friends, but only to himself, and that in secret. But there are things which a man is afraid to tell even to himself, and every decent man has a number of such things stored away in his mind. —Fyodor Dostoevsky

"Do you believe Dostoevsky?" McMucker asked. "Do you believe that's true of every man?"

Mark pondered the quotation for a moment. "For the most part, it's probably true. But every man? Probably not. There are exceptions to every rule, right?"

"Not this one, Mark." McMucker got up from the table and retrieved a bottle of brandy and two small snifters. "Every single one of us wears a mask to hide their true selves, divulging only what we want others to see. Correct?"

"Agreed."

"Dostoevsky is just taking that concept one step further. Whether or not we want to believe it, deep down inside every one of us, there are monsters. But he's teaching men like us a very important lesson: that we can hide behind masks even from ourselves." McMucker leaned forward, lowered his voice, and spoke in a tone Mark had not previously heard. "In this business, you may be called upon to do unpleasant things for the greater good. I implore you to never do those things as Mark Landry. Instead, create an identity known only to you and hide from yourself behind that mask. Keep the two separate. One day you will thank me for this advice. Give your monster a name and make sure that you can summon him at will. Understand?"

Mark cleared his throat. "I understand," he answered, his voice a bit shaky.

The two men sat quietly for several minutes before McMucker broke the silence. "Have you given him a name?"

Mark nodded. "Yeah."

"Good," said McMucker, raising his glass. "Then go forth and do great things. And may you be in heaven half an hour before the devil knows you're dead."

. . .

"No, thank you," said Kenny. "It's a long ride back to Boston and Mark doesn't like to stop."

"Suit yourself," said McMucker. He put the coffeepot back on the kitchen counter and returned to his chair next to Mark in the living room. "What was the name again? Oleg Borodin? If he's been around as long as you say and not much is known about him, I'd be very careful. Guys like that worry me. High-profile types who shoot their mouths off, not so much."

"We'll be in Berlin in a few days. Hopefully the Germans have some new information on Borodin for us. At least that's the plan," replied Mark. "You about ready, Kenny?" Kenny was looking out the window watching as Murphy ran around with McMucker's dogs. "What about you,

McMucker? Are you bored up here? Want to join us in the hunt for this Russian guy? We could use you."

"You sound just like Dunbar," said McMucker. "Indeed. A chip off the old block."

Even the most attentive observer would have missed the evanescent spark in the spymaster's eye. Mark would have missed it too had the flash not been meant for him specifically. McMucker could grip men he'd just met with a well-spun pub tale, while simultaneously having a separate, silent conversation right under their noses. When McMucker had said Mark sounded just like Dunbar, he wasn't simply saying it was the kind of thing Dunbar would ask. He was saying that Dunbar had offered him fieldwork *recently*. McMucker probably didn't want to talk about the legendary former boss in front of Kenny, whom he had just met. He was glad to see that Mark had received the message and knew better than to ask questions. Instead, Mark just casually reiterated the offer. "Just know the door is open if you get restless."

McMucker smiled. "Thanks. I have to admit that I do miss the field, and sitting around watching my mistresses get old is depressing. But I still have a few things I need to take care of before I could take off for any extended period of time. Thatcher and Churchill," he said, pointing out the window at the two black German Shepherds chasing after Murphy, "go back to their New Hampshire State Police K9 handlers at Alpha Troop next week. And I'm still trying to find a good home for that fine specimen right there," he said while pointing to Bolo, who was lying at Mark's feet with his chin resting on his foot. "He certainly likes you, Landry. Bet your kids would love him."

Mark looked down at Bolo. "No way, McMucker. Don't even think about pawning this guy off on me. My wife is annoyed enough with me lately. It took her long enough to warm up to Murphy. She'd kill me if I came home with another dog."

The three men walked outside together. McMucker whistled for the dogs. Kenny said goodbye, climbed into the passenger seat, and called the office to check the status of several missions Mark had been asking about. Mark gave McMucker a firm hug. Then he opened the door and

Murphy hopped into the back seat. "Thanks for giving Murphy a much-needed tuneup. The kids are dying to have him back home again."

"I'm sure they are. Hey, Mark, what ever happened to that Breitling I so generously gave you?" asked McMucker with a quizzical smirk on his face.

Without missing a beat, Mark patted the bulge in his breast pocket. "Right here where you just put it," he answered matter-of-factly. "Take care, old man." McMucker laughed and watched the Range Rover pull out of the driveway and drive off into the thick woods on its way to the main road.

"I guess I can't fool him anymore, Bolo," he said, looking down at the dog leaning against his leg, half asleep. He reached down and scratched the dog's head. "Don't worry, my friend. We'll find you a proper home. But it wouldn't kill you to put a little pep in your step when I'm trying to show you off."

Mark and Kenny spent the first part of the ride back to Boston answering messages and getting caught up on calls. When they hit I-93 south, Mark reached into his breast pocket to retrieve his watch. But when he looked into his hand, he didn't see the stainless steel Breitling he had worn for years. Instead, he was holding McMucker's gold, ruby-encrusted Rolex. An attached note written in elegant cursive read, "Time for an upgrade." Mark laughed quietly. Then he fastened the new chronometer to his wrist and shook his head.

Still a sneaky little bastard, aren't you, McMucker?

CHAPTER TEN

Wellness Check

Mark arrived home too late to spend time with the kids. They were already asleep and Luci was working late with the new detective she was training. Mark walked the nanny to her car before going back inside and lying down in bed with each of the twins for a few minutes, taking great care not to wake them. He hated being away from them and considered his long periods of separation the worst part of the job. He could handle the danger, but he felt guilty for not being around as much as formerly.

He went downstairs, grabbed a beer from the refrigerator, and took a sip as he looked around. The house was quiet and felt empty.

I don't know why Luci gives me so much shit for working too much when she's not here anyway.

On the counter was an invitation for Luci to participate in a two-day seminar on issues concerning women in law enforcement. A big "Yes!" was scribbled across the top. Next to the invitation was a catechism pamphlet from the local Catholic parish. The kids were soon to begin Sunday school, something Mark wasn't crazy about. "It's Sunday school, they're not joining Opus Dei," Luci had quipped when he started to push back against the idea. Religion hadn't been particularly important to either of them, but since the kids were growing up and starting to ask questions, Luci wanted to provide some direction. And since they had both been born and raised somewhat Catholic, it made sense to her. He simply nodded and let it go, not wishing to cause further waves in their relationship.

Things weren't bad per se, but the past few months had felt different. Less intimate. Nights when both were at home were often spent on their respective sofas, each of them working or entertaining themselves with little interaction between them. And Mark was still a bit ticked off at something Luci had done the previous week.

Both of them worked dangerous jobs and knew that every shift or mission contained potentially lethal risks. As a matter of family policy, they always made sure to hug each other and the kids and tell everyone how much they were loved prior to leaving the house. But last week, Luci had left to work a night shift without saying a word. It happened after a disagreement over her post-retirement plans. She had floated the idea of running for Congress some day; instead of simply listening and letting the impulse dissipate on its own, he had pounced on it and rattled off all the reasons why it was a terrible idea. Maybe he had been too harsh. But it still bothered him that she had left without saying goodbye. Mark made a mental note to take some time off soon and focus on rekindling the relationship. He didn't think it would be too difficult once he had the time. They had been through plenty of ups and downs since meeting back in their teenage years. Still, it felt a little different this time.

Next to the church pamphlet was Luci's completed paperwork declaring her candidacy for Essex County Sheriff. It had been finished for a few weeks but she had yet to file. This was an idea he supported. Soon she would retire from the local police department and leave behind all of the inherent dangers that went along with being a cop. The sheriff job was mostly administrative; it would be a ton of work, but Mark was still busy with his career and the twins, now in grade school, required far less attention than before. Luci was still relatively young and not ready to simply retire. Besides, she had the experience, credentials, and reputation to win. Mark was all for it. He wondered why she still hadn't filed the paperwork.

The Sunday edition of the *Lawrence Eagle-Tribune* was still on the kitchen table. One of the main articles was a lengthy interview with an outspoken district court judge named Christina Brannigan, who had been making a name for herself by publicly slamming law enforcement officials over the past few months. This particular article referenced a case the judge had thrown out a few weeks earlier after declaring the arresting officer's search unconstitutional. In the interview, Judge Brannigan mentioned the officer by name—Detective Sergeant Luci Landry—and described her actions as "overzealous, pushy, and downright authoritarian." The quarter-pound of cocaine found in the suspect's pants was barely mentioned. Luci was still fuming over it. Mark shook his head in a mixture of disbelief and disgust. Outspoken judges had become much more common across the country since Justice Midas had been sworn in to the Supreme Court. Those at the top of the food chain set the tone for the rest. Local judges seemed to figure that if Midas could make inflammatory public statements and get away with it, they could too.

Mark tried not to overthink the potential fraying of his connection with Luci. Instead he chalked it up to their collective workloads, post-retirement jitters—being a cop had been her life for two decades and that was about to change—and perhaps a sort of midlife crisis as they both inched their way toward age fifty. Public criticism from a local sitting judge didn't help.

The image of an acerbic Judge Midas caused Mark's thoughts to shift to his mother, Senator McDermott. The past few months had been almost unbearable for her, and he needed to check on her. He went upstairs to bed. Mark would be up before dawn to depart for Washington, D.C. as Luci would finish her shift. They would pass like two ships in the night. Again.

. . .

The next morning, Mark called Luci while battling the Washington, D.C. traffic.

"Jesus Christ, I'd kill myself if I actually had to live in this town," declared Mark. "I've been driving for an hour and I swear I've only gone like three blocks." When the car in front of him hesitated, he quickly maneuvered around it only to stop immediately. There was no reply on the other end of the call.

"Luci, you still there?"

"Yeah, I heard you. Traffic sucks. You're glad you don't live in D.C."

She sounded either pissed or distracted. Lately, Mark had had a hard time telling the difference. But he knew better than to ask what was wrong. Either she would tell him sternly that nothing was wrong, and that if anything ever was wrong she would inform him, or it would open a can of worms that he didn't have the time or patience to deal with.

Mark's mother, Senator McDermott, had been uncharacteristically laconic and sounded more depressed than usual the last time he spoke with her. Toward the end of the conversation he could barely hear her and had to ask her twice to raise her voice. He was worried and decided to stop in unannounced to see for himself how she was doing.

First he had to finish with Luci. "Listen, I'm about to pull into the parking garage where I'll probably lose my signal," he said. It was a plausible but unlikely excuse since his phone, a modified Boeing Black model, was always connected to the top-secret Joint Worldwide Intelligence Communications System (JWICS) network. He had been to some pretty remote places and had yet to lose a signal. Again, no response from his wife. He could hear a computer keyboard clicking and visualized Luci's perfectly manicured red fingernails tapping away.

"So I'll talk to you later, okay? I'll try to call tonight before the kids go to bed."

"Yeah, please do that. Listen, I'm gonna be slammed here today. Lots of paperwork and reports. I need some sleep so I'll talk to you later."

"Okay, no worries. Have a—"

The line went dead. Mark shook his head in frustration. Luci had been busy as long as he had known her. But lately things just seemed different. Something was off. Distant. He blocked it out of his mind. At the next light, he turned and entered Senator McDermott's parking garage.

"Hello? It's just me," Mark called out after letting himself into the senator's apartment. There was no answer. She might be taking a nap in her bedroom. The apartment was dark. The curtains covering the sliding glass door that led to the balcony were closed. He crossed the family room and opened them. The sun was shining brightly. Mark looked at the sofa and coffee table and shook his head. They were cluttered with her favorite newspapers and magazines—none of which had had anything nice to say about McDermott since Justice Midas's confirmation to the Supreme Court. A picture of CNN's Jeffrey Toobin lay on top of the stack with its face scribbled out and horns added to his head.

Why does she do this to herself?

She had been put through the wringer more than anyone in recent memory. The fact that she was still in the Senate was a miracle. The sustained onslaught of pure hatred that she was enduring would have caused many to resign and disappear from public life. He wondered whether the masses would let up if they knew how much damage their constant harassment was causing. Mark had questioned a few times whether she was a threat to herself but dismissed the possibility. She cared too much about him, his kids, and his sister Megan, whom he had never met and who was still unaware that she had a brother. And she was naively optimistic that one day they would all live as one big happy family. She would never hurt herself, no matter how bad the pain got. But something felt different—call it a presence—in the apartment and he couldn't put his finger on it. He was worried but didn't know exactly why.

Mark picked up one of the magazines and flipped through it as he slowly paced toward the kitchen. Any minute she would emerge from the bedroom, force a big smile, and say how nice it was for him to stop in. He would chat for a few minutes and then tell her for the thousandth time that things would get better, even though he wasn't so sure anymore. Then he would put his mother out of his mind and go back to work. He glanced at his new watch and hoped the situation would get better soon because he had things to do. A breeze came through the open balcony door. He turned his head. Sunlight reflected from something small on the kitchen floor.

Click.

Mark squinted. It looked like a piece of broken glass. He moved closer. There was broken glass all over the kitchen.

What happened? And why had she not cleaned it up? It wasn't like her to leave a mess. And where the hell is she anyway?

He quickly looked around at the broken glass. When he turned to look at the pile of awful media coverage on the coffee table, an alarm went off in his head. Maybe he had been wrong. Maybe she had been pushed too far and finally lost it.

Oh shit! No. No. Please, no.

Mark released the magazine from his hands. He was sprinting toward McDermott's bedroom before the magazine hit the floor—hoping to God he wasn't too late. The door was ajar. He pushed it open and scanned the master bedroom. Nothing. Light leaked through the space at the bottom of her bathroom door.

"Hello?" he called out. No answer. He twisted the knob and opened the door a few inches. The shower curtain was drawn. He could hear a slow dripping sound. He entered fully prepared for the worst. Halfway there, he was surprised by a familiar voice from behind.

"Oh, hi, honey. I didn't know you were stopping by."

McDermott was standing behind him in the bathroom doorway, wearing shorts and a T-shirt. Her hair was tied up in a bun. She was thinner than he had ever seen, and her eyes looked glassy. She was cradling a bandaged hand. Mark breathed a sigh of relief and dropped his shoulders. "Thank God," he said. "I saw the mess and the broken glass and got worried about you."

McDermott looked confused. Mark's words didn't seem to register immediately. "Oh yeah, the glass," she said, holding up her bandaged hand. "I broke a glass."

"Who are you talking to, Mom?" asked an unfamiliar voice from behind the shower curtain.

"It's just Mark," she answered cheerfully.

"Who the hell is Mark?" A set of eyes peered around the curtain and settled on Mark standing just feet away. They popped wide open and were followed by a scream. "What the fuck is that guy doing in here? Get him out! Fucking pervert! Call the police, Mom!"

Mark held up his hands in the universal sign of surrender. "It's not what you think, Megan." He kept his hands up and turned his back toward his sister. McDermott looked as if she was out to lunch. Mark ignored the screaming behind him and approached his mother, put his hands on the senator's shoulders, and looked into her eyes. "I'm leaving. I think it's time you had that talk with Megan."

"What talk?"

"Seriously? I have to explain this? Listen, tell her about me. About us. Do it now before she does something stupid like calling the police or tries to kill me. Step aside."

McDermott slowly moved aside and Mark briskly made his exit. He had always known it was a matter of time before he and Megan actually set eyes on each other. But he had not envisioned it playing out like this. She had been out of the country for several years, and although she was due to return, he wasn't expecting her today.

McDermott grabbed a towel from the rack and handed it to Megan behind the curtain. "You can stop screaming now, Megan. He's gone."

"Would you mind telling me who the hell that guy is and how he got all the way into your private residence?"

"Yes. I know it seems weird right now but we need to talk about that, honey," she answered matter-of-factly. "His name is Mark Landry. And he's not a pervert. He's your brother."

CHAPTER ELEVEN

Crimson Tide

"Here you go," said the waitress, placing the dessert in the middle of the table along with two long spoons. "Can I get y'all anything else?"

He shook his head and focused his eyes on his much younger date. Heather Mays dipped her finger into the whipped cream topping and smiled back as she licked it off. Then she handed him a spoon. "Better dig in because I'm about to strap on a feed bag," she said softly. She knew he was already enamored. But he was trying to play it cool, so she threw in a wink that nearly sent him over the edge. He reached for ice water.

Heather Mays was not the first girl he had met online. But she was the first whose profile photo did not come close to doing her justice. She was stunning. He guessed that her true age was very close to her claim of twenty-five. The slow batting of elegant lashes over her pale blue eyes was hypnotic. And he loved the way she twirled her long brown hair as he talked about what it was really like to be a venture capitalist. "Most people think that because I have tons of money I'll just throw it around. But nothing could be further from the truth," he declared. He placed several crisp bills into the check holder and handed it back to the waitress. "Thank you, sweety. All set." He redirected his attention to the bombshell sitting across from him. "I always expect a return on investment."

He rambled on about himself as she finished most of the dessert. Then she sat back with both hands on her belly. "I'm stuffed," she said. He nodded slightly and continued talking about himself.

"It's not just the money. It's the experience that we VCs have to offer. We've been there, done that. Believe me, if I were advising Zuckerberg, Facebook wouldn't be in the world of hurt it's in now. But these young tech guys think they know everything and just don't listen. You know what I mean? Of course you do," he answered for her. "That's why you're here with me and not out with one of them, right?" he added, laughing at his own joke. "Tech companies are starting to bore me anyway. Do you want to know what the next big sector is going to be? I'll give you a free tip if you do." He took a sip of his swanky after-dinner liquor and waited for an answer.

"Do you want to get out of here and go back to my place?" she asked.

Caught off guard by her assertiveness, he froze for a moment. Then he finished the drink, placed the empty cup off to the side, and leaned forward. "Why yes, young lady. Yes, I do."

"One condition," she said, pulling out her phone. She scrolled to the photo she wanted and stretched out her arm for him to see. He gently grasped her wrist and moved the screen further away from his face until his mature eyes adjusted. "This is me and my boy. I call him my little Crimson Tide," she added, smiling like a proud mother.

"He's adorable," he answered awkwardly, unsure of why she was showing him the photo. "You both are. Congratulations. Now what's the condition?"

"He is the center of my universe. That will never, ever change. And you need to always respect that? Understand?"

"Absolutely," he answered. "I wouldn't have it any other way."

"Promise?"

"Of course."

"Say it," she demanded, playfully.

"Okay. I promise," he answered somewhat reluctantly. He was not used to his dates making demands.

"Good. Then you've earned it," she said, a coquettish smile stretching ear to ear.

"Earned what?"

The smile disappeared. "The best blow job you've ever had," she declared, with a stone-cold seriousness that sent chills up and down his spine.

He handed the valet a $50 bill. Then he slid behind the wheel of his classic blue Porsche 356 Speedster convertible and waited for her to retrieve her own car from the public lot adjacent to the restaurant. He would follow her home. He looked down at his phone to check his messages. A vehicle came to a quiet stop next to him. The driver honked twice. "You ready?" she asked through the open passenger side window of her black Tesla Model S. She didn't wait for an answer. The tires squealed as she tore out of the lot and turned onto the main road. He quickly followed, now more intrigued than ever.

He had offered to pick her up for their blind date, but she said she preferred to meet at the restaurant. When he bragged to her about what kind of car he drove and how nice it would be with the top down, she still declined. Now he was struggling to keep up with her as she weaved in and out of the unusually dense evening traffic—seemingly unconcerned with whether or not he kept up. It all made him want her even more.

After ten minutes of racing south on the highway in the far left lane, she jerked her car hard right, barely making the exit. They drove two more miles through a small town. When the homes started getting bigger and the spaces between them longer, she pulled into a wide driveway. An electronic gate closed slowly behind them. She was already opening the front door by the time he parked and got out of his car. "I'm just going to change and check on the little guy. Meet me in the kitchen straight ahead. Help yourself to anything." She disappeared, leaving the door open.

He strolled up the brick walkway and noted the meticulously manicured landscaping. Inside the door was an entryway that rivaled his own, complete with a hanging chandelier that cost more than the average car. He was confused. Why would a girl driving a fancy car and living in a beautiful home be looking for dates on a site known for linking older, affluent men with young, attractive women? Usually they were looking for sugar daddies. But she obviously didn't need money, so why the older men? *Daddy issues*, he said to himself. *Who cares—let's get to the blow job and I'll be on my way.*

He was drinking a beer he had found in the industrial-size, stainless steel refrigerator when she entered the kitchen wearing a tight gray University of Alabama T-shirt and equally snug black shorts. She had the body of a serious athlete. He didn't care which sport and didn't bother asking. "Is this your house? Do you, like, live here alone? Just you?"

She nodded. "Just me and my little boy. My little Crimson Tide," she answered. Then she took a slow sip of his beer and placed the bottle on the counter. "And I just sent the sitter home."

"The sitter?" he asked. She gently clasped his face with both hands and kissed him softly on the lips. When he clumsily pushed his tongue into her mouth, she pulled back. "Follow me to the family room," she said, taking him by the hand and leading him into the next room. She pushed him playfully onto the sofa. "What kind of music do you want to listen to while I go down on you?" she asked, sauntering toward a large entertainment center.

"Uh, wow, uh, you are direct. I like that. And anything is fine with me," he answered, his words quivering with anticipation.

"How's this?"

"Perfect. That's perfect," he declared, even though his heart was beating so loud he couldn't hear the music.

She straddled him on the sofa, grabbed a handful of his hair, and pulled his head back. Then she passionately kissed up and down his neck. He jumped a little when she buried her teeth into his ear lobe and growled playfully. "Sorry. Should have warned you," she whispered. "Sometimes I nibble."

"Honey, you can nibble on anything you want," he gasped.

"Hold on. I'm going to go put my hair up and check on him really quick. I want to make sure my little Crimson Tide is still sleeping," she said, standing up. "I'll be right back."

He watched her leave the room. Raising an eyebrow, he reflected silently on how odd it was that she had to check on him again at that point. When she returned, he was scrolling through the messages on his phone. Without a word she unfastened his belt and pulled his pants and boxer shorts down past his knees. He was ready. Then, to his surprise, she took his phone away and thumbed her way to the video camera. She pressed the record button, handed it back, and got started. He inhaled fast and sharply, as if he had just jumped into a freezing cold ice bath. Then he watched her work through the camera as it recorded. "Holy shit," he said. "Where the hell did you learn how to do that?" Her mouth full, she looked up at the camera and winked.

After a few more seconds, he tossed the phone to the side. "I can't hold onto this thing anymore," he said. He reached up with both hands and grabbed the long bar that ran along the top of the sofa. She looked up, stopped, and straddled him again. Then she reached under one of the cushions and removed a pair of handcuffs.

"I have an idea," she said, holding them up. "Let me put these on you."

He looked at the cuffs. "I don't know about that. I mean, why? I'm having a great time as it is. Those aren't necessary." He tried to push her head back down. She resisted.

"So am I. But these make me horny as hell. So I'll give you a choice. I'll finish what I'm doing now and you can leave. Or you can let me slip these on and I'll fuck your brains out all night. It's up to you."

He looked at the cuffs again, then into her pale blue eyes. Breathing heavily, she licked her lips. "Fine. Go ahead. Put 'em on me. But not too tight." She gently grabbed one of his wrists and kissed it before securing it with one of the cuffs. Then she raised both of his hands to the bar above his head, swung the remaining cuff over the bar, and fastened it around his free hand. Once he was shackled to the bar, she kissed her way back down and swallowed him whole.

"God damn!" he said aloud.

She stopped abruptly. "Shut up!" She covered his mouth, quickly snapped into an upright position, and cocked an ear toward the other side of the house, straining to listen. "I think I just heard him. Maybe I should check on him again."

He exhaled loudly. "Are you fucking kidding me? Check on him again? Why?"

"Why?" she asked, a shocked look on her face. "I told you earlier he was the center of my universe. You said you understood."

"Can't he wait like five minutes!"

"He's my life and you said you'd always respect that. You promised! Did you lie to me?"

"For the love of God, your little Crimson Tide is fine! Trust me," he exclaimed. "it's just a fucking dog anyway!"

Her face became a blank slate. She reached into his pants, crumbled up below his knees, and retrieved his car keys. Then she covered his private area with a blanket, grabbed his cell phone from the seat cushion next to him, and powered it off.

"Okay, fine. Whatever," he said. "Game over. Just undo these cuffs and I'll get out of here."

"No."

He pulled hard at the handcuffs and raised his voice. "Get these fucking things off me or I swear to God you're going to be sorry."

"No. And I don't want to talk about it anymore tonight. You've upset me. So you're going to sit right there and think about what you did," she said in a stern, motherly tone. Then she turned the lights off and left him in the darkness alone.

CHAPTER TWELVE

Probable Cause

"Look at them, man. It's the walking dead out here. You'd think they'd be working a bachelor party somewhere or something," said Goodie.

"I've arrested the one on the left before," said Luci, pointing through the windshield of her unmarked cruiser at two women on the far side of the intersection. When the light turned green, she turned right, into an area that cops called the Black Hole—a block with boarded-up storefronts and mostly broken streetlights.

"Prostitution, I assume?" asked Goodie.

"Yes. And endangering the life of a child. She was out here working in the middle of the night, walking the streets with an infant in her arms. I've see my share of shit over the years, but that one set me off." Luci thought about her own kids for a moment—both sound asleep at the nanny's house, since she had to work and Mark was traveling again. She hated it when they had to stay there on a school night. But since ants were on a mission to take over their garage and basement, she had to have the house fumigated and so the nanny's residence was a convenient refuge. Murphy, the Landry family's German Shepherd, had been forced to vacate the premises as well. He was spread out across the back seat of the car. Luci reached back and rubbed his belly.

"Seriously? She had a kid with her out here? Jesus, what the fuck is wrong with these people?" asked Goodie rhetorically, shaking his head in disgust. "Not exactly good for business either, I imagine."

Luci was annoyed by his comments. But since Goodie was a new street detective and she was his field training officer, she didn't rebuke him as she might have done to a more experienced cop. Instead, she chose her words carefully and treated it as a teachable moment.

"Keep a few things in mind. First, none of these women want to be out here. So let's dispense with any myths of consent. Most are in the throes of addictions that will eventually kill them. And between now and then, they will do things that they never—even in their worst nightmares—could have imagined doing."

Goodie started to speak up—presumably to walk back his comments—but Luci held up two fingers and kept talking.

"Second, forget any stereotypes of supposedly good men just looking for a little company or bachelor party entertainment. Johns are scumbags at any hour, but especially at this time of night. Any guy out right now looking for girls is a straight-up predator and scum of the fucking earth. The worst of the worst. It's not the sex that turns them on—it's the vulnerability of these poor women—and they thrive on it like sharks after chum."

Goodie was nodding his head throughout Luci's speech. "Totally agree," he replied when she finished. "Totally agree. It's a big problem."

Luci pulled into a parking space in front of a rundown building and killed the headlights. From there, she and Goodie had a clear view up and down the block. The streets were dead silent. Not a soul in sight. She checked the time and fired up a portable laptop. "It's quiet tonight. Call Sawyer and see if anything's up. I heard him earlier so I know he's working tonight. Sometimes they stay off the radios and talk on their phones." Sawyer was the regional Drug Enforcement Agency (DEA) task force commander. Luci had a good relationship with him, but sometimes the feds kept local law enforcement in the dark on sensitive investigations and raids until the very last minute. The better to prevent leaks, they would say—which was a nice way of saying they didn't trust local authorities not to blab in advance and blow the mission. Luci understood why they did it, but it still pissed her off.

Goodie made the call while Luci tossed a treat to Murphy in the back seat. He caught it in his mouth, and she reached back and scratched him under the chin. "What a good boy. Who's mama's baby? Are you mama's baby?" Murphy barked and Luci gave him another treat.

This part of the Merrimack Valley in Massachusetts—located north of Boston and bordering New Hampshire—was a designated high-intensity drug trafficking area (HIDA). As a consequence, it was under intense scrutiny by a federal Organized Crime Drug Enforcement Task Force (OCDETF) made up of elements from the DEA, ATF, FBI, IRS, ICE, U.S. Marshals, and the U.S. Attorney's office in Boston. When petty disagreements, turf disputes, or key leaders' egos got in the way, OCDETF was just an idle resource functioning at considerable taxpayer expense. But lately, spurred on by the release of another Trinitario execution video—this one featuring a captured undercover narcotics enforcement officer—the team was firing on all cylinders and hell-bent on avenging their colleague's grotesque death.

The hideous video had been released the day before. It opened in the same way as the first one, with a closeup shot of the conscious officer strapped to a chair in a bright white room. The camera panned out to reveal two figures dressed in blue jumpsuits and clown masks with bright red hair—each holding a Louisville Slugger baseball bat. Then the soundtrack started. *"Who you trying to get crazy with ese? Don't you know I'm loco?"* echoed throughout the room, followed by the well-known hip-hop beat and opening lyrics of Cypress Hill's *Insane in the Brain*.

To da one on da flamboyant tip
I'll just toss that ham in the fryin' pan like spam
Get done when I come and slam
Damn, I feel like the Son of Sam

The officer saw the clowns and started to convulse uncontrollably. Fully aware of what was about to happen, he screamed and begged for mercy. The clowns smacked their palms with the bats in sync with the music. His futile pleas morphed into barely decipherable shrieks as he shifted from begging to sending a final message to those whom he would leave behind. He called out his wife and kids' names and declared how much he loved them. The clowns danced to the beat and jokingly mimicked the dying man's words. Then they commenced batting practice until he was unrecognizable.

Wanton violence like this was not uncommon and almost expected in underdeveloped narco-states plagued by violence. But this level of orchestrated savagery was rarely seen in the United States. The U.S. Attorney for the District of Boston immediately declared the Trinitarios a Consolidated Priority Organization Target (CPOT). Its members were either running or hiding and the OCDETF was on the hunt.

"Sawyer says the whole team is on the streets tonight," said Goodie. "But it sounds like they're all closer to Boston. They rounded up a ton of street-level distributors and are squeezing them for info on the execution tapes. One of his teams raided a place in Lowell about an hour ago. All they found was a few baggies of heroin and a few dozen pills. On the bright side, they also found a dead guy shot twice in the back of the head, execution-style. He called it a public-service homicide. Sawyer's words, not mine," Goodie quickly added.

Luci nodded. She didn't like casually dismissing or celebrating anybody's death, but she wasn't able to muster much sympathy for a dead drug dealer. "Okay. So that means we're out here mostly alone tonight."

"That means I get you all to myself," replied Goodie. "Just the way I like it."

Luci turned her head and shot him a stone-cold look. "What does that mean?"

"Nothing untoward," he replied, raising his palms in the air to emphasize his innocent intentions. "It's just that I won't be working with you forever and I want to learn as much from you as possible before you retire. If I can be half as good a detective as you are, I'll be golden. That's all I meant. Bad word choice, I guess. Sorry." He lowered his arms, placed his palms on his knees, and bowed his head in mock shame like a child apologizing to his mother.

Luci laughed out loud. She reached over and pushed his shoulder playfully. "Get your head up. We won't catch any bad guys with you looking at the floor. And don't be sorry. It's not you. It's me. I've been anxious as hell lately. Lots on my mind."

Goodie smiled and pretended to wipe the sweat from his brow. "Whew! Thank God. Thought I blew it for a second. Still partners?"

"Partners? Hmmm. Technically, no. We're not partners. I'm training you," she answered, patting him on the shoulder a few times. "But if it makes you happy, go ahead and call me your partner. I won't object as long as you've got my back. I'm assuming you know how to take care of yourself. You're not going to melt like a snowflake if things get dicey, right? You know how to take care of yourself," she asked sarcastically.

Goodie smiled from ear to ear as she chided him. "Of course I can handle myself. But who cares when we've got this guy?" he added, nodding toward Murphy spread out on the back seat.

"He's good company and he has skills just as good as any of the department's K9s. But Murphy's a civilian. So he stays in the car tonight unless I let him out to do his business."

"No worries. You got me and that's good enough." Goodie pulled out his cellphone. "Did you ever see any of my fights on the ice back when I was in the NHL? There's a bunch of them online. I saw a montage of my scuffles the other day. Let me see if I can find it for you. You'll love it." He started searching YouTube.

"Really? You played hockey?" Luci asked sarcastically, rolling her eyes. "Because you never talk about it." She started to laugh but stopped when light spilled from around a corner a block away. "Headlights up ahead. We've got company." She looked at Goodie, who was still searching for the highlight reel of his hockey fights. "Heads up, Goodie. Pay attention."

The vehicle turned the corner and slowly headed toward their position. The driver had the windows down and the music turned up. It was a red Honda Civic with lightly tinted windows and thick titanium mag wheels. As the vehicle drew closer, Luci and Goodie's seats vibrated from the stereo's bass. Luci always felt like a sitting duck when sitting in a parked cruiser—marked or unmarked. She unfastened her seatbelt and reached under her sweatshirt to grip the handle of the Smith & Wesson M&P 9mm with Crimson Trace laser sights that she carried on duty.

"Can you see a plate?" she asked Goodie.

"No. The asshole's high beams are washing out my vision."

The Civic rolled closer, at what felt like a snail's pace to Luci. The driver, a young Hispanic male, slowed down even further as he approached. It appeared that he was going to stop when he was alongside the unmarked cruiser, but instead, the driver hit the gas and sped off. Luci squinted in the rear-view mirror and read the license plate backwards, committing it to memory. It was a skill she and Mark had practiced all the time until it was second nature. When they were driving with the kids, they'd make a family game out of it.

"Rhode Island plates. This guy is a long way from home. It's 2 a.m. and he's in an area known for drug trafficking. I could probably pull him over right now, but I'm going to follow him a little to see what he does. Run the plate." Luci recited the license plate number to Goodie as she made a U-turn. The driver of the Civic saw them coming, made a hard right turn, and gunned the engine. Rubber squealed. "That didn't take long, did it?" Luci hit the blue lights.

...

"Do you mind stepping out of the car for a second, Mr. Vasquez?" asked Luci. She waited for an answer and looked at Goodie, who was standing on the other side of the Civic, shining his flashlight through the windows. He shook his head to Luci, indicating that he hadn't seen anything incriminating in plain view.

"Why?" answered the young man, gripping the wheel to keep his hands from shaking. "What's the problem?" He tried to play it cool, but his voice was breaking up.

"There's no problem. Your license and registration came back fine. I just want to talk to you. Do you mind stepping out?" she asked in a neutral, non-confrontational tone that sounded more likely a friendly request. "Do you mind? We can stand right in front of your car and chat."

Vasquez nodded reluctantly, slowly unfastened his seatbelt, and exited the vehicle. Luci led him into the glow of the headlights, since there were no working streetlights for blocks. She stood several steps away and at a forty-five-degree angle from the subject's left side—the classic police interview position. Assuming that he was right-handed like more than eighty percent of people, that position would keep her gun out of his immediate reach and give her some much-needed time and space to react if he tried to throw a punch. Luci looked him up and down but did not touch him. "Do you have anything on you I need to worry about?" She watched closely for his reaction to the question.

"No."

"Mind if I pat you down just to make sure?" she asked in the same non-confrontational voice she had used to get him exit the vehicle by his own volition.

"I told you I don't have nothing on me." Luci said nothing. She just stared into his eyes and waited. Uncomfortable with the silence, he quickly consented. "Yeah, fine, whatever. Just get it over with. Hands on the hood?" he asked.

"Yes, please."

When she didn't discover anything she tapped him on the back. "Thank you. You can turn around."

"Told you I didn't have nothing," he muttered aloud.

"So tell me. What brings you to this neighborhood at this hour?" she asked.

He gave her a song-and-dance about taking care of a sick family friend who lives in the area. He must have taken a wrong turn somewhere and got lost. Now he was worried. She was home alone and he wanted to get back to make sure she was all right. When Luci asked why he was out at 2 a.m., he said it was to get some air. When she asked for the friend's name and address, he became flustered. "Why do you need that? That ain't none of your business," he protested.

"Okay. I was gonna offer to send a car over to check on her. She's really sick and you're worried about her, right? That's all." Luci eyed him closely. She didn't smell alcohol and his pupils looked fine, but he was growing increasingly nervous. "I can see you want to move on. So do we," she said, nodding in Goodie's direction to remind the young man that she was not alone. "Do you mind if I take a quick look in your car so we can make that happen?"

He immediately stiffened up. "I do not consent to any searches, officer." The words rolled smoothly off his tongue.

"What's that?" she asked.

"I do not consent to any searches," he repeated, exactly as he had been taught.

"Just get the fuck out of the—" began Goodie.

Luci silenced him with a raised hand, without taking her eyes off the subject. "Okay, no problem. Here's the thing. I want to take a look in your car and you're not giving me consent. So I'm going to call for a K9 and we'll leave it up to the dog. If he detects something, I'll have probable cause to take a peek in your car. If not, you'll be free to go."

The threat of a K9 sniffing around their vehicle always rattled subjects. If they had nothing to hide but weren't cooperating just to make a point of exercising their civil liberties, the thought of standing on the street and waiting God-only-knows-how-long for an available K9 to arrive and clear them was usually enough for them to cave in and give consent. If they did have something to hide, the mere mention of a K9 sent their hearts racing. Luci watched him closely. His breathing quickened and he started to fidget.

"I do not consent to any searches," he repeated.

"Fair enough," said Luci. "Just know that it's a busy night so it could be a while before a K9 is available."

"Man, you don't have any reason to search my car. So I don't—"

"Yeah, I know. You don't consent to any searches. I got that part. You've been coached well," she added. "Do me a favor. For my protection and yours, put your palms on the hood and keep them there."

She told Goodie to call in the K9 request and ask for a backup patrol car in case they needed to transport the subject to the police station. Goodie returned to the cruiser while Luci kept her eyes on the young man. Small beads of perspiration were forming on his forehead and the cheeks of his clean-shaven face. She stood quietly several arm lengths away and let him sweat for a few minutes before addressing him again.

"If there's anything in the vehicle that I need to know about, now would be the time to tell me, Mr. Vasquez. If you're straight with me, I might be able to help you out. But if you lie and I have to learn things the hard way, I won't." She heard the cruiser door shut, followed by Goodie's approaching footsteps. The subject became visibly agitated. His sweat started to drip onto the hood of his vehicle.

"Bitch, I told you I don't consent to no searches!" he said in a raised voice. Then he pulled his hands away from the car as if it was a hot stove, turned aggressively toward Luci, and took a step. She reflexively backed up and reached for her weapon, anticipating the assault. But Vasquez froze in place. His eyes were wide as saucers and his gaze was fixed on something other than Luci. She sensed movement from behind. Then she heard an aggressive bark followed by a black and tan blur in her peripheral vision as Murphy flew through the air toward the subject.

"Slow down, buddy!" Goodie jerked back on the leash. The German Shepherd's powerful jaws snapped shut just inches from the threat's face.

"Hands back on the hood, now!" ordered Luci. But the subject was still frozen in a state of shock. Before he could process what had just happened, Luci had him bent over the hood and his wrists handcuffed behind his back. She took a few deep breaths before leading him by the shoulder to the sidewalk. "Sit here on the curb and don't even think about moving. You move—I taze. Got it?" She slapped him on the back of the head to snap him out of his daze. "*Comprendes?*" He nodded and she moved toward Goodie and Murphy.

"What the hell are you doing?" she asked Goodie.

"What? Relax. The patrol car backup will be here in a few minutes, but it was gonna be like two hours for a K9. So I thought we'd rattle him a little. Plus, I figured Murphy might want some fresh air," said Goodie, smiling.

"I'm not laughing. Does it look like I'm laughing?" she asked, pointing at her own face. "I told you earlier, the dog stays in the car."

"Fine. Sorry. I honestly didn't think it was a big deal. I thought it would speed things up," he snapped defensively.

"Goodie, I've done this shit a thousand times. He would have eventually given me consent on his own. All I needed to do was sweat him for a few more minutes. Now you scared the shit out of him and his head is all fucked up." She quickly scanned up and down the street. "If anybody saw that or—even worse—shot a video of it, it'll look like we were harassing and trying to intimidate the guy. Do you have any idea what kind of liability you're opening us up to with this kind of shit?" Luci had spent her career operating by the book. She wasn't about to put her pension and reputation in jeopardy on the verge of retirement.

"I'll put him back in the car," said Goodie, turning his back.

"Do it quickly." She approached the curb and redirected her attention to the subject. "You're fine. Just relax and think about what I said before. I can't help you unless you help me first."

"Fuck you," he said under his breath.

"Fuck me? Okay, then. Don't say I didn't warn you," she said, stepping back from the curb. Luci wondered what was taking the uniformed backup so long to arrive. She pulled out her phone and started to dial a number but stopped when she heard Murphy start to bark again. It was not his typical excited barking; rather, it was much deeper with a slow, deliberate cadence. She turned away from the subject to see Goodie standing behind the Civic, holding the leash. Murphy was up on his hind legs, thumping his front paws on the top of the trunk as he barked. He was sending Luci a clear message that he had detected something.

"You think he found something?" asked Goodie.

Luci ignored the stupid question and told him to back up with the dog. Then she called to inquire about the K9 request. The two police dogs on duty were busy tracking suspected gang members along the Merrimack River. Their handlers would get back to her when they had more information, but they made it clear that her request was not a priority. Luci ended the call. "Shit."

"I told you they were all tied up," Goodie said. "Your dog smells something, right? So why don't we just search the car?"

"I'm thinking," she answered, reaching both hands behind her head to tighten her ponytail. "Murphy knows what's he's doing, but he isn't a police K9. It's not like we can just use any dog and if he happens to bark we magically have probable cause. He's just a pet." Luci looked over at the handcuffed subject sitting on the curb with his head down, about thirty feet away. "I already have enough to arrest this guy for disorderly conduct or maybe even attempted assault and impound the car. We can just have a K9 come to the lot and sniff around whenever one becomes available. God damn, Goodie. Why didn't you just leave Murphy in the car?"

"Listen, we know the K9 is going to detect something. So why not save time and just search the car now?"

"Because there's no rush. He'll be in jail and the car will be impounded. We have plenty of time. And if we find anything to charge him with, a good defense attorney will argue that since the assault took place on the street we had no authority to search the vehicle. Better to wait and not give him the argument. Don't take chances. You never know how judges will rule these days."

Goodie pointed to the defendant. "That guy's going to have an overworked public defender who will do anything to avoid a trial. He'll plea out like everyone else. Let's at least pop the trunk. How do we know he doesn't have a person tied up in there? Exigent circumstances, I say."

Luci looked back and forth between the suspect and the vehicle. She was tired. It was already late and she didn't want to put more hours between her and her bed. She looked at her watch and shook her head. Then she walked to the rear of her cruiser and popped open the trunk.

"So what are we gonna do?" asked Goodie.

"I'm gonna get some gloves and a mask. Then I'm going to pop the trunk."

Lucy snapped on disposable nitrile medical gloves and slipped the protective mask over her face. She tried not to think about the long list of potential substances, some microscopic, that cops had to fear inhaling or touching during routine searches. Satisfied that she was sufficiently protected, she went to work. The trunk lid wouldn't stay open on its own, so she held it open with one hand. The main compartment was empty except for a window ice scraper and a set of jumper cables. She used her free hand to lift the trunk bottom and search around the spare tire well. When she didn't find anything, she let go of the trunk lid. It slammed shut on its own.

"Not normal," she said aloud. "Too heavy. Get me a screwdriver, Goodie."

A marked cruiser turned the corner a block away and sped to a halt in front of the Civic. A uniformed officer hopped out. He said a few words to the suspect and then checked in with Luci to see how he could help. Goodie handed Luci a screwdriver. She used it to pry away a square metal plate from the bottom of the trunk lid. As it popped off, dozens of baggies filled with white powder and an old snub-nosed revolver fell into the trunk.

"There it is," she said, turning to the uniformed officer. "Would you be so kind as to inform Mr. Vasquez that he is under arrest for assault and possession of whatever the hell this stuff turns out to be? Probably heroin. And since it's unlikely he has a license, throw in a firearms charge for good measure. Thanks."

"My pleasure," replied the cop.

"You see how sloppy this false compartment is, Goodie? This one is pretty bad but you'd be amazed at how creative they can be. I've completely missed them before, but thankfully other cops noticed and pointed them out. A car is only so big but it still seems like they never run out of ideas. Know what I mean?" she asked. When she heard no reply, she turned around. "Goodie? Goodie, where'd you go?"

Goodie was standing on the street next to Luci's cruiser. The back door was open and he was pointing inside. "Hey, Luci. I think you'd better come here for a second. It looks like there's something wrong with your dog."

Luci approached her car and looked through the open door. Murphy had fallen off the back seat and was lying on his side on the floorboards. He had thrown up the treats she had fed him earlier. Now he was dry-heaving. She lifted his head and quickly examined him. His eyes were closed, and his breathing was slow and shallow as if he was under anesthesia. She said his name several times. Murphy's eyes flickered open and she noted his pinpoint pupils.

"Oh, shit!" she said loudly, turning to Goodie with a horrified look on her face. "Get me some Narcan!"

"Narcan? Why?" he asked.

"Just do it, Goodie!" She pointed in the direction of the uniformed officer. "Ask him if he has any. Do it now!"

CHAPTER THIRTEEN

Return to Berlin

"Cable," said Billy into his phone, loud enough for Mark and Kenny to hear him in the back of the plane. The Gulfstream G280 was cruising at thirty-three thousand feet above the Atlantic Ocean. Flying just over five hundred miles per hour, they would arrive at Ramstein Air Base in southwest Germany by dusk. They would refuel and be back in the air within an hour and would land in Berlin later that evening.

The meeting with German intelligence officials was scheduled for the following morning. Mark was anxious to learn what, if anything, they knew about Oleg Borodin that he didn't already know. Heike, the German operator with whom he had a prior history, insisted that the trip would be worth it for him. Still, he was skeptical because they had already scoured through every shred of data they could get from the entire alphabet soup of U.S. intelligence agencies. Besides, the German and U.S. governments had a close intel-sharing relationship. If she had information that the CIA or FBI didn't have, it meant they were holding out. If that was the case, he wondered why.

"Cable," said Billy forcefully, looking back over his shoulder at Mark and Kenny and rolling his eyes.

"Who is he talking to?" asked Kenny.

"No idea," Mark answered. "And this is the last time I'm reading through this file," he added, referring to the Oleg Borodin dossier he and Kenny were reviewing for the umpteenth time.

"We already know it by heart. Nothing ever changes and I'm positive we aren't missing anything. This guy dots his i's, crosses his t's, and covers his tracks like nobody I've ever seen. Let's hope Heike has something useful for us."

"I'm looking forward to meeting her," said Kenny.

Mark closed his laptop and looked at Kenny in the seat across from him. "Yeah?"

"Yeah. I'm just curious. That's all. I've heard her name a few times over the years."

"Billing!" shouted Billy in the front of the plane.

Kenny and Mark both looked up at Billy, then back at each other and shook their heads.

"He okay?" asked Kenny.

"He's got a lot on his mind," answered Mark.

"So, Mark," Kenny began, awkwardly. "About Heike."

"What about her?" asked Mark with a raised eyebrow.

"Well, I know you two have worked together before and I've been through everything we have. But even our files are heavily redacted and confusing as hell, which, I imagine, is not an accident. So it's hard to get a real understanding of what you guys did together in Berlin way back when. Would you mind filling in the blanks for me?"

Mark placed his computer in his bag and slid his reading glasses to the top of his head. He took a few deep breaths and considered Kenny's request. "Okay, we can do this. Tell me what you know and I'll fill in the blanks. Keep in mind it was like ten years ago."

"Okay, I get the crux of the dilemma. U.S. chemical weapons had somehow fallen into the hands of some neo-Nazi group in Germany. But I don't see how that's possible, since we got all our chemical weapons out of Germany and destroyed them back in 1990."

Mark tried not to laugh. "Technically, you are correct. But, Kenny, stranger things have happened. We've had inspections of our entire nuclear arsenal where half of the weapons failed to meet basic safety standards—despite knowing about the inspections in advance. We've lost track of nukes for days and even weeks. We've somehow mistakenly armed bombers with live nukes and flown them around the country, letting them sit on tarmacs unguarded for weeks, before anyone noticed. Missiliers have been caught sleeping in their launch capsules with the doors open. And that's the big stuff. You'd shit if you knew how many times we've done the same with smaller stuff. It doesn't surprise me at all. I'm not knocking the boys, just saying that shit happens. And sometimes that shit is big."

"So how did a neo-Nazi group end up with half a dozen U.S. 155mm artillery shells filled with some kind of chemical weapon? And how did we find out before they had a chance to do damage? This is completely new to me."

"The Germans used to protest the presence of chemical weapons on their soil all the time. But they usually did it outside U.S. military installations that didn't even house any of them. The bad stuff was secretly kept at a small depot in Clausen, Germany near the French border. President George H. W. Bush promised Helmut Kohl that we'd get rid of them, so the chemical guys secured them all in these funky-looking, vapor-proof containers. Then they were trucked to the coast under heavy guard and finally shipped on boats to somewhere in the Pacific to be destroyed. Except that somehow a few ended up on a different U.S. base in Heidelberg. Nobody knows how or why, but more than likely it was just a huge fuckup because they sat there for a few decades before some second lieutenant stumbled across them during a special munitions inventory. I'd give anything to have seen the look on that butter bar's face when he found them. He must have nearly shit his pants," said Mark, smiling.

"What were they exactly, and how did they get from his inventory to neo-Nazis?" asked Kenny.

"Nasty stuff. Sarin and VX. The lieutenant should have reported it immediately. But he was inventorying in advance of a major DOD inspection that the base commander's third star was riding on. He didn't want to be the turd in the punch bowl. So Lieutenant Snuffy, or whatever his name was, panicked and got creative." Mark leaned forward, clearly animated by the memories. "He drove them to the rifle range and dumped them next to the amnesty box with a note."

Kenny looked confused, so Mark explained the concept of the military amnesty box that soldiers learn about on day one in the military. After being issued their gear and signing all the requisite paperwork in basic training, soldiers are told to stand at the foot of their assigned bunks. Drill sergeants then place large trash barrels marked with bright red signs reading "AMNESTY" throughout the barracks. Recruits are told that if they have anything in their possession that they shouldn't have, this is their final opportunity to get rid of the contraband without penalty. If they are caught with contraband any time after that, punishment would be swift and harsh.

Having given this instruction, the drill sergeants leave the barracks. When they return ten minutes later, the barrels—typically loaded with candy, pornography, drugs, and weapons—are dragged away and disposed of, with no questions asked.

"Amnesty boxes are also found on most rifle ranges. Soldiers have to shake themselves down and return every single round of ammunition before leaving the range. But just in case, there is usually an amnesty box nearby where a soldier can drop rounds they somehow missed during the shakedown. As long as they don't leave the range and return to the barracks with whatever they found, no foul."

Kenny opened two bottles of cold water and handed one to Mark. "But there's a world of difference between a couple of rifle or pistol rounds and 155mm chemical weapons. This is still hard to believe."

"Believe it, my friend. Lieutenant Snuffy scoured the rules and regs and couldn't find any exceptions or restrictions for the amnesty box. None. So he loaded the shells into the back of a Humvee. Then he drove to the nearest rifle range, dropped them off next to the amnesty box, and drove away fully cleansed. Free of sin, if you will. Born again. From there, it all eventually got picked up by a German civilian hired by the DOD to collect dangerous waste on base twice a month and dispose of it in accordance with German domestic environmental law. Turns out he was hired without a background check and nobody ever noticed or cared about the questionable significance of some of his neck tattoos."

"Seriously? Holy shit. Then how did we find out where it all ended up?" Kenny asked

"Initially, a German law enforcement informant embedded in the neo-Nazi group sent a red notice to his handlers. He personally saw six 155mm shells. He got a good look at the markings of five of them and they were Sarin and VX. But the numbers he reported on the sixth were confusing. Either he got the markings wrong or it was actually a biological weapon, which would make things even worse. A chemical weapon is bad enough and can cause a world of hurt, but biological weapons are living organisms and can self-replicate. So if you have one, you have a stockpile. Unfortunately, it was impossible to verify the numbers because the informant was found dead in his apartment a week after reporting on the shells. Suicide by poison. I didn't enter the picture until after they had the leader of the group in custody."

"What was your role?" asked Kenny.

"My role was—"

"Representative!" yelled Billy. Now he was standing in the front of the plane, screaming into his phone. "I said representative, Goddammit!" He threw the phone against the cockpit door. It bounced off and slid down the aisle to the back of the plane. Mark reached down and grabbed it, then brought it with him as he tried to figure out the problem.

"What's up? What happened? Who were you yelling at?" he asked Billy.

"Nothing. Sorry about that. Cable company," Billy answered, taking deep breaths to cool himself down.

Mark handed Billy his phone. Amazingly, it was still intact. The cockpit door opened and Bode, the pilot, poked his head into the cabin. Bode had recently retired from the U.S. Air Force and had been Mark's primary pilot for only a month. As his final job in the Air Force, he flew one of the U.S.'s four Boeing E-4B Doomsday planes, mobile command posts for the National Command Authority, out of Offutt Air Force Base near Omaha, Nebraska. He was happy to have a post-retirement job where he would actually fly instead of spending his shifts sitting on a runway, engines humming, hoping he would never have to take off and direct a nuclear war from the sky.

"Everything okay back here?" Bode asked. Mark shrugged his shoulders. Bode nodded and returned to the cockpit, unconcerned. Mark took a seat next to Billy, who was now sitting quietly and staring at his computer. On the screen was his soon-to-be-ex-wife's Facebook profile. She had just posted a picture of herself with another man, cheek to cheek on the back deck of Billy's former home.

"I just realized I'm still paying the fucking cable bill back in Oklahoma," he said in a low voice. "Normally, something like that wouldn't set me off so bad. But that," he said, pointing to the picture. "That boils my blood, man. She's been seeing this guy for a lot longer than we've been separated. And the comments. Ah, fuck. The comments from people who I thought were my friends are too much. I'm sorry, man. I lost my cool." Billy was embarrassed.

Mark smacked him on the shoulder. "What are you apologizing for? Look around." Mark pointed around the interior of the Gulfstream's cabin. "It's only us here, man. Just don't do that tomorrow at the Bundesnachrichtendienst." Seeing Billy's face go blank, he clarified the long name. "Sorry, the BND."

"Thank you," Billy replied, cracking a smile and apparently calming down. "No need to speak Kraut. We're not on the ground yet." He pointed at the screen again. "I should have known, man. I should have known. There were signs. She started cold-shouldering me over a year ago and I blew it off. Then there were little things. About six months ago I was back home for a week. That first night back we grilled some steaks and drank our favorite wine. Everything seemed normal, but when we went to wash the dishes, she took off her watch and wedding ring. She had a little tan line around her wrist from the watch but nothing on her ring finger. Which meant she hadn't been wearing it. She just put it on because I was home. I saw it. I knew what it meant. But for some reason I blocked it out of my mind. Now this shit is right in my face," he said, pointing to the screen again. "It's enough to make a guy lace up his Bruno Maglis."

Mark winced at the O. J. Simpson reference but couldn't help but laugh. "Oh, dude, don't even say that. That's terrible."

"You know what I mean," added Billy, trying unsuccessfully to stifle his own laughter. "After twenty years of bliss she drops a shit bomb on me out of nowhere. She was lonely and this asshole"—again he pointed to the screen—"comes along, gives her the attention I wasn't, and boom, my fucking marriage is done just like that," he said, snapping his fingers for emphasis. "I gotta stop looking at this stupid shit or I'll never get over it."

"Agreed," said Mark. "It ain't helping. Thankfully my kids are too small for it and Luci has never had any interest in this social media crap."

"She's may not be very active, but she has an account at least." Billy scrolled down and pressed a few keys. "See, there she is. Luci Landry."

Mark pulled his glasses down over his eyes and looked at Luci's Facebook profile on the screen. He had never seen it before. He grunted at the profile picture. She had obviously snapped it while sitting at the desk in her home office. She was alone but smiling ear to ear as if she had just won a Grammy. "I don't get this shit at all, man," Mark said under his breath. "I'll leave you alone with your O. J. thoughts and get back to talking with Kenny. You good?"

Billy nodded, then shook his head. "I was driving her away and didn't even know it. I took it for granted. You and Luci have something special. Hold her tight, man."

"Break out the emergency whiskey if you need it, and don't forget to share."

Mark returned to his seat across from Kenny and reclined it as far back as it would go. He crossed his feet at the ankles and laced his hands behind his head. Kenny raised an eyebrow and pointed up toward the front of the aircraft with his chin. "He's fine," said Mark.

"So how did you get pulled into the chemical weapons thing in Germany ten years ago?" asked Kenny, eager to continue the conversation.

"I was already in Germany. It all came to a head the same time as the annual Munich Security Conference. National security officials from more than fifty countries attend this event. There were a ton of credible threats surrounding the conference, so Dunbar had some of us there working dark. A bunch of muckety-mucks were attending a production of the Bavarian State Opera at the National Theatre Munich. Sadie and Billy, dressed in formal evening gown and tuxedo, were working the inside of the theatre while I, having lost the coin toss, sat, bored shitless, on a rooftop with some snipers overlooking the building. That's where I was when Dunbar called me and told me to pack my shit and get to Berlin ASAP. The Germans had already picked up the leader of the neo-Nazi group, a well-known troublemaker known as Neo Helmut. They had him on surveillance talking about the artillery shells. Worse, he claimed they had extracted and repurposed the payloads and an attack on the Berlin transit system was imminent. So they snatched him off the street and were trying, to no avail, to find out where the weapons were before it was too late. He wasn't giving them anything. That's where I came in. I helped get the information."

"How? What'd you do?" asked Kenny, trying to hide the fact he was on the edge of his seat. He had been dying to know the details of this mission for years, and now he was about to find out.

"I just helped find the proper"—Mark thought long and chose his words thoughtfully—"...leverage."

"What did you do to him?"

"Him? Nothing. The Germans had him locked down tight. I couldn't get anywhere near the interrogation. So Heike and I had to get creative."

Mark stared at the ceiling of the plane for several moments. Kenny figured he was reflecting on the story and waited for him to continue. When he didn't, Kenny tried to prompt him. "Okay, define creative. What did you guys do?"

Before Mark could answer, a loud beep came over the plane's intercom system, followed by the copilot's voice. "Mark, you're going to have a call from the National Security Advisor's office coming through in about thirty seconds."

The interruption was welcome. Mark was not in the mood to recount the rest of the story. He wasn't sure how Kenny would take it. He patted Kenny on the shoulder as he walked by on the way to the plane's secure phone. "I have to update Johnson on some things. We can talk more later."

CHAPTER FOURTEEN

Lawyered Up

Luci had just put the twins to bed and stepped into the shower when she heard the doorbell. She hastily toweled off and pulled on a sweatshirt and yoga pants. Then she scurried to the door before he could ring the bell again and wake the kids. It had taken forever to get them to fall asleep. If they heard the doorbell and knew that a strange man was in the house, they would never go back to sleep. She pulled open the front door and held her finger to her lips.

"Shhhh. If you wake them, I will kill you," she warned. "And I told you to give me half an hour. That was about ten minutes."

"Sorry, I guess I just couldn't wait to see you," answered Goodie sarcastically. "Or maybe it's because I spent the entire day cooped up in the station writing reports and can't call it quits until you've signed off on them," he offered, holding up a stack of paperwork.

"Fine. Give me a minute to grab my stuff," said Luci. "Wait for me in the kitchen."

Luci disappeared upstairs and Goodie made his way to the kitchen. He dropped the paperwork onto the countertop and spent a few minutes looking at the collage of family photos that covered the refrigerator. He noted how photogenic Luci and the kids were. They wore ear-to-ear smiles in every picture; in contrast, Mark's expressions were often much more subdued, as if his mind were somewhere else. Goodie shrugged. Then he casually opened the refrigerator door and browsed through its contents. A low growl from behind got his attention. He turned to find Murphy crouching, his ears at full attention and the hair on his back standing straight up.

"Hey, buddy," said Goodie. "How are you doing? Feeling better after your little scare?" He started to bend down and reached out his hand to pet Murphy on the head. The dog showed its teeth and growled louder. Goodie got the message and backed off. "Okay, got it. You're still a little sore."

Murphy walked into the adjacent family room. He crouched low on the floor next to the sofa and kept his eyes trained on the guest. Goodie had his nose in the refrigerator when Luci arrived. "Can I help you?" she asked.

"Yeah, can I have this?" he asked, holding up a sixteen-ounce can of Mark's favorite beer that he ordered direct from a small brewery in North Carolina. "It's the last one."

Luci placed her items on the counter and started to flip through the reports Goodie had brought. "Of course. By all means. Come to my house for the first time and drink my husband's last beer."

"Was that a yes? I can't tell."

"What do you think?" she answered, without looking up from the papers she was quickly initialing. The refrigerator swung closed, followed by the familiar pop and fizz of a beer can opening. She looked up with an expression that said, Did you really just do that?

"What?" Goodie smiled wide and gestured around the house. "He's not here. When's he even coming home?"

"No idea," she answered, returning her attention to the task at hand.

Goodie took a long sip of the beer and exhaled slowly. "Now that's good. I can see why he likes this one. I guess your husband has good taste in a lot of things."

They spent ten minutes quickly reviewing reports and completing paperwork. Luci acknowledged that the bureaucratic requirements of the job seemed to get worse every year and she didn't see it getting better any time soon. "I can't say I'm going to miss any of this," she added, noting that her retirement ceremony was only weeks away.

"You won't have time, you'll be too busy missing me," he joked.

Luci ignored the comment and pushed the pile of completed work toward Goodie. She cocked an ear toward the ceiling. "I think I hear one of the kids. Look these over to make sure I didn't miss anything and I'll be right back."

Luci left the room and Goodie started flipping through the stack of papers. Everything seemed to be in order. He swallowed the rest of his beer in one gulp. Luci's cell phone was charging on the counter next to the toaster. It started to ring and vibrate. The screen lit up. Goodie looked at the phone. It said "Call from Mark Landry." He reached down and declined the call, sending it directly to voice mail. A moment later Mark called again. "Don't worry, buddy," Goodie whispered as he playfully tapped the red button again with his index finger. "I'll take good care of her."

"What's next? Are we finished?" Luci asked as she reentered the kitchen.

"Just one more thing." He tossed the empty beer can into the recycling bin. Then he sat next to her, pulled his chair close, and lowered his voice. "I was over at the courthouse today. We may have a little problem with one of our cases."

Goodie's sudden occupation of Luci's personal space felt awkward, but she resisted her instinct to pull back. His change in demeanor and tone intimated that he had something serious to tell her. She wanted to hear it and figured that leaning away from him to create space or getting up from her seat might seem rude. Instead, she endured the discomfort and waited for him to speak. After several long seconds of silently looking her in the eyes, she prodded him along.

"What problem? Which case?" she asked impatiently. He was smiling at her. When he exhaled, she smelled the strong scent of her husband's favorite brew. His proximity was starting to make her feel claustrophobic.

"Vasquez. The guy we collared the other night for heroin possession with intent to distribute, illegal possession of a firearm, and disturbing the peace." He paused. Luci gave no reaction. Goodie pointed to Murphy, who was watching them both closely from the other room. "He was out with us. Remember?"

"Yeah, I remember," she answered. "I remember having to give him Narcan because someone didn't leave him in the car like he was supposed to. What about Vasquez?"

"We were expecting him to end up with a public defender and figured he'd cop to some kind of plea and that would be the end of it." She nodded. "Well, he showed up in court with a lawyer from Brown & Brown. He either has a bunch of money of his own or someone he works for is footing the bill. He's out on bail. They entered a 'not guilty' plea and have already filed a bunch of pretrial motions. The DA's not offering them much because of Vasquez's record, the large quantity of heroin, and the firearm. Not to mention the DA is up for reelection and there's been a wave of fatal overdoses lately. If they don't get offered a substantial plea agreement, they'll be going over everything with a fine-tooth comb. Which means—"

Luci cut him off. "I know what it means." She got up and walked to the other side of the kitchen. She rinsed off several plates and loaded them into the dishwasher.

"I'm not worried," he said confidently. "I still don't think it'll ever see trial. My guess is that the lawyer is just going to make noise until he gets the best plea deal he can. Brown & Brown is one of the best groups of defense attorneys in the state, with much bigger cases to worry about. And the DA's office is stretched thin as hell. So I wouldn't even worry about them getting a chance to rip our report apart in front of a judge."

Luci bristled at the mention of the arrest report. She didn't share Goodie's optimism. Vasquez's lawyer, she guessed, was already ripping their case apart. Expensive lawyers are expensive for a reason. Thinking back on the evening of the arrest made her anxious and paranoid. Murphy could have died after suffering a transdermal absorption of fentanyl through one of his paws. Luckily, the uniformed backup officer who arrived on the scene had been carrying Narcan and Luci had been able to administer enough of it intranasally to reverse the effects of the synthetic opioid. She never told Mark because she knew how the conversation would go. He would lecture her on all the ways the situation could have been avoided. Then she would get pissed off and remind him that if he had taken care of the fumigation issue when she had asked him weeks earlier, Murphy would have never been in the car with her. The dog was fine anyway. Telling him would just cause more friction in the relationship. He didn't need to know. She was much more concerned about any close scrutiny of the arrest report.

"I'm not worried," Goodie added dismissively.

Luci shot him a look out of the corner of her eye as she wiped down the countertop. Of course you're not worried, she thought to herself. As the junior detective, he may have written the report, but Luci, as the senior detective and mentor, had officially signed off on it when he presented it to her. Standard reporting procedures and department policy for arrests involving K9s stipulated that one should first list the K9 and handler by their names and badge numbers, then give specific details on how the dog detected and signaled its find. Goodie simply skipped the first part and jumped right into the details. As a result, the report gave the strong impression that an official police K9 had responded to the incident. The defendant wouldn't have known the difference and the uniformed cop who showed up would never squeal. "Nobody will even notice," Goodie argued. "And if anyone does, just say it was an oversight. Say you have a lot of paperwork and you didn't notice the omission." Luci had a reputation for being a strong, independent woman, but Goodie could be convincing and pushy when hung up on something.

She still couldn't believe she had gone along with it. But after more than twenty years of operating by the book, Luci had signed a report she knew to contain false and misleading information. And she didn't really understand why. She wanted to blame Goodie for everything, but she was the senior officer and mentor, which meant that the buck stopped with her. She had been hoping to God the case would never see the inside of a courtroom and had been trying not to think about it. Filing a false report and fudging probable cause were serious offenses. And depending on which judge received the case, the rebuke could be painful enough to stain the end of her career and hurt her future chances of being elected as Essex County Sheriff, should she choose to run. With only weeks until retirement, she now had reason to worry about her reputation and future. This was not the conclusion of her career that she had imagined. Again, she resisted the urge to blame Goodie. This was all on her.

"I bet you fifty bucks this guy gets processed like ninety percent of all cases and this all goes away," said Goodie, after a few moments of awkward silence. "I bet she never hears a word of any of these pretrial arguments."

"She? Who is she?" asked Luci.

"Christina Brannigan. The judge assigned to the case."

Luci leaned against the sink and bowed her head. Of all the district court judges who could have been selected to hear the case, it had gone to the very judge who had publicly criticized Luci as "overzealous, pushy, and downright authoritarian." That was the last thing Luci needed.

"But just in case it goes forward, we should come up with a plan on how to handle things. I kind of know Brannigan. Maybe I could talk to her," Goodie offered. Luci shook her bowed head vigorously back and forth, indicating no. "Okay, so you just want to let it play out and see what happens?" he asked. Luci nodded yes.

She obviously didn't want to talk about it. Just thinking about it made her cringe. And the last thing she wanted was Goodie stumbling around trying to fix a problem—a problem he had created in the first place—with a judge who already seemed to have it in for her. That could only make things worse. Luci finished rinsing a glass and turned to face Goodie as she toweled it dry. He knew she was not happy, so he tried to redirect the outrage.

"It's ridiculous we have to even worry about something like this. Drugs are tearing this country apart, but judges are more concerned with nitpicking and frying the police than they are with putting drug dealers behind bars where they belong. So we end up walking on eggshells while the scumbags get emboldened to the point where they're making snuff movies of cops being executed. It's friggin' ridiculous."

Although she couldn't help but agree with Goodie's general sentiment, Luci was not comforted. It wasn't Judge Brannigan's fault that they had disregarded well-known policy and procedure and filed a fraudulent report. It was theirs alone. Goodie could see that Luci wasn't buying it. True to form, he defaulted to his cute routine.

"Hey, look on the bright side. At least you still get me to yourself for a few more weeks, right?" said Goodie, flashing a wide smile. He was trying to lighten the mood, but he came off more like someone who failed to grasp the seriousness of the moment. Was he naïve, Luci wondered, or just completely oblivious to his own recklessness? His smile and jovial locker-room-buddy personality may have kept him out of trouble in the past, but this was serious territory. Luci was leaning back against the kitchen sink with her arms folded. He approached slowly.

"Listen, I'm going to get out of your hair," he said. "I just wanted to get your John Hancock on this paperwork and let you know what was going on. And don't worry." He placed a hand on her shoulder and looked her in the eyes. "I always got your back. Someone has to, right?" He looked around at the empty house for emphasis. "I'm here if you need me for anything. Understand?"

Luci mustered a smile and nodded. She watched through the window as Goodie drove away. Then she fixed herself a plate of leftovers, sat at the kitchen table across from Mark's empty chair, and began to cry. She had never felt so alone.

CHAPTER FIFTEEN

Leverage

Mark's team spent less than an hour on the ground at Ramstein Air Base before continuing on to Berlin, where two plainclothes USMC embassy guards were waiting for them. The team had originally planned to stay in a hotel, but several ongoing missions in different time zones required close monitoring. Accordingly, Mark sent Bode and the rest of the airplane crew to the hotel to rest and decided that he, Billy, and Kenny would stay at the operations center located in the basement of the U.S. Embassy. The embassy bunker had secure communications and several small private rooms with everything they would need.

Billy leaned forward from the middle of the back seat and small-talked with the Marines during the thirty-minute drive from Schönefeld Airport while Mark and Kenny checked messages and viewed Berlin through the one-way bulletproof glass of the embassy's custom SUV. Mark had been hoping for a quick voicemail or text message from Luci, at least a check-in to let him know everything was okay, but his in-boxes were all business-related. The stress at home was starting to bother him, making it more difficult to compartmentalize things. This was a new feeling. His career success as an operator had always hinged on his ability to mitigate stress and solve problems under the worst of conditions. But, he reminded himself, he had been single during the first twenty years of his career, so the things he had to compartmentalize weren't personal.

Things were different now. Being married with children brought more than just extra balls to juggle. His wife and kids meant the world to him. He put his phone away and hoped they knew that he hated being away just as much as they hated not having him there.

Berlin is a city with a heavy history. They drove by the Brandenburg gate—where Napoleon triumphantly rode through on horseback, the Nazi party marched with torches, and Ronald Reagan stood strong and demanded that the Soviet Union tear down its wall. Which it did, but not until after Mark's first visit to Berlin with his adopted mother, Agnes, in spring 1989. He remembered them standing side by side, arms linked, on the west side of the wall, gazing at the famous gate. Then he remembered the advice she had given him on that occasion—advice that he wished he had heeded more closely. She awkwardly tried to explain, as best a nun could, that society was much more liberal in Europe and that young people of Mark's age regularly consumed alcohol and partied at Berlin's famous nightclubs. Always a pragmatic person, Agnes got directly to her point: "Mark, just remember sometimes it's better to stay up all night than to go to bed with a dragon."

The SUV entered the U.S. Embassy through the side gate and drove to the rear of the building. Both Marines escorted Mark, Billy, and Kenny inside and down two steep flights of stairs, after which they boarded an elevator and descended two more floors. When the doors opened, they walked briskly down a long hallway. The senior Marine punched a passcode into the security keypad and the thick steel door clanged open. "Have a good evening, gentlemen," said the gunnery sergeant.

On the other side was another long hallway with several rooms on each side. The first room was the largest. In it, roughly a dozen people were scattered about, watching monitors and talking quietly on secure lines. Mark and his team were greeted with a few nodding heads and no questions. They carried their bags to a private room at the end of the hall, equipped with secure communications, beds, and a full bathroom.

Mark immediately picked up an embassy line and dialed the hotel where he had originally intended to stay before deciding to join Billy and

Kenny at the embassy. He explained to the clerk that his travel arrangements had been interrupted and that he needed to cancel the reservation. The clerk obliged. Then Mark asked if his wife had already checked in. The clerk explained that since the reservation was in his name only, it would be impossible for anyone, even his spouse, to check in without his knowledge.

Mark laughed softly. "I understand that," he explained, "but my wife and I were to meet in Berlin tomorrow night to celebrate our anniversary and it wouldn't surprise me if she arrived early and checked into my room just to surprise me." The clerk, as Mark had anticipated, insisted that such a thing was out of the question. "Of course, but my wife can be very persuasive. You may want to send someone to the room to inform her I won't be arriving tonight. Vielen dank."

Kenny looked at Billy with a confused look. "Wife?"

"Heike," replied Billy.

Kenny waited until they were a bit more settled in before asking Mark to finish his story about first meeting Heike. Mark laid back on his bed and laced his fingers behind his head. He didn't feel like talking about it, but Kenny was obviously not going to let it go. "Where did we leave off?" Mark asked.

"I know how things started and ended, but you still haven't told me exactly how you helped find the chemical weapons before they could be deployed. They had this guy, Neo Helmut, in custody but he wasn't giving them anything. So how did you get him to give up the location of the stolen artillery shells? What did you say to him?"

"To him? Nothing. I never saw him. There's no way I could have gotten into the interrogation room. There were too many officials from all the different German intelligence and law enforcement agencies who, according to Heike, seemed more concerned with government oversight and protecting Neo Helmut's rights than averting a disaster."

"Sounds familiar," scoffed Billy.

"It was starting to look hopeless until Heike made a comment about Neo and his son. Something about the apple not falling too far from the tree. I thought to myself, 'Bingo, there's our leverage.' But I had to get to the son and she had to somehow clear the interrogation room and get her cellphone in front of Neo so he could see that I had junior."

"You used his son for leverage?" asked Kenny.

Mark sat up, turned sideways, and planted both feet on the floor. "Yeah, I did. But he wasn't a kid. He was nineteen or so. I was in a Ranger battalion at the same age; he was a budding leader in the neo-Nazi movement. He already had multiple arrests for violent behavior and was wearing an ankle bracelet for his role in the rape of a fifteen-year-old Syrian refugee. Just as repulsive as his father, maybe worse. I never thought twice about it."

"Amen," muttered Billy as he pulled a clean T-shirt over his head and laced up his shoes.

"The only thing I didn't know," continued Mark, "was whether the old man cared more about his cause than about his son. But it was our only play and the clock was ticking." Mark could sense Kenny's weariness and didn't see the point in dredging up something from almost a decade earlier. He decided to redact his own story while giving Kenny enough to satisfy his curiosity and put the whole thing behind them.

Mark explained that the ankle bracelet was keeping Neo Helmut's son restricted to his high-rise apartment building, where he lived with several other neo-Nazis. The building was under constant surveillance, so waltzing in through the front doors was not an option. Through a combination of threats and bribes, Heike convinced a local news channel's helicopter pilot to drop Mark on the rooftop. From there, he would have to work his way down to the lower levels and find Neo's son.

Mark could remember descending toward his target. He recalled sharing the world's slowest elevator for several floors with an elderly German couple. He remembered their outfits and the way the woman had smiled at him as she exited on their floor. And he remembered clicking as soon as the doors crept open on the basement level of the building. He neutralized two threats before even exiting the elevator; then he quickly isolated the target in the boiler room and started streaming video to Heike.

Kenny asked if Heike was on board from the beginning or had to be convinced. Mark let Billy answer for him. "You shittin' me? She was turned on. Probably hasn't slept a night without dreaming of Mark since."

"Turned on?" asked Kenny with a sour look.

"Yeah," answered Mark. "I didn't pay much attention to it. Turns out Agnes was right about that dragon thing." Kenny looked more confused than ever. "I'll get to that part," Mark assured him.

"I know the rest of the story," said Billy, rising to his feet. "I heard a rumor there's a twenty-four-hour chow hall in this embassy and I'm starving. That's where you'll find me," he informed them on his way out the door.

Mark started reading his emails. After a few minutes, Kenny spoke up. "So what happened?"

"It worked. Neo caved within three seconds of seeing his son bound and gagged. Heike caught a ration of shit for unauthorized access to the detainee, but since the disaster was averted her career survived. Everything worked out."

Mark closed his laptop and said he was going to see if Billy had any luck finding the cafeteria. Kenny expressed his interest in going too, but Mark asked him to first make sure that all the arrangements for their meeting the next day had been made. If German officials gave them any actionable intelligence on Oleg Borodin, he wanted to be able to exploit it ASAP.

"You got it. I'll doublecheck everything right now," answered Kenny. "Can I ask one more question? You said something about dragons."

Mark paused at the door. "For obvious reasons, standard procedure is to leave town after a mission. For the first and only time in my career, I didn't. I like Berlin so I stayed for a few days. I spent those days with Heike. I got to know her. And I wish I hadn't."

Heike's Swedish mother had been an aspiring actress from Gotland, a large and strategically located island in the Baltic Sea off Sweden's coast. She was mentored by another famous resident of the island: Ingmar Bergman, a famous Swedish filmmaker who often spoke of the great things she would accomplish in film. And she likely would have, had she not visited Berlin and fallen in love with Heike's father—a handsome young aide-de-camp to an East German general.

He was instantly smitten with her and used all his charm to convince her to marry him and move to East Berlin. She balked at the idea of voluntarily migrating to a country whose own citizens were clamoring to get out. But he convinced her that life for them would be different. He was quickly rising through the ranks, and life as the wife of a senior officer in East Germany would be glamorous. He also promised her that she could continue to act and would be able to travel and visit Gotland often. He knew none of this was true, but he sold it with a wide smile and blue eyes overflowing with love. She believed it because she wanted it to be true. The reality was much worse. Over time, Heike's mother fell into disillusionment and depression, exacerbated by her husband's alcoholism and frequent abuse.

Heike's childhood and upbringing were a sick version of "good cop, bad cop." Her mother would shower her with love, affection, and inspiration for a better future while her drunken father would simply ignore their distress. When he couldn't ignore them, he would beat them into silence. After his wife died a long, slow death due to breast cancer, Heike was left to endure the abuse alone—sometimes thinking her mother had been the lucky one for dying.

Then, one evening in December 1989, she left the house and started walking west with only the clothes on her back. She was going to cross the border into West Germany or die trying. But history unfolded as she made her way toward the wall. By the time she reached the Brandenburg Gate, the East German government had collapsed. Heike walked right through the previously impenetrable wall and never looked back.

There was no need to share any of this with Kenny. He did not need to know Heike's life story. "Suffice it to say her father fucked her up good," Mark summarized. "She never had much of a chance. It's a wonder she didn't kill herself or end up swinging around a pole in Berlin's red-light district."

Mark left to find Billy while Kenny made his final preparations for the morning. He was glad to finally know the story, but something wasn't sitting right with him and he couldn't put his finger on it. He felt there was more to the story, that it couldn't have been that clean. But he told himself to let it go. It wasn't his business and it had happened long before he joined Mark's team. Besides, over the past few years he himself had participated in plenty of missions that crossed legal—and many would argue ethical and moral—lines. But he knew that those people, like the hacker SocraTeez, had deserved whatever they got. In for a penny, in for a pound, he told himself. After all, from everything Kenny could see, if the American people could get an unfiltered look inside Mark Landry's operation and the things he did to help protect them, they'd be more likely to demand that he be given a medal than to call for locking him up.

CHAPTER SIXTEEN

The Shithouse

Billy and Kenny were waiting in the SUV with the same two Marines. Mark was the last to leave the café. His eyes darted back and forth from behind mirrored sunglasses. Halfway to the SUV, a late-model BMW screeched to a halt in front of him. He stopped short and almost spilled the cup of coffee-to-go in his hand. The window came down and Heike smiled from within. Her long, blond hair was down. With two fingers, she she pulled her sunglasses down to the tip of her nose and looked up at Mark with her sparkling green eyes. *"Guten morgen*, Mark. I missed you last night."

He imagined her in his hotel room, laying naked in the bed, the previous night as some unlucky member of the staff informed her that her husband had canceled his reservation. It made him cringe a little, but the point of his trip to Berlin was to get as much information out of her as possible. Showing up at the hotel and having to reject her personally could have poisoned the well. "We got in late. Change of plans." He knew she wasn't buying it, but the excuse helped her save some face.

"Hop in. We can talk on the way," she offered.

"Thanks. But I have some things to take care of so I'll meet you there."

"Fair enough. Just some advice then. Be patient and don't get frustrated by the official briefing this morning. Your trip will be well worth your time and effort. I promise you," she said. Then she waved to Mark's team in the SUV and sped away.

"What was that all about?" asked Billy.

Mark settled into the back seat and sighed audibly. "I'm not sure, but it sounds like she's lowering expectations. This trip better not end up being a waste of time. If it does, I'm gonna be pissed."

. . .

"You pissed yet?" whispered Billy.

Mark's eyes remained locked on the man who had been giving them a presentation in English for the past ninety minutes. "If I don't hear something new soon, I will be. We didn't come all this way for a refresher on information warfare, Russian active measures, and KGB anecdotes from the Cold War. This better get interesting soon."

"You want me to be the asshole?"

"Not yet. Give her a chance," answered Mark, glancing at Heike who was sitting on the other side of the room. She had barely taken her gaze off Mark. Her arms were folded tightly in front of her. She knew it was not going well. Almost an hour had passed before any of the dozen or so representatives from the Bundesnachrichtendienst (German Federal Intelligence Service), the Bundesamt für Verfassungsschutz (Federal Office for the Protection of the Constitution), and the Bundeskriminalamt (Federal Criminal Police Office of Germany) in the room even mentioned Oleg Borodin. And so far, they seemed to know even less about the man than the U.S. intelligence community.

In fact, the only new information Mark had ascertained was that apparently nobody in the room, except Heike, Billy, and Kenny, knew he spoke fluent German. On the few occasions when Heike had interjected a comment in German, the speaker had quickly silenced her objection, as if Mark and his team weren't even there. If she disputed a fact, the speaker reiterated that these were the facts all departments had agreed upon beforehand and then continued the presentation. If she offered an additional piece of information, it was summarily dismissed as uncorroborated. Billy, who didn't understand more than three or four words in German but could read a room as well as Mark, had commented early in the meeting that Heike appeared to be in the shithouse with respect to her colleagues.

Just as Mark was about to lose his mind, the door to the secure conference room opened. The room went momentarily silent as a tall, thin gentleman in his mid-forties entered, wearing a dark suit. He had black, slicked-back hair and a smooth face. His complexion was a shade darker than everyone else's and his eyes looked like two blood-red saucers. The newcomer apologized to the woman speaking at the time for his interruption and encouraged her to continue before taking a seat diagonally across the table from Mark. The two men locked eyes and gave each other a subtle nod of familiarity. Kenny, sitting behind Mark and Billy, squinted and examined the man's appearance more closely. Leaning forward between Mark and Billy, he whispered, "Is it me or does that guy have red eyes?"

"It's not you," Billy answered over his shoulder.

"Do you know him? Who is he?"

Billy looked to Mark for a nod of approval before answering. "The Turk."

Kenny started to ask another question. Mark turned his head to the side and beckoned Kenny closer with his hand. "We can talk later." Kenny slinked back in his seat, a little embarrassed at his eagerness. Mark was right—there would be plenty of time to debrief and ask questions later. Right now, it was time to shut up and listen.

The female speaker quickly finished her part of the presentation, after which two more presenters spoke. Then the Turk apologized for his late arrival and asked politely if it would be okay for him to add a few things before the meeting adjourned. Hearing no objection, he addressed Mark directly. "Mr. Landry, you are no doubt familiar with the famous quote from Rolf Wagenbreth, director of disinformation operations for the former East Germany. He said, "Our friends in Moscow call it 'dezinformatsiya.' Our enemies in America call it 'active measures,' and I, dear friends, call it 'my favorite pastime.'"

Mark nodded.

"Oleg Borodin was cast in the same mold. An old-school

gaslighter who enjoys the psychological and physical pain he causes. He thrives on it. Inflicting pain is his fuel. This makes him much more dangerous than the men who wage war for ideological purposes. For him, gaslighting is not a means to an end—it is the end. His goal is never simply to confuse his targets by promoting false narratives or fake news, but to induce a psychological disequilibrium where they begin to question their own sanity, see everything as a threat, and doubt everything they thought was real. In such a world, a world without truth, life is unlivable.

"Unfortunately, the creation of the Internet was a boon for people like him. What used to take years or decades can now be accomplished in weeks, days, or even minutes. His goal, if he could achieve it, would be for no historical event to ever live up to scrutiny—or, as Arendt so eloquently wrote, a world where nothing is true but everything is possible. He has an army of gaslighters including highly skilled bloggers, social media manipulators, journalists, hackers, and dark-web criminals. And he has an endless supply of violent thugs willing to engage in the most vile forms of violence imaginable at his order. He is a very sick man. And as long as he roams free, liberal democracies like ours are in danger."

"Why must we make our enemies out to be ten feet tall?" Heike asked rhetorically in English. "Borodin is five feet eight at best." The Turk turned his head, focused his red eyes on her, and muttered something in Arabic as he rose and buttoned his suit jacket. Then he excused himself and left the conference room.

"What did he say to—?" Kenny started.

Mark cut him off. "No idea."

Billy looked eagerly to Mark. "Asshole time?"

Mark was fuming. "Do it."

Billy smiled from ear to ear. Then the Oklahoma native rose to his feet and rapped his knuckles on the mahogany table as if he was trying to wake the dead. "Okay, thanks very much for all of that. We really appreciate it. It was great, really. But we still have two questions you folks can hopefully help us answer. Y'all ready? Okay, does anybody know why Oleg Borodin was in Boston earlier this year? And does anybody know where he might be right now?" The room was quiet for several long moments. "Okay, maybe we should do these one at a time. Does anybody here have any idea—at this point we'd settle for a hunch—as to why Oleg Borodin was in Boston earlier this year?" Still no response. "Okay, I'll put you all down as 'no' for that one. Good, we're makin' progress. Next, does anybody have any information as to Oleg Borodin's whereabouts right now or do you have any kind of plan on how to find him?" Again, nobody spoke and most of the room was now avoiding eye contact with the Americans. "Okay then, I guess we're done here. *Muchas gracias.*"

Heike didn't catch up with them until they were already out of the building and walking down the sidewalk toward the waiting U.S. Embassy SUV. "Mark, wait!" He ignored her and kept walking. "Mark, I told you this morning that I would make your trip worth it." Mark told Billy and Kenny to go ahead, then turned around to face Heike.

"Yeah. Well, you didn't. The only thing you gave me was an open-source introductory course on disinformation and gaslighting. Otherwise known as shit I could have Googled. You wasted my time. The only thing new I learned is that you evidently don't get along very well with your colleagues." With that snappy conclusion, Mark turned his back and walked away. Heike pursued him.

"Wait!" she screamed. "Those people are not colleagues. They are conference-room warriors who have never heard a shot fired in anger."

"All of them?" he remarked, without mentioning the Turk by name.

"He was never scheduled to be there," she said dismissively. "The rest are paper pushers who question the judgment of field operators like you and me. I am just as frustrated with them as you, Mark."

"Let's be clear. I am not frustrated with them. I am pissed off at you. Goodbye."

Heike grabbed his hand as he reached for the SUV door handle. "Borodin wants to defect," she said. "All we need is the right approach and incentive. I am sure of it."

Mark gently pulled his hand from hers and considered her statement. His orders were to capture or kill Borodin. Should he be captured, Mark had low expectations that they would ever get any useful information out of him. More than likely he would simply clam up or send his captors on endless goose chases as he rotted away in a cell. But defections were different. Much different. In exchange for safety, the defector has to give up the keys to the city. Mark wasn't buying her claim. "Bullshit. Guys like that don't defect. Why would he be different? What makes you so sure?"

"Because I have a deep source I have been working for almost a year. A deep source I refuse to share with any of the paper warriors in that building," she said. "That is why they hate me. Because they know I do not trust them. And deep down, they know I am right not to."

Mark listened silently. Her excuse was plausible. Generally, he and his team shared information freely with their American counterparts in all the three-letter agencies. But there were occasions when they kept their cards closer to the vest. Luci had experienced the same thing when working with feds at the local level. They had legitimate fears of local authorities leaking sensitive information, so they kept it to themselves.

"I want to hear everything about your source," he told Heike. "Don't hold back a single detail, including his identity."

"Would you prefer to hear it straight from him? I can arrange a face-to-face for as early as this evening. Just say the word."

Mark pursed his lips and considered the surprising offer. He would never have made the same offer. Cultivating deep sources and building trust took a long time, and the biggest challenge was to convince them that their identity would be protected at all costs. Bringing an extra person unannounced to a clandestine meeting could blow everything. Heike was a strong, confident, and very capable operator, so the tinge of desperation he saw in her eyes would normally be a red flag. But after what he had just witnessed in the conference room, it made sense. Being in the shithouse with colleagues when you know you're right was demoralizing. She needed a win. "Set it up," Mark said.

"*Sehr gut*," she replied, suppressing the urge to smile. "The meeting will be late. Perhaps we can discuss it over dinner beforehand?"

"No. No dinner. Just set up the meeting." Mark jumped into the waiting SUV and sped away. Heike watched until the vehicle disappeared. Then she continued down the sidewalk, grinning from ear to ear.

151

CHAPTER SEVENTEEN

The Source

Heike picked Mark up in a different car from the one she had been driving earlier in the morning, before the disastrous briefing. He didn't catch the make, but it was an older-model sports car with uncomfortable bucket seats. Each time she turned sharply to weave through the traffic, his body would shift and the full-size Sig Sauer 1911 chambered in .45 caliber and holstered behind his right hip at the five o'clock position dug into his back. This was one of the main reasons he preferred to carry in the appendix position. But he hadn't liked any of the compact pistols available in the U.S. Embassy's armory, and once he attached the tactical light and reflex sight, the full-size .45 was too big to carry in front.

Heike screeched to a halt at a crosswalk and tapped her hand on the steering wheel impatiently as a large group of Middle Eastern men took their time crossing the street. Then she slammed the gear shift into park and crossed her arms. "Globalization and multiculturalism are killing Germany," she said. "I feel like a stranger in my own country." Walking behind the men at a much slower pace was an even larger group of women wearing full burqas. *"Diese Menschen sind schlimmer als Zigeuner,"* she muttered under her breath loudly enough for Mark to hear. He gave no reaction to the double slur, loosely translated as "These people are dirtier than Gypsies." Instead he looked out the passenger side window and rolled his eyes.

Jesus, where the hell did that come from, Heike?

They continued driving for several minutes before Heike swerved into a row of open parking spaces in front of a high-rise apartment building. "You remember my old place?" she asked, leaning over into the passenger seat and pointing up at the massive structure.

"Uh-huh," answered Mark. "Thirteenth floor. If you need to run in and grab something, I'll wait here."

"Actually, I moved recently to a much more exclusive neighborhood. I'd love to show it to you," she offered, placing a hand on his thigh. "It won't take long."

"I don't think—" he began, only to be cut off when she leaned in quickly and pressed her lips against his. He resisted the impulse to pull back quickly, worrying that such a blatant rejection might impact her willingness to cooperate and share vital intelligence. He could feel her tongue softly probing for an opening into his mouth. She moved her hand from his thigh to his groin. After a soft squeeze, she started to rub along his beltline.

After a few seconds, Mark brought a hand to her cheek and gently pulled away. "Maybe later," he whispered. Heike smiled, but Mark could see in her eyes that she wasn't buying it. She knew it wasn't going to happen. "Right, we have work to do," she replied unconvincingly.

They continued driving for another twenty minutes before Heike parked again and pointed to a large, rectangular brick building two blocks ahead. It reminded Mark of the textile mills in the Merrimack Valley of Massachusetts, most of which had been repurposed into condominiums and office space after manufacturers left in search of cheaper labor elsewhere. When Heike opened the door, he looked up at the thick wooden beam high above them that ran the length of the third-floor studio apartment. Above the beam, it was another five or six feet to the ceiling. Mark felt as if he could have been in Lawrence or Lowell.

Heike removed her black coat and tossed it over a chair. Then she pulled an elastic band from her pocket and tied her hair into a ponytail while Mark quickly verified that no one else was in the apartment. With only one large room and a small bathroom off to the side, there was practically no place to hide. "How long do we have before the source gets here?" he asked.

"Are you ready?" she asked. Mark nodded. Heike smiled. "Then I will signal as such."

Mark glanced at his watch as she exited the apartment. In the old days, her signal to the source that the coast was clear to enter could have been something as simple as a chalk mark against the building, or turning on a specific combination of lights that the source could see. These days, it was probably just an encrypted text message. But since the apartment was more than likely an intentionally constructed dark spot for digital communications, she may have needed to step out to send word to her source.

At least that was what Mark had assumed when she left. But, after she had been gone for three or four minutes, his cellphone rang. He declined the call from an unknown number and sent it directly to voicemail. Whoever it was called back immediately. He declined again. Then a text message arrived.

ANSWER YOUR PHONE

On the third try he answered the call and simply listened. He could hear someone breathing on the other end. "Ja?"

"Yes. Mr. Landry?"

"Wer ist das?" he answered. *Who is this?*

"You know very well who this is, Mr. Landry," answered the voice. "After all, it was you who went to great lengths to arrange this call. It is Oleg Borodin."

Click.

CHAPTER EIGHTEEN

Confusion

Mark held the phone to his left ear and popped one of his ear buds into the right. Then he reached behind his hip to the five o'clock position and pulled his jacket and shirt out of the way so that he could draw his .45 quickly if necessary. He rapidly scanned the apartment again, looking for anything out of the ordinary.

"May I call you Marco?" asked Oleg.

"No."

"Why not?" pressed the Russian.

"Because it's not my fucking name."

"I see. When I agreed to this call, I did not assume you would be so pusillanimous," Oleg remarked, hinting in his tone that he was somewhat insulted. Mark didn't reply. "Pusillanimous, it means—"

"I know what it means."

"You do? Good. Now then. What do you say we, as they say, cut to the chase?"

"Sounds good to me," answered Mark, his eyes darting in every direction as he tried to figure out what was going on. He could hear Oleg cover the phone with his hand and mumble something in German. It sounded as if he was clarifying his order with a waiter or waitress. "Where are you?"

"Closer than you may imagine."

"Then why don't we get together and talk face to face?" offered Mark.

"Hmmm. I don't think so. Not yet, at least. I need to hear your offer first."

What offer? And where the hell is Heike? Did she know Borodin would be calling? Is that why she left? Or did the source somehow arrange for this call without her knowledge? If so, how did they get this number? Shit.

Mark was confused. Heike had stated with high confidence that she had good reason to believe Oleg Borodin wanted to defect. If that was the case, Oleg should be the one making offers. Mark remained silent and tried to think of what to do next.

"You seem confused, Mr. Landry, as am I. Tell me, is Heike there? If so, perhaps she can shed light on our collective perplexity," Oleg suggested. After several moments of silence, he continued. "I see. It seems my time has been wasted. Then I shall simply leave you with this. I have thought long and hard about—"

Mark's phone dropped the call and the apartment simultaneously plummeted into darkness. He quickly stuffed the phone into his pocket and froze. Through the amplification of his ear bud, he heard a key being inserted into the apartment door, followed by a metallic click. The door squeaked slowly open. Backlit by an exit sign in the exterior hallway operating on emergency power, he saw what appeared to be a masked figure about to enter the apartment. When the door fully opened, enough light spilled in for Mark to regain his bearings. He stepped onto the sofa with both feet, crouched down as low as he could, then exploded upward in a vertical jump with all his might, his outstretched arms reaching for the wooden beam high overhead.

Shit.

Mark knew he had badly misjudged the distance before his head even smashed into the beam above his right eye. His arms flailed as he fell backwards and crashed into the solid mahogany coffee table below. The bulk of his weight landed directly on the pistol holstered near the small of his back, and his head smacked against the table with a deafening thud. Conscious but stunned, he lay motionless for several seconds before mustering all the strength he had to lift his head. As he did, the lights came back on just in time for him to see the hooded figure get taken down hard to the tile floor from behind, his attacker wrapped around him like a boa constrictor. Then he heard a familiar voice.

"Mark, get the door." When he didn't instantly pop up from the coffee table, he heard the voice again. "Mark, if you can, close the door," said the voice, firmly yet calmly.

Mark shook off the cobwebs as best he could and tried to ignore the intense pain from his mishap. He stumbled to the door and locked it just as he heard the unforgettable sound of air escaping from a punctured lung. The latecomer rolled off his victim and, although Mark's vision was blurry, he could make out the handle of a dagger sticking out vertically from behind his unconscious would-be assassin's collarbone. The victor of the struggle rose back to his feet as if a demon had slipped him on like a glove—his red eyes locked on Mark. "Are you hurt?" asked the Turk.

Mark looked at him and took several deep breaths before answering. He was trying to take it all in. "I don't know. I don't think so … banged up … but I'll be okay. Who the hell is that?" he asked, pointing to the corpse now lying motionless on the floor.

The Turk didn't answer. Instead, he reached down and pulled on the dead man's black ski mask until it slipped off his head, revealing a tattoo-covered face and floppy blond hair. He moved his prey's head from side to side and noted several neo-Nazi tattoos on the man's neck. "Nobody I know. You?"

Mark shook his head no. "Care to fill me in?" he asked, even though he was already piecing things together. Heike had obviously flipped and sold him out. "How long have you known about her? Why didn't you warn me?"

"I have suspected her for several months, but I had to be sure. And I did warn you," the Turk replied. Mark started to reply but stopped himself. He had thought the Turk's unexpected appearance and his visible contempt for Heike at the morning briefing had seemed odd. But now it made more sense. The two men's careers had crossed paths several times in the past. They knew and respected one another. He had crashed the meeting to send a subtle warning to Mark as a professional courtesy. It was Mark's fault for not seeing it for what it was.

Additionally, Heike had made comments to Mark about feeling like an outsider in her own country and how much she loathed multiculturalism. Maybe she had been trying to deliberately tell him something. Or maybe her subconscious was trying to explain to Mark what she knew he would eventually learn—that somehow she had betrayed her country when in fact it felt very much the other way around to her. Regardless, her bigoted comments had been a red flag to which Mark should have paid closer attention.

The Turk grasped Mark by the arm and asked again if he was hurt. Mark shook his head no. "Then you need to go now. Get some air as quickly as possible," he instructed, as both men moved toward the door. Mark thanked him and the Turk paused before opening the door. "One more thing. I was asked by a mutual friend to deliver a message to you directly."

"What's the message?" asked Mark.

"That nothing is as it seems. Nothing."

"Not exactly useful. Who sent it?"

"Dunbar. Now go quickly. I'll handle this mess," he said, motioning toward the dead man.

Mark hobbled down the three flights of stairs as quickly as he could, wondering the whole way why the hell Dunbar—his old mentor and retired boss, whom he hadn't spoken with in months—would have sent such a cryptic message through an intermediary instead of simply telling him personally. But Dunbar must have had a good reason. Mark pushed it out of his mind and focused on the immediate tasks that needed to be accomplished.

He exited the building through an emergency side door and quickly scanned the scene. His back was aching and he knew his right eye would soon be swollen shut. Detecting no threats, he limped down the street and pulled the phone from his pocket. Billy answered on the first ring.

"Talk to me, Jefe," Billy said cheerfully.

"Call Bode and tell him and crew to get to the plane ASAP. Then grab all of our shit and come get me. I want to be wheels-up in an hour."

CHAPTER NINETEEN

Special Projects

Senator McDermott leaned against the wall of the Red Room and acted as if she was listening to the First Lady's remarks. All three parlors on the State Room floor of the White House were humming this morning. But a rare appearance by the first lady to push her autism initiative necessitated removal of the Red Room's furniture to accommodate the standing-room-only crowd. Although Senator McDermott was among the special invited guests, she still felt out of place and self-conscious regarding her degraded appearance. The First Lady made a self-deprecating joke about her reclusiveness. McDermott mustered a fake smile and nodded her head along with the crowd a few times before returning her gaze to her phone. She was texting with Peggy, using an encrypted app that deletes messages immediately after they are acknowledged by the recipient. It was an easy way to keep their conversations private. The two hadn't actually spoken since the last time Peggy delivered her meds. McDermott could tell that her oldest friend was increasingly concerned because she kept asking the same questions.

"Can we please talk like normal humans? This is getting old," Peggy texted. McDermott replied, "Not a good time." Then she snapped a quick picture of the First Lady standing at the podium and attached it to her reply. "Then text me your answers," Peggy quickly replied. She was not letting up. She wanted to know about McDermott's prescriptions.

How were the adjusted doses working out? She also wanted to know if McDermott had heard from Megan and when she planned on telling Mark the truth about his father.

McDermott explained that the adjusted medication doses seemed to be making a big difference. The somnolence and cloudy-headedness had lifted more than she would have expected at this stage of her illnesses. She was feeling cognitively clearer than she had in months, today at least.

As for Megan, she hadn't heard from her since the night Mark surprised her during a shower. After that unexpected encounter, McDermott sat down with Megan and provided a long-overdue explanation about Mark Landry, the child to whom she had given birth as a teen and given up for adoption. Megan was predictably outraged, as McDermott had expected. Megan had always been a hothead. The majority of her teachers, coaches, and professors would wholeheartedly agree on that fact. As she grew into her twenties and early thirties, she had fewer tantrums; their intensity could be disturbing but she would always pull back before completely losing it. Not this time. Upon hearing that she had a forty-seven-year-old brother, Megan came totally unglued. Then she packed her things and, before walking out the door, turned and asked McDermott a most unexpected question.

"Did dad know?"

McDermott stood in front of her daughter shell-shocked, unable to speak. She had spent all her time preparing to handle Megan's temper. She had never thought about the obvious questions someone would be likely to ask upon receiving such stunning news—like whether Megan's late father, McDermott's husband for nearly two decades, knew about Mark. Tears welled in the Senator's eyes. Then she bowed her head in shame, unable to look her daughter in the eye. The answer was clear. She had never shared that secret with her husband, and she never could have imagined having to confess that decision to their daughter. Megan squeezed out a few breathless sentences, but the only two words McDermott could make out through the Charlie Brown "mwa-mwa-mwa" were "betrayal" and "liar," so it took Megan a few tries to get her message across. She was leaving for good. Just thinking about that night made

McDermott feel like a fraud.

Peggy still felt that Megan would eventually come around. In the meantime, she thought, McDermott should immediately tell Mark about his father. "The longer you take, the harder it will be," she argued. McDermott said she'd wait until he got back in town. According to Luci, Mark was in Germany for a few days. At least that's what Luci had said when she finally responded to McDermott's text.

Years earlier, their relationship had started out warmly but chilled over time because Mark did not show much enthusiasm for anything closer than an arm's-length relationship with his mother. McDermott knew Luci was a generous, loving wife and mother and couldn't blame her for barely keeping in touch or even giving her the cold shoulder; she was simply following her husband's lead. McDermott couldn't remember the last time they had actually spoken to each other. She had to settle for an occasional text.

McDermott kept her head down and funneled out of the Red Room with the rest of the crowd. She didn't want to speak with anyone. *Nobody ever mentions the fifty thousand refugee babies I once helped rescue*, she thought to herself. Not ever. An occasional Republican might quickly express thanks for her vote to confirm Justice Midas and for doing what was "best for America." Or a stray Democrat, citing that very same vote, might actually mutter "sellout" or "traitor" in her hearing instead of just thinking it. But most of the time she was simply ignored. Today was one of those days. The rest of the herd was looking for valuable face time and photo ops. McDermott was just looking for the nearest exit when the National Security Advisor gently grasped her by the elbow.

"These people are going to take forever, Senator. Come with me and I'll get you out of here quicker."

"And let me guess. You'd like to small talk about SSCI subpoenas?"

"I confess the topic may come up. Along with anything you may like to talk about," he added quickly. "How about we catch up for a few minutes in my office on the way out?"

McDermott looked at the traffic jam of bodies blocking the main exits. "Lead the way." NSA Johnson unhooked the red velvet security rope and nodded for her to pass.

It was a short walk to the NSA's West Wing office. The outer office was filled with staffers and humming with activity. Ever the multitasker, Johnson answered questions and gave orders to his team as he escorted Senator McDermott across the main salon and toward his private office. She was more focused on keeping her composure and projecting whatever strength she could muster to pay attention to the humming going on around her. But then she heard two specific words she never would have expected to hear anywhere—let alone in the office of the National Security Advisor.

"Mark Landry."

She froze in place and took a few deep breaths, telling herself that she was just imagining things. Then she heard it again and looked up to see who said it. A fit staffer with a closely cropped military haircut was holding a cellphone to his ear and talking to NSA Johnson at the same time. He was saying that Mark Landry was in the bird on his way back and needed to speak with him. Johnson said to have him return to Washington to deliver a personal briefing in Johnson's office. He always preferred face-to-face discussions on sensitive matters.

"Are you okay?" asked Johnson, looking back at McDermott.

She waved off his concern, but she could feel the building pressure within and knew what was coming. Right now she just felt hollow. The ramp-up would be gradual, like the metallic clicking of a chain link bringing a roller coaster train to the top of its initial hill. Then there would be a brief moment of peace before she was dropped like a stone and whipped through banked turns and loops. She knew there was nothing she could do to stop the ride. She just hoped to hold it off for as long as she could. She breathed deeply, thanked God her meds had been tuned up, and focused on what she needed to know, keenly aware that this might be the only opportunity.

NSA Johnson motioned for her to sit and fetched her a glass of water. Standing behind his desk, he held up a stack of folders, each one containing a subpoena from the Senate Select Committee on Intelligence

(SSCI) aimed at government personnel whom the NSA would prefer to keep in the shadows. The battle had been mostly behind the scenes, but at some point one side would have to give or a judge would have to rule. They were nearing that point, so NSA Johnson was making a last-ditch effort to avoid unnecessary public and journalistic scrutiny. It was a nonstop balancing act in National Security and he was getting tired of it. They bantered back and forth about the subpoenas. During one of his replies, he paused for a second longer than usual and she pounced.

"Now tell me about Mark Landry," she demanded.

Johnson shrugged his shoulders. "Are we done talking about these?" he asked, pointing to the folders.

"Maybe. Does Mark Landry work for you? What does he do?"

"Senator, you'd be doing me a big favor if we could stick to the open cases, at least for a moment. That seems reasonable to me."

McDermott shrugged her shoulders and pointed to the folders. "You want these killed? Talk to me about Mark Landry and I'll kill them for you. I probably still owe you a favor or two anyway." Seeing that Johnson looked stunned, she pounced again. "Look, you asked me in here because you want these subpoenas killed, right? I'm saying okay but you have to talk to me about Mark Landry first. Do we have a deal?"

NSA Johnson gazed expressionless from across his desk and took a few moments to digest the unexpected offer. Could she deliver? Yes. The only reason Democratic Party leaders left her on the SSCI was her ability to be a colossal pain in the ass to Republicans. Whichever subpoenas she lacked the ability to kill outright, she could use arcane Senate rules to effectively delay action forever. She could definitely deliver. NSA Johnson wondered why information on Landry was so important to her that she would wipe the entire slate of subpoenas clean, but he knew a good deal when he heard it.

She waited patiently for his answer. Finally he tapped his fingers on the folders and nodded in agreement.

"What does he do for you? He's headquartered out of Boston, right?"

"Yes. He works on special projects and reports directly to me."

"Does the Gang of Eight know about these special projects? Do you brief them?" she asked, referring to the top four elected members of Congress from each of the major parties, plus the chairs and ranking minority members of the Senate and House intelligence committees.

"I could. Or I could just call the *Washington Post* directly and save time."

"Give me an example of a special project."

"Like highly classified intelligence gathering, some analysis work, you know—special things. Whatever comes up. No two work days are alike." He was trying to keep things as vague as possible.

"Is he authorized to use force?"

"Seriously? You mean like 'licensed to kill,' Senator?" he asked, using his fingers to put the words 'licensed to kill' in air quotes. "Let's not get too dramatic," he added condescendingly.

McDermott took the jab and answered with a wallop of her own. "Don't patronize me. I expect you to bullshit me. I expect you to arrogantly hand me an Authorization for the Use of Military Force from twenty years ago. But I won't be patronized. So you can choose to either answer my questions or not. I'll eventually get answers. I'd prefer to get them from you. I can help keep a lid on things if need be."

NSA Johnson came around from behind his desk and sat in the chair next to McDermott. "I had almost forgotten how tough you are, Lois. One of the toughest in the Senate."

"I learned from the best. I miss our coffees. Do you miss the Senate?"

"No, I don't. And let me apologize for the comment about being dramatic; it was unnecessary and you deserve more respect than that. You've earned it."

McDermott wasted no time in returning to business. "What's he doing in Germany?"

NSA Johnson smiled and contemplated whether to acknowledge that Landry had been in Germany. Then he checked the time on the clock over McDermott's head. He had other national security fires to put out, so he decided to cut to the chase and satisfy McDermott as quickly as possible. Landry was in Germany on a fact-finding mission, he explained. He was working side by side with our closest allies to bring down Oleg Borodin, a Russian SVR officer with a career's worth of grotesque psychological operations under his belt. Someone every NATO country agreed needed to go.

McDermott nodded her head along with his words. Her body felt like a pressure cooker of competing physiological responses brought on by emotions that were changing too quickly to label. Mark Landry. Boston. Germany. There was little doubt that they were talking about the same person. She was getting crushed in the middle of two colliding worlds, and the cold sting of humiliation was starting to settle in. She felt as if the rest of the world had been laughing at a joke nobody would ever let her in on because she was the punchline. Life had consistently dealt McDermott bad cards, and she had always played them as best she could and never quit. But she had just felt the earth move under her feet, and this time things were different. The stoic mask covering her face—a mask that had served her well for so many years—was dissolving like an Alka Seltzer. Soon it would break apart and McDermott's true self would leak through the cracks. But she had no intention of letting anybody see it happen. She had enough strength in her for one more question and wanted to remove any doubt that they were talking about her son. She knew Mark had traveled to London in the not-so-distant past.

"What about London? What do I need to know about that operation?" she asked vaguely. NSA Johnson shrugged his shoulders and was about to say he had no idea what operation she was talking about, but McDermott cut him off. "The hacker who disappeared from the Venezuelan embassy" rolled off her tongue. They looked into each other's eyes. NSA Johnson wondered how much she already knew about Operation Hemlock and if she was testing him. McDermott was hoping he couldn't tell that she knew nothing and had just pulled "London" and "hacker" out of the blue. She had no idea where the words had come from. Maybe her meds were working even better today than she had thought.

"SocraTeez is a piece of human trash," he muttered.

"Agreed. But he is still human and we have international and domestic laws to honor. That means sometimes having to fight our enemies in the daylight."

"The same outfit conducted direct action missions against human traffickers who prey on refugees in the Eastern Mediterranean. There's no telling how many men, women, and children we've saved. Do those missions sit better with you?" She nodded her head in agreement. "Because they rub up against the very same laws," he continued. "I'm curious, what would you say if you had to publicly explain why the use of U.S. military force is justified in that scenario but not the former?"

McDermott crossed her arms and thought hard before answering. "It depends. Off the record, I'd just concede your point and save time. But on the record," she said, trying to suppress a grin—"on the record, I'd probably just use a bullshit interpretation of an Authorization for the Use of Military Force from twenty years ago."

Both laughed, then gave themselves a quiet moment to enjoy the camaraderie. "Our sides want to get to the same place," Johnson said; "we just differ on which routes to take. People like you and me help to keep things from becoming too unbalanced. That's all the special projects unit does, just on a bigger scale. They help to keep the balance, Lois."

McDermott felt a sharp pain behind her eyes and knew it was the onset of a bad migraine. She had to get out of there quickly. NSA Johnson saw a flash of panic on her pale face and asked if she was okay. "We have a physician right down the hall if you want to see her," he offered.

McDermott declined and composed herself. Then she looked into his eyes one last time. She wanted to tell her old friend how special he was to her and how important it was for the country to have men like him watching over them. She wanted to tell him that he had given her hope in some of the darkest times of her life. And she wanted to tell him that his affection meant more to her than he could have ever imagined. But she quickly discarded any notions of more talk. He already knew all those things. He was smiling, and this moment captured exactly how she wanted them to remember each other: a woman who gave all she had for as long as she could, and a dying breed of southern gentleman the country desperately needed.

McDermott exited through the East Wing of the White House to avoid the reporters who usually monitor the West Gate. She had several texts and missed calls from Peggy. She ignored them and spoke to no one during her commute home, feeling as if her head could explode at any minute. The armored SUV weaved its way through the thick D.C. traffic. In front of McDermott's apartment building, someone was illegally parked in the space reserved for drop-offs and pickups. Instead of waiting for someone to clear out the space, McDermott told the driver she'd rather walk fifty extra feet than stay in the vehicle a second longer than she needed to. McDermott and two bodyguards popped out of the vehicle as soon as it stopped. In less than sixty seconds she was safely inside her apartment building. It all happened so quickly that she hadn't noticed the car parked in the restricted space in front of the building was Megan's. And Megan had been too busy scrolling through her messages to notice her mother's sudden arrival.

McDermott immediately opened the sliding glass door to the balcony and breathed in the fresh air. It was a beautiful windless day and she could hear the bustle of D.C. traffic floating up from the street four stories below. Another text from Peggy. She ignored it and thought back to the deal she had made to save fifty thousand refugee children in exchange for confirming a Supreme Court justice she despised. Why had she really made the deal? Did she do it for those children? No. She now realized that she had done it entirely for herself—to somehow convince herself that she wasn't a horrible mother for giving Mark up as a baby and never being truly honest with Megan. Keeping a secret as big as Mark's existence meant that she had never shared herself completely with her family. In Megan's eyes, it was a deep betrayal. McDermott had once been proud of her role in achieving passage of the Refugee Act; now she assumed that her children saw through her grandiose attempt to overcompensate for her own shortcomings and she felt embarrassed at how obvious it must have looked to them. She went back inside, removed the eyeglasses perched on top of her head, and pulled out her earrings, placing them on the kitchen counter. Then she grabbed a bright red linen handkerchief, monogrammed with the initials M.M., from a kitchen drawer. It was the only thing Megan had left behind when she stormed out.

Mark's coolness toward her had been difficult to criticize because McDermott had always felt that she had failed him. She gave him life but had never been a part of it until he mysteriously showed up in her life one evening. And even then she failed to tell him the truth about his father. Mark had plenty of reasons to resent her, yet it didn't make his behavior any less shocking. *How was he able to trick me so easily?* she wondered. McDermott had always tried to keep her cool around Mark, but it was impossible not to tell how badly she longed for his love and forgiveness. So it was inconceivable that he didn't know. He also knew she was an ill woman. Who didn't? And yet his response to her outstretched hand had been to hover precariously, never letting his own hand get close enough for her to actually grasp yet never fully pulling away, as if deliberately trying to keep her in a state of psychological limbo. Was this some kind of a game to him, or did he just not care?

As a controversial public figure with too many enemies to count, Senator McDermott was necessarily a vigilant woman. How then, she wondered, did Mark manage to deceive her so easily? She already knew the answer. Peggy had intuited something early on, but McDermott had been so blinded by love or hope that she refused to see what had been floating in front of her face the whole time. How did Mark do it? Mostly with a straight face. But sometimes with a playful, boyish grin timed to flash and fade at just the right moment. He had a generally cool demeanor but could turn up his emotional dial for a passing moment, in a way that in retrospect now seemed noticeably methodical. He could coax and prod without appearing to pressure. He could lead you exactly where he wanted you to go, all the while making you feel as if you had chosen the destination. And he did everything so smoothly and effortlessly that even with the benefit of hindsight, the trickery was tangible but difficult to quantify objectively—much like her experiences with Mark's father. Peggy had been right. McDermott blocked the discomforting similarities from her mind. She desperately wanted to know what kind of person Mark

Landry really was, and she immensely regretted that she would never find out.

Now the house phone was ringing. It was probably Peggy. McDermott wanted to pick it up and tell her lifelong friend how much she adored her, but Peggy already knew that, and the senator didn't want to do or say anything that might suggest what was about to happen was anything other than a horrible accident. She felt that her whole life had been spent fighting off wave after wave of attack, but deep down she had always known this was her likely fate. The war was finally over. There would be no more waves. Resolved, she wiped the tears from her cheeks for the very last time with the red handkerchief and walked toward the balcony with her head held as high as her frail neck muscles would allow.

She slipped off her shoes and climbed barefoot onto the tall chair that sat beneath the wind chimes. After polishing one of its pieces with the handkerchief, she reached up and rotated the security camera until it was pointing in the opposite direction, something she was known to do on occasion. Eventually, somebody from her security detail would knock on the door and ask permission to come in and fix it, but this time no one would be there to answer their knocks.

With her back to the street, she released the handkerchief from her fingertips and bowed her head. "Megan," she whispered. "I failed you and betrayed your father. ... I pray that one day you will find it in your heart to forgive me. Mark ... at least I had my son for a little while ... I hope you get what you want ... good luck keeping the balance." Looking skyward with outstretched arms, Senator McDermott fell backward and into the inescapable arms of fate.

. . .

Megan was happy. She had been job-hunting for only a few weeks and she already had two solid job prospects in D.C., at the ACLU and the Brookings Institution. She was a little worried that the ACLU was more interested in having someone on staff with access to a sitting U.S. Senator than in her actual abilities, and she thought Brookings might be a little too conservative for her ideological tastes, but both jobs were otherwise good enough to put the bounce in her step that she so desperately needed. The less stress she had about work, the more she could focus on reconnecting with her mom, which she knew was best done with a home-cooked meal. She knew it wouldn't be easy, but she loved her mom with all her heart and was ready to start over.

She had turned to the bags of groceries on the floor of the back seat and started to organize what she would need to cook dinner when she saw something appear out of the corner of her eye. It was red and crumpled and had blown onto the hood of her car. She leaned forward until her nose was inches from the glass and squinted her eyes to get a closer look. *Is that my handkerchief?* she asked herself. A moment later— something crashed into the car.

When Senator Lois McDermott's body hit the hood, the sound on the street was enough to turn heads. But inside the vehicle, it felt and sounded like an explosion. Screams of recognition erupted from the small group of onlookers who had already started to gather by the time Megan managed to get out of the car, uninjured but clearly in a state of shock and confusion. *What the hell just happened?* she kept asking herself. People were moving around and talking, but she didn't know what they were doing and their words all sounded like the adults on Charlie Brown. She caught a quick glimpse of her car. The hood was a bloody mess, but whatever or whoever had hit it eventually ended up on the pavement where the crowd was already growing.

But the red handkerchief was still sitting on Megan's windshield. She took it into her hand and looked skyward to the sea of balconies overhead. Then she looked at the ring of cellphone-wielding spectators encircling the victim and deduced that her worst nightmare had just come true. Her mother was dead before she had a chance to apologize. And bloodsucking demons with cameras were there to document it.

Everything started to fade. Megan stumbled slowly toward the crowd, flailing her arms and screaming at the top of her lungs before passing out into an EMT's arms.

CHAPTER TWENTY

The Man Kennel

The prisoner could have watched the show from the basement window, but he decided against it this morning. He would have had to get up on his tippy toes and perform a half chin-up just to get his eyes to a grass-level view of the backyard, and he wasn't sure how many more times, if any, he could swing it. Besides, he didn't have to see to know what was going on out there. Heather Mays would begin by parading to the center of the sprawling lawn and announcing the arrival of her champion to an imaginary crowd. "Ladies and gentleman, here he is, the reigning National Dog Show champion and supreme emperor of all Irish setters, Little! Crimson! Tide!" Then she would spend half an hour training. The dog would perform poorly, and she would shower him with praise anyway.

She had not been so patient with the prisoner's training sessions. He looked down at his naked, battered body and the chain that kept him moored in the corner of the cold, dark dungeon, and he wondered how much more of this he could take before losing his mind.

The basement door opened and she took her usual seat on the middle step. Louis Vuitton sunglasses were perched atop a new look. She had cut off her long blond hair and it was dark now. As she chatted softly on a cellphone, it sounded as if she was switching back and forth between different languages, but one of his eardrums was badly swollen, making his hearing at that distance unreliable. He closed his eyes and tried to sleep until he heard the clicking of stiletto heels approaching his corner of the basement. She put the stainless-steel feeding bowl on the ground next to his water dish. He could smell the juicy leftover steak tips that she had mixed in with his usual small pellets of dry dog food. She called out to him from the bottom of the stairs.

"This is a special meal for a special day. I think you've learned your lesson. You're going home today," she announced.

He lifted his head up from the floor and looked at her, surprised. He knew better than to speak like a human, having learned that lesson early in his captivity. The prospect of getting out of this hellhole had never come up before. He had been close to resigning himself to dying alone in a basement, covered in his own waste. "I am leaving in three minutes. If you have eaten your breakfast by then, you'll go home today. This is a big day and you'll need your strength. If you don't eat, you'll have to wait until tomorrow. I'll get your clothes."

He heard the jingle of car keys and started to get excited. *Are those my keys?* he wondered. Then he looked at the bowl and took a big whiff of the special meal. It smelled delicious, but this was so out of the ordinary that he wondered if she was somehow testing him. "Two minutes left," she called out from upstairs. He looked at the bowl and began to panic. It was a lot of food. He started scooping it into his mouth and forcing himself to swallow as quickly as he could. The juices from the steak tips helped to moisten the dog food, but the dry pellets were still hard enough to scratch and cut his throat as they traveled down to his empty stomach.

He distracted himself from the pain by thinking about how the rest of the day would go. She said she was going to get his clothes. Would she make him bathe first? Would she just let him walk out or drop him off somewhere? Where the hell was his car? What about his phone? Would he get them back? How does she know that he won't go directly to the police? How would she think she can get away with this? Maybe to her this is just a freaky sexual fantasy. Did she think they were role playing? That this was somehow consensual?

"One minute." He heard her slowly descending the stairs and strained to eat quicker. By the time she got to the bottom, he had ingested it all. He forced himself to lap up the remaining juices from the empty bowl so she wouldn't think he was ungrateful. Now she was casually small-talking with someone on a different cellphone as she watched him. His mind continued to spin. His hatred for her was white-hot and he would have his vengeance. She would get what she deserved. She knew he was a man of means and resources. Did she think he was going to just let this whole thing go?

The room spun around a few times before she clapped her hands to get his attention. When he looked up, she blew him a kiss and mouthed "bye-bye." It was the first time he had seen her smile. He knew he was done. He glanced at the empty bowl, wondered what he had just ingested, and hoped it would be quick.

The first jolt of pain knocked him off his hands and knees and into the fetal position. His whole body was suddenly aching. He tried to stifle the moans. He started to cough, then sneezed violently. Blood began to flow from both nostrils and every muscle in his body was rapidly contracting and releasing. He convulsed for a few more seconds before deflating like a popped balloon.

She retrieved the stainless-steel bowl and whistled as she climbed the stairs. "It never gets any easier," she said aloud.

CHAPTER TWENTY-ONE

After the Fall

Megan saw Mark approaching the swinging doors at the end of the hospital hallway and was suddenly thankful for the group of cops and federal agents standing guard. She turned her back slowly enough for the attending physician to pivot with her as he explained Senator McDermott's condition. A brief moment later, the physician looked over Megan's shoulder and stopped in mid-sentence. Megan felt a gentle touch on her back, followed by a soft voice.

"I need a quick word."

"How did you get in here?" asked Megan, after furrowing her brow at Mark's fresh black eye.

Mark kept eye contact with her and held out his federal credentials for the doctor. "Doc, can you just give us about sixty seconds, please?"

"Not necessary," she said.

"Yeah, it is," Mark insisted.

Megan looked confused. When their mother had finally told her about Mark the half-brother's existence, she had mentioned that he was some kind of private security contractor. But now he was flashing a big, shiny federal badge. The stare-down was making the doctor nervous. He pulled his clipboard against his chest.

"Let's split the difference," he offered. "I'll grab a quick cup of water at the other end of the hall and be right back. Can I get one for either of you?" He hovered for a response that never came, then gave up and scampered down the hall. Megan dropped her gaze to her sneakers. She was still in the sweaty workout clothes she had been wearing when she arrived at Senator McDermott's residence. She had been replaying the horrible scene over and over in her head for hours. She was exhausted, overwhelmed, and frightened at the prospect of being alone in the world, except for the brother she never knew existed and who was now standing in front of her. Since she didn't know how to process all this, she defaulted to fighting.

"Megan," he said softly. No response. After he said her name twice more, she looked up with shiny eyes.

"Get out," she whispered. She cleared her throat, pointed to the door, and spoke louder. "Just go." Her chest rose and fell with each nervous breath. Mark looked as if he had no intention of budging. "Listen, I don't know who you think you are. And I don't really care. Right now, I just want—"

"Sorry to interrupt, but how do you think I felt?" Megan's circuits were already being overloaded by the tragedy at hand. Mark's unexpected question threw her off and confused her even more—exactly as he intended. Megan had a reputation for being ornery under normal circumstances. Add in the medical emergency and the sudden appearance of a sibling she never knew she had, and Mark knew that his first real encounter with Megan would likely be full of pyrotechnics if he let things play out on their own—which he had no intention of doing.

Mark would need Megan to confirm his family status to the physician in charge so that he could have unfettered, confidential access to the senator and her doctors. He also needed her to extend him a modicum of courtesy during the process. So he decided in advance to grab her by the horns and take control from the very beginning. He had practiced aloud how he wanted the conversation to go, experimenting with different words and tones, on the way to the hospital. He was going to try things the nice way first, but if push came to shove, he didn't have time or patience to play games.

"How do you think I felt?" he asked again.

"About what?"

"When I first found out I was adopted. How do you think I felt that day?"

Megan thought for a moment. Then she opened her mouth to speak, but nothing came out. Mark held an index finger just inches from her lips. "Hold that thought and I'll help you out. Confused. I was confused as hell. All the other kids talked about their moms all day. But mine was someone I never even met because she gave me away. Why would someone carry me for nine months and go through hours of labor, just to give me away as soon as I took my first breath? Throughout my life I often wondered: *Where is she now? Does she have a family? Does she ever think about me?*"

Megan stood frozen. Mark inched closer and said what he thought had the best chance of shutting her up. "Listen, I don't know much about you. But you know even less about me. Which means that you are not pissed off at me for anything I have done—but simply because I exist."

Megan was too stunned to speak. Mark grasped her by the elbow and the two slowly paced down the empty hall. "I didn't ask for any of this, Megan. I wouldn't have wanted it in a million years. But I played the cards I was dealt and that's what you and I have to do now—play the cards we were dealt, as best we can. And that all starts with you discretely telling the doc about my relation to the senator as soon as he gets back. Because like me or not—and that's not a decision you have to make right now—we're family."

. . .

Megan listened as the attending physician started from the top. All three of them were standing in the doctor's private office. There was no new information for her, so she had time to observe Mark. His words in the hallway had been effective, but there was something she didn't like about him. Still, she had to admit they shared more than a random resemblance to each other in looks and personality. They had the same eyes. Both carried themselves confidently. Or maybe she was just looking for reasons to warm up to her estranged half-brother and was deliberately searching for bits of herself in him. Regardless, it didn't work. She refocused on the physician, who was just wrapping up.

McDermott's prospects were bleak. When she arrived at MedStar Georgetown University Hospital, she was barely alive. Emergency physicians didn't need to wait for a CAT scan to confirm the skull fracture. Her pupils were big as saucers, and the clear fluids draining from her ears and nose were sufficiently reliable signs. A neurosurgeon tapped on one side of her head and listened through a stethoscope from the other side. The familiar "cracked pot sound" confirmed that she had brain abscesses and excessive cerebrospinal fluid exacerbating the swelling. She was unresponsive to painful stimulation, indicating that she could be brain-dead. Specialists were still trying to determine the extent of the damage to her major organs, and there were too many broken bones and torn ligaments to count. The long bone fractures had been stabilized with external fixators while the orthopedic surgeons argued over where to begin, assuming that they ever got the chance. Machines were currently pumping McDermott with replacement blood units and high doses of decadron for the brain edema. They added a tsunami of diuretics and corticosteroids in an aggressive attempt to decrease the volume of fluid swirling around inside the senator's broken body. She was currently intubated and doctors were already talking about a tracheotomy.

Mark read Megan out of the corner of his eye. She either didn't understand any of this or was foolishly holding out for a miracle. Nobody—not even a much younger, stronger person—had much of a chance against these odds, and McDermott had been frail and sick to begin with. He wanted to tell Megan that their mother was not coming back and that she should plan accordingly. But she was actually holding things together pretty well for a person who had just gone through seeing something horrible, and he didn't want to be the one to push her over the edge when he might still need her for something. Mark thanked the doctor and started to excuse himself.

"You're leaving? Don't you want to see her?" snapped Megan.

Mark looked into her eyes. Her defiant mask and body language weren't fooling him. Inside she was scared to death of ending up alone in the world, and right now she wanted to share the misery. She was reaching out the only way she knew how. Mark was about to decline when the physician interrupted and saved him the trouble.

"Actually, right now is not a good time. There are a number of specialists in there right now. Later would be much better for everyone."

"Fair enough," answered Mark. "I need to get back to Boston and see my wife and kids. I'll come back when I can. Until then, you both have my number. Thank you."

Mark got a call from an unknown number as he was exiting the hospital. He declined the call and descended the stairs to the bottom floor of the parking lot. He checked the time and figured he could still get home at a reasonable hour as he had promised. Luci said she needed to talk to him about some things but gave vague answers when he pressed for specifics. He was dreading what kind of mood she would be in but was excited as ever to go home and hug the twins. Especially since there had been a moment in Berlin when getting to do that again was in question. But tonight he would get to tuck his kids into bed—all thanks to the Turk.

As he was backing out of his space a text arrived. ANSWER YOUR PHONE. Pulling out of the garage and joining the one-way stream of traffic, he took the call.

"Hello, Marco. This is Oleg Borodin. I was hoping we could pick up where we left off, but you sound stressed. Is everything okay?"

CHAPTER TWENTY-TWO

Think about It

Mark's plane landed at Logan International Airport after sunset and taxied to a private hangar. Twenty minutes later, he was driving north on I-93 between the colorful spot-lit cables of the Leonard P. Zakim Bunker Hill Memorial Bridge. Luci had texted that she was putting the kids to bed. Mark was pissed. *Seriously?* he thought. *They can't stay up half an hour longer so they can say good night to their dad?*

The ride home gave him time to think. Oleg Borodin's second unexpected call, although not a complete surprise, had put him on edge for good reason. The last time Oleg called Mark, the lights suddenly went out and someone tried to kill him.

Kenny and the rest of the technical team were busy trying to identify where the call had originated from. It was not an impossible task, but it certainly wasn't easy considering the efforts Borodin put into masking his whereabouts, which sometimes included inserting barely perceptible and seemingly random background noises for his pursuers to waste time analyzing. Tracking the call would take time, and the chances of him still being there once they determined his location were zilch. The location and means of communication would be noted and added to Borodin's profile, but they would likely bring Mark and his team no closer to catching the master spy.

Mark would let the technical operators do their thing while he concentrated on the content to see what he could glean. He was listening to the recorded conversation through his vehicle's sound system for the umpteenth time, paying particular attention to Borodin's tone, pace, and word choice for clues. Normally this was a routine task for someone as experienced as Mark. The overwhelming majority of human beings cannot completely contain their subconscious thoughts. Their true intentions often leak into the conversation unintentionally and manifest themselves for anyone looking closely enough to see. With a normal person, you could take that leakage to the bank. But Mark knew he was dealing with a master of deception. If he spotted any leakage in the conversation, there was a strong possibility that it was intentional.

According to Borodin, Heike had approached him, claiming that American intelligence officials had been considering giving him the opportunity to defect and receive amnesty from prosecution for his crimes in exchange for his complete cooperation. They sent her to float the idea and test the waters. It had taken Heike months, but she had finally convinced Borodin to at least entertain a conversation.

"I agreed to the call but was shocked to find that Heike was not with you. And after considering your obvious surprise when I rang, it became clear that she had not been entirely honest with me. I should have trusted my instincts, Marco. We Russians generally know better than to trust Germans, but she can be very persuasive, as you yourself well know. So before I move on, let me just state that I was not responsible for setting up anything that evening. Regardless, I am glad that we have been introduced, even if so clumsily, but I would just as soon remove the middleman if that's okay with you."

The story Heike had told Mark was much different. She claimed to have knowledge through a deep source that Borodin himself was fishing for some sort of a deal worth flipping for. And she offered to introduce Mark to the secret source who would confirm it. Mark agreed—a decision that almost cost him his life. The original story she had told Mark about Borodin no longer mattered. The Turk had confirmed her treachery after showing up and saving Mark's skin. Heike, wherever she was, could not be trusted.

Mark shared none of that evening's events with Borodin. For all he knew, Heike was sitting right next to the Russian. Borodin sensed that his American counterpart was not going to share much. So he launched into his soliloquy.

Borodin claimed that over his decades-long career, American intelligence operatives had given him multiple opportunities to share his secrets in exchange for safety and an easier life. The alleged offers, which Borodin knew damn well were nearly impossible to corroborate, had never interested him. "Not even for a nanosecond," he declared proudly. "But time passes and weather changes, Mr. Landry. And I would now like to rekindle those talks with you."

"Why?" asked Mark. "What's changed? Midlife crisis?"

"Too much has changed. Not me, I assure you. But the world has changed drastically and there are some things of which I am now certain. The Russia I once loved has left me and is gone forever, which, I must admit, was not a total surprise. Our relationships with our lovers are not unlike our relationships with our countries, you know. Early in both, we subconsciously pick up on things that bother us, but we are so blinded by love or nationalism that we ignore our intuition and delude ourselves into thinking everything is fine. Not until we are betrayed can we see what had been in front of our faces all along. The state does not love us back. It can't. And so the very same state that selected, trained, and deployed us eventually turns its back on us. Shame on us for thinking it would end any other way. The same goes for the lover's betrayal. You married a coquette—what did you expect?"

Borodin cleared his throat, then continued. "Modern Russia, once a great power, has devolved into a corrupt society of chain-smoking drunkards ruled by ignorant wolves. I am also certain that the international system and all its moving parts—which has long been unsustainable—is finally on the verge of collapse. When that happens—not if, when—the wolves and those like them around the globe will be unleashed and we will enter an era of violence and uncertainty not seen since the Middle Ages. I am simply looking for the strongest manor from which to weather the storm. In exchange, I will share with you everything I know and—perhaps most important—pledge to assist you in the future. I have learned much about you. You are not weak, Mr. Landry. To the contrary, you are a surprisingly brutal man with powerful friends. But you will need a friend like me to help you navigate the future."

Mark replayed Borodin's pitch a few more times and snickered at the apocalyptic picture he had painted. Mark doubted he meant a word of it. He could seriously be testing the defection waters, but there was no way he actually believed the sky was falling. Only paranoid people wasted time worrying about such a total collapse. It made Mark laugh out loud. Borodin sounded like a nutcase conspiracy theorist. Mark expected him to continue with remote possibilities like nuclear weapon–induced electromagnetic pulses plunging the world into darkness.

"You don't really believe that bit about the Middle Ages, do you?" Mark replied.

"I do. And I believe it enough that if I had children—and I am quite happy that I do not—I would ensure that they had the skills necessary to survive in the world I just described, because it will be here very soon."

"It sounds like you've put a lot of thought into this, Oleg," Mark replied somewhat sarcastically.

"A wise man once taught me that a man without a plan is not a man."

"Okay, I'm convinced. Let's get together and talk about it," suggested Mark.

"In due time. Right now we are just two dogs sniffing each other and I am enjoying learning about you. You have many enemies, Mr. Landry. But the antidote for fifty enemies is one friend like me. Think about it. And enjoy your dinner."

As he reviewed the recording, Mark noticed numerous parts of the conversation that contained possible leakage or intentional misdirection. Specific phrases and word choices by Borodin would need to be pondered and further scrutinized later.

Mark exited the highway, turned off the radio, and opened all of the windows. Fresh air flooded the vehicle as he weaved his way through the state forest. He needed a few minutes to decompress and collect his thoughts before dealing with Luci. He had already made up a lame story about Billy hitting him with a door to explain the black eye. And he'd make something up on the spot for the dark purple bruise on the small of his back if he had to. But since their schedules were often different and intimacy between the two had all but disappeared recently, she probably wouldn't see it anyhow.

CHAPTER TWENTY-THREE

Deep Fake

"Do they still think it was an accident?" Luci asked, after placing the hot casserole dish on the chopping block and turning off the oven. "What are the Capitol Police and feds saying? Have they ruled out suicide? What a shame the whole thing is."

Mark had expected a lukewarm reception when he arrived. But he had also expected Luci to be more somber about Senator McDermott's fall. She was generally empathetic, the type of person who cried during sad commercials. But he could see that although she had made an effort to appear concerned about McDermott and asked a few questions about Megan, she wanted to get the topic out of the way as soon as possible, as if it were a distraction from more important things. Maybe a career of policing fatal car accidents and other tragedies had finally desensitized her.

Mark commented that the kids' recent report cards looked great. Luci pointed out that the report cards had been sent home two weeks ago. She said it matter-of-factly, but an ever so slight snarl of contempt flashed on her lips. Mark wanted to say he was very much aware that the report cards had been sent home two weeks earlier, because he had picked the kids up from school that day. He wanted to remind her that he had chatted with their teachers before hand-carrying said report cards home and placing them on the counter. But he knew it wouldn't change anything. A storm was coming. When she inhaled and turned in his direction, he braced for it.

"You must be hungry, baby. I cooked lasagna. Have a seat and I'll bring you a plate," she said, gesturing toward the table with the warmest smile she could fake. There was something she was dying to say or know, and she wanted him in the hot seat. She looked as if she were about to burst.

Mark dug into the lasagna, wondering how long she could keep up the charade. Luci was a good interrogator, but her husband had plenty of experience on both sides of the interrogation table under high-stakes circumstances. He could read most people. If she had something to tell him, she was better off just saying it.

"So I'm prepping for that conference on women in law enforcement that's coming up in Boston. I mentioned it before. You probably don't remember. Anyway—"

"I remember. You said you thought it was going to be at the Hyatt Regency Boston Harbor, but you weren't sure."

"Well, now I am. That's the confirmed location," she answered, trying not to sound agitated. "Anyway, I got to wondering if you have many female operators in your unit. You've mentioned you have like thirty to forty operators but I can't recall you ever talking about any women in the ranks. Are there any?"

Mark considered the question. What the hell was she getting at? Is that what she's been so pissed off about lately, equality in the ranks? "About a third are women," he answered.

"Really? I would have guessed far fewer," she replied. She sounded legitimately surprised by the number. "So do you work closely with them?"

"Yeah, I work closely with everyone in the unit. That would obviously include the women," he answered, putting down his fork and resting his forearms on the edge of the table. "Why are you asking me all this, Luci?"

"If it makes you uncomfortable, we don't have to talk about—"

"I didn't say it made me feel uncomfortable. That's ridiculous," he snapped back. "I just want to know where all this is coming from and you keep beating around the bush. Say what you have to say, Luci. What is it that you want to know?"

"Okay," she answered. Then she grabbed her laptop from the counter and set it on the table in front of her husband. "Is this whore with her tongue in your mouth and a hand on your balls one of your operators?" she asked, pointing to a crystal-clear photo of Heike leaning into the passenger seat of her car and kissing Mark while they were parked in front of her old apartment building in Berlin. "Who is she, Mark? Is this who you've been spending all your time with?"

Mark had not expected to see that awkward moment captured on film. And he never thought his wife would be asking him to explain something regarding another woman. But he was most shocked by how reflexively and easily he lied about it. It felt as natural as brushing his teeth or winding his watch. McMucker had taught him well.

"What the hell is that?" he asked, looking closer as if completely unfamiliar with the scene shown in the photo. "Oh my God. Who made this?" He started to laugh out loud, then stopped himself and pulled out his phone. "Hold on a second."

"No, Mark! I won't wait a second. I confront you with something like this and the first thing you do is pull out your phone. I want an answer to my question. Is she one of your operators?"

"No! I have no idea who that is. I've never seen her before in my life. She may not even exist, for all I know." Luci's phone vibrated against the granite countertop on the other side of the kitchen. "You're going to want to look at the video I just sent you. I think you'll find it enlightening."

Mark waited as Luci watched a montage of deep fake videos Kenny had made of himself, including him scoring a goal in the World Cup and occupying the grassy knoll in Dallas during the Kennedy assassination. The newest clips included one of Kenny being swarmed by paparazzi while leaving a posh D.C. restaurant with Monica Lewinsky on his arm.

"Are you saying Kenny made this?" she finally asked.

"No, I don't know who made it. But I'm telling you it's not real. Somebody is fucking with me, and when I find out who I'm going to beat their ass. That stuff"—he pointed to Kenny's fantasy highlight reel—"is funny. But this one of me is way over the line. Too far. What if I hadn't been here to prove it was fake? You might have believed it was real. What if my kids had caught a glimpse of this? I don't know who thought this would be funny, but if it came from anybody on my team, I'm going to nip this shit in the bud. These technologies aren't novelty toys."

Luci's phone started to vibrate in her hand. It was Goodie. She declined the call and sent it to voicemail. Then she looked at Mark. "Okay," she sighed. "I gotta say I felt pretty shitty when I saw that picture, Mark. My stomach sank and my legs went numb. But I'm glad you were here to clear things up."

Mark returned to the table and Luci went upstairs to make a phone call. Goodie answered on the first ring. He needed to talk to her about something important. "Okay," she said. "What do you want to talk about?" He said it was so important that they had to talk about it face to face. "But don't worry," he added, "it's great news." She asked where he wanted to meet, then demurred. "No, not your place. Where are you right now? Okay, I'll be there in thirty minutes."

Normally Luci wouldn't consider leaving the house at night unless it was an absolutely necessary part of the job. But tonight was different and she was in a bad mood. Maybe good news and fresh air were exactly what she needed. She wiggled out of her gray sweatpants and pulled on a pair of jeans. Then she let her hair down and brushed it while scanning her walk-in closet for comfortable shoes. She had plenty of lipstick in the car, she reminded herself.

Mark was downstairs booting up his computer on the marble-topped kitchen island. Furious and confused, he tried to collect his thoughts. Someone—either Heike or Borodin or both—had sent a salacious photo to his wife in a deliberate attempt to sabotage his family. Disaster had barely been averted. But that was not the target that his instinctive sights were focused on. It was her reaction to Mark's explanation. It was clear that the matter had deeply disturbed her. It was equally clear that she accepted the explanation that the video had been digitally engineered; she said so herself. But she also seemed just a touch deflated, as if a part of her had wanted it to be true.

The keys in Luci's hand jingled as she descended the staircase and made her way to the kitchen. He was engrossed in something. She kissed him quickly on the cheek. "I need to go in and meet with another detective for a little while. I won't take too long and I could use the air anyway."

"Okay," he replied. Then he typed a few more sentences. When he turned to say goodbye to his wife, she had already departed, leaving behind a confused husband and a trace of her perfume in the air.

CHAPTER TWENTY-FOUR

The Penalty Box

"She'll be here any minute, Sully," said Goodie to the bartender after ordering another Jägermeister shot and a beer.

Sully didn't react to the announcement or the drink order. Instead he pressed his palms on the bar and leaned forward. "So when can I expect my money, Goodie?" he asked.

"Oh God, will you stop! You'll get your money soon. You know I'm good for it."

"Do I?"

Goodie rolled his eyes. "You gotta be joking, Sully. We've known each other for years. Listen, I promise you you're going to get your money in the next few days. I promise. Just don't mess with me tonight, okay? I'm begging you, for your own sake, don't get me in a bad mood. Not tonight. I've worked hard for this."

Sully placed Goodie's shot on the bar and filled a frosted mug with Samuel Adams. "Don't look now," said Sully, nodding his head toward the entrance of the nearly empty Penalty Box Sports Bar & Grill. "But I think your girl just walked in."

"Don't tease me," replied Goodie with a flash of excitement on his face.

"Straight black hair? Smooth mocha complexion? Bright red lipstick?"

"That's the hat trick right there, but please go on. You're good at this."

"I've been robbed more times than I can count; giving accurate descriptions is a skill I've acquired," Sully turned to face the entryway and continued the description from head to toe. "Shoulder-length hair, large hoop earrings, denim jacket over a black sweatshirt, snug jeans, and Timberland boots."

"Stunning, no?"

"Just like you said—right down to the lips and hips. Is this one married too?"

"Some retired military guy who travels a lot," Goodie replied with a dismissive wave of his hand. Then he smiled at Luci and pointed to an empty booth in the back corner of the bar.

"Hey, Luci. How you doing? Ever been here before?" he asked.

Luci looked around the dingy, dimly lit bar and tapped the thin wood paneling that enclosed the booth. "Never. You?"

"Once or twice. I had just got here when I called you," he replied, although his breath and slurred speech suggested otherwise. Instead of taking the seat across from her, he made her scoot over and slid into the booth right next to her. Feeling awkward, she scooted to the far side of the booth.

"What? All of a sudden you don't want to sit next to me? Are we gonna need a wider cruiser for these last few weeks?" he asked, putting her on the spot.

"Bad mood," she replied. "It's not personal."

"I know just the fix," Goodie replied. Sully was watching them closely from behind the bar. Goodie tapped his mug and gestured for two more.

"Actually, I'm good," said Luci.

"Just have one, it'll take the edge off." She shook her head. "Come on, just one. One and done. You deserve it."

"Fine," she relented, sensing that he wasn't going to let it go if she continued to refuse. She would sit and talk with a beer in front of her if it would shut him up, but she had no plans to drink it.

After Sully delivered their mugs, she got to the point of the meeting. "What was it that you needed to talk to me about? You said you had good news. Let's hear it."

"I just wanted to personally inform you that the thing we were worried about is all taken care of. We're good. It's over. I took care of it." He was smiling proudly—almost gloatingly—from ear to ear, but Luci had no idea what he was talking about. Was he drunker than she thought?

"Perhaps you could be more specific," she suggested.

"The Vasquez case. Remember the night your dog got a little sick?"

"A little sick? You mean the night I told you to leave Murphy in the car and you ignored me? The night he almost died? Is that the night we're talking about?"

Goodie nodded. With that reminder, Luci's memory of the incident quickly came back to her. They had been worried that the high-dollar private defense team someone was bankrolling for Vasquez would have a field day with their use of a private dog to establish probable cause for a search of the defendant's vehicle. The last time Luci and Goodie had spoken about the case was after it had been formally assigned to a judge who had rebuked Luci's investigative work previously. Luci had been anxious ever since. She was only weeks away from retiring with a spotless record, and this would be more than a blemish. It would certainly impact her viability as a candidate for Essex County sheriff should she choose to run.

"Judge Brannigan denied the defense's motion to dismiss this afternoon."

"I thought that didn't go to her for another week or two."

"She heard private arguments this afternoon in her chambers. A girl I know who works in her office said Brannigan listened for maybe three minutes before ruling."

Luci perked up at the news. "Really? Man, that's a surprise I didn't see coming. It's definitely a bounce in our direction. But I wouldn't say it's completely over. You never know how an appellate judge will rule these days."

"There's no appeal. You don't understand. When I said it was over, I meant done. After the motion got denied, whoever was paying Vasquez's legal bills must have decided they had better use for their money than trying to keep him out of prison. His defense lawyers negotiated the best plea deal they could and were on their way out of town by the end of the business day."

Luci pumped her fists. "Yes! Wow. Seriously? Holy shit, that was lucky. This never happens. Man, I'm going to buy a lottery ticket on the way home." The good news instantly changed the trajectory that Luci's career was likely to take during her final weeks on the job. Things would go a lot easier than what she had been bracing for. It certainly rejuvenated her enthusiasm for the sheriff's race, although she was still keeping those cards close to her vest.

"Don't waste your money, Luci. It wasn't luck," he said, tapping his chest. "I told you I'd take care of it and I did."

Luci was confused. She remembered Goodie once mentioning that he somehow knew the judge but she hadn't thought about it again. "What do you mean?" she asked. "How did you take care of it?"

"I told you I knew her from a few years back when I was still playing hockey. I knew the case was coming up and decided it would be a good idea if I stopped by her chambers to say hello and maybe soften her up to our case a little in advance."

"You thought that was a good idea? It's not. It's a terrible idea," said Luci, her voice starting off strong, then lowering to a whisper. She instinctively scanned the bar and checked over her shoulder to see how close the nearest people were sitting. "I would have never supported that move. You could have made things a lot worse."

Goodie sensed her concern for privacy and made a lame wisecrack that he had already scanned the bar for wiretaps. "But just to clarify, I didn't make things worse. I solved the problem, just like I said I would."

"I know. My God, is everyone a Bruins fan but me?" she asked rhetorically.

"I didn't meet her when I played for the Bruins, actually," Goodie replied. "I met her back when I was still playing for BC. She was a star prosecutor at the time, and let's just say she was an enthusiastic supporter of mine."

Luci cringed at the comment but looked away and sipped her beer instead of showing her discomfort. Goodie was definitely drunk, but Luci figured he had probably been a lot more worried about the case than she had realized. He was blowing off steam and celebrating, so she cut him some slack. Besides, he probably felt guilty about the whole incident but just wasn't the kind of guy to show it, she reasoned.

Luci wanted to leave, but Goodie started telling a funny story about one of his first hockey fights. She tried not to smile and nod too much, because she didn't want to encourage him to talk all night. But the story was so hilarious that she ended up bursting into laughter.

When Sully came over to take their empty mugs, Goodie ordered another round. Luci protested and said she needed to get home and finish a few things before bed. "One more drink. You deserve it." Goodie kept pressing, but she didn't give in until he bemoaned how sad it was that their time working together was almost done. Then she considered that the kids were sleeping soundly in their beds and her husband was probably on the couch watching an old Magnum P.I. rerun. On that basis, she decided she wasn't missing anything at home. She sent Mark a text.

LUCI: I'm working with another detective. Don't wait up.

"You're right. I do deserve this." She took a few sips from her mug and slid her phone into the breast pocket of her denim jacket. Then she looked Goodie in the eyes and smiled. "Thanks for reminding me."

CHAPTER TWENTY-FIVE

Death Row

"Mark, I got the Turk on speed dial whenever you want him," said Billy. "Do you want to see it all one more time or do you just want to talk to him now?" Billy extended his arm and offered Mark the phone.

"Why bother?" asked Mark. "We know it's all bullshit." He was referring to the brand-new information on Heike, complete with a video package, that Mark had received from German intelligence an hour earlier. They had officially declared Heike dead, but nobody in Boston was buying it. Even Kimberly, the newest member of the team, could smell bullshit.

"Are we seriously supposed to believe Heike stayed completely invisible for as long as she did and then suddenly did this?" she asked, pointing to the video with the remote control. "The location is a private boating marina in northwest Lithuania on the Baltic Sea. In the opening seconds of the footage, Heike appears on the dock. Then she takes out a cellphone that she knows is being tracked and makes a ten-minute encrypted call. After that, she joins a man inside a brand-new cabin cruiser, where she sits for over an hour before finally lifting anchor and traveling west." Kimberly switched from the marina security footage to the night-time drone footage. "A six-man team of German SEALs was inserted in the boat's path about fifty kilometers off the coast. Then this happened," she stated ominously. The tranquility of the nighttime images of Heike's vessel was violently interrupted when a blast in the belly of the boat disintegrated most of the deck and released a fiery orange ball that lit up the sky. The explosion instantly killed the German SEALs, who had just reached the hull of the boat when it detonated.

"The footage is all real," Kenny interjected. "There's no evidence of digital engineering. But they're going have a hard time convincing us that Heike is dead without giving us something more concrete than this. The chances that she spent a career in intelligence learning how to hide only to suddenly abandon those skills when she needed them most are zilch. She's not that stupid or desperate. My guess is she faked her death and now she's looking for a hole to crawl into."

"More like a closet," said Mark before extending his hand toward Billy to accept the phone. Then he retreated to a corner of the conference room and sat down to talk to the Turk. "You mean to tell me you actually believe this crap?" he asked right off the bat.

"That is not what I said. You know me better than that. I said the official position of the German government is that she is dead. I imagine it was the most efficient decision for the politicians tasked with intelligence oversight. Or maybe they truly are that stupid. Either way, resources have already been reallocated. Officially, Heike is a dead issue."

"What about unofficially?" asked Mark.

"We've known each other a long time, Mark. Officially, Heike is dead. Unofficially, I have no idea because there's no body. But I can confirm that six of our SEALs are going home in pieces. If you happen to find Heike alive, remember who saved your life and please consider repaying my favor from Berlin. It would give me and their families a modicum of peace."

"Where do you think she went—Russia?" asked Billy, accompanying Mark down the hall and into his office. Kenny was following close behind.

"No way. She knows that no matter what Borodin says, if she enters Russia they may never let her leave. Just like the East Germans never allowed her mother to return to Gotland," he added, pointing out the big Swedish island on the map displayed on the touch-screen monitor that covered his office wall. "Which brings me back to the closet comment

I made a few minutes ago. Kenny suggested that she had faked her death and was looking for a hole to climb into, but that's backwards. She would have decided where she would ultimately go long in advance."

Mark leaned back in the soft leather chair behind his desk and pushed a few of the buttons located under the armrest. The chair vibrated softly and he let the mechanical fingers knead his lower back for a few seconds before continuing.

"When we first met, Heike told me a lot about her childhood. Too much, actually. I remember her describing a map of Scandinavia she had pinned to the wall inside her bedroom closet. If her dad went on a drinking binge or her parents fought, she would hide inside the closet with a flashlight and dream of traveling to Gotland one day or some shit like that. If you ask me, she slipped out of the boat early—maybe even before it left the marina—and headed west on her own, all the way to Gotland. She knows she can't win. But she also knows she doesn't have it in her to run from me forever. Knowing her, she probably still has one or two cards up her sleeve. But those cards won't matter if she eats a bullet before she gets a chance to play them. So she's flipping the script. She aims to draw me in and get me to listen. That's her strategy: go to Gotland, hope I show up, and pray that she gets a chance to speak before I kill her."

Kenny looked confused. "Huh? That doesn't make sense. She just faked her death. Why would she want you to show up?"

Mark nodded to Billy, who then turned to Kenny and presented his explanation. "Two reasons. One, she's bat shit crazy. And two, she's bat shit crazy about Mark Landry. Obsessed, really. Always has been. Or had you seriously not started to pick up on that yet?" Billy asked sarcastically.

Mark needed to make several important calls. Billy and Kenny headed back down the hallway to update the team. They were to immediately refocus all available resources on Gotland. If Heike was there, Mark wanted to move on her quickly.

"Man, I'm tired as hell and my head is spinning. There's way too many mind games going on these days for my tastes," said Kenny. "I'm having a tough time keeping shit straight."

"You ain't the only one."

"It's getting tougher to distinguish between a total coincidence and something that actually might have been deliberately done for effect."

"Not following you," replied Billy.

"Like the guy who tried to kill Mark in Berlin. Did Heike and Borodin just hire a guy for the job who happened to be neo-Nazi? Or did they deliberately hire a neo-Nazi for the job? Or could he have been one of the three guys Mark wounded and left behind in the basement of that huge apartment building back when he and Heike first met? How difficult would it have been to track any of them down this many years later?"

"Impossible."

"Maybe not. I know Mark said he didn't recognize the guy. But he did have Nazi tattoos on his neck, and people's appearances change over time. Maybe he was one of those guys but looks a lot different now, and Mark was too rushed to make the connection."

"Impossible for two reasons," Billy snapped. "One, Mark would never miss easy shit like that. And two, he sent all three of them up the chimney." Kenny looked confused. Billy leaned in and continued in a whisper. "You would have done the same thing if you'd seen the walk-in-refrigerator-sized furnace in that old building. It was a no-brainer. Mark knows better than to ever give anyone a second chance to kill him. So he tossed 'em in the furnace as if they were kindling and never looked back. It was the right thing to do."

Kenny nodded as if in agreement, but inside he was shocked. He knew that Mark had been holding back some details and that those details likely weren't pretty, but he never would have expected Mark to throw live bodies in a furnace. Regardless, Kenny wasn't a shrinking violet. He had been around for a few years and seen his share of violence. Once he had a chance to think about it, he'd probably be okay with torching neo-Nazis. Why the hell not?

But something else was bothering him. Kenny wondered why Mark had decided not to share the whole story with him in the first place. He feared that he was somehow slipping from Mark's good graces and was willing to do anything to stop his fall.

CHAPTER TWENTY-SIX

Comfortably Numb

Billy was wiping down a 12-gauge Mossberg 590 tactical shotgun and telling stories to two of the younger operators when Mark opened the hatch and entered the berthing area of the medium-sized cargo ship. The Danish captain had put the vessel in a tight holding pattern northeast of Gotland while Mark waited for confirmation from Sadie that she had completed her difficult assignment on the nearby island of Faro.

"I just spoke with Sadie," Mark announced to Billy and Quincy. "She has completed her task without incident. Smooth work. We will pick her up on the way to the objective, and she will be taking a well-deserved vacation as soon as we get home, so don't schedule her for anything else. Now let's talk through everything one more time before our final equipment check and departure. Quincy is coming with me. Bring extra darts just in case."

Quincy patted the nylon pouch attached to his belt where he kept his syringes, indicating that he had it covered.

"Billy will stand by right here on the Love Boat with a quick reaction force just in case anything goes wrong with the lead team. Tonight is Heike's first night in this new location and it has a special significance for her. So let's hit her before she has a chance to settle in and harden her position. Make sure everyone knows not to take any chances. If she makes a move, pull the trigger. If not, let's hold off on popping her until we're sure we've gotten everything we need from her, okay?"

. . .

Heike turned her back on the spectacular rooftop view of the Baltic Sea and paused to inhale the cool breeze one more time before closing the door to the widow's walk. Then she descended the winding stairs to the ground floor of the seaside mansion. A portrait of the home's original owner, famed Swedish director Ingmar Bergman, peered down from above the fireplace. Heike removed her clothes in the laundry room and walked naked past the portrait to the master bath.

After a long shower, she wiped the steam from the mirror with a hand towel. Then she probed her moist scalp for an appropriately flat area. Using a straight razor blade, she made a tiny incision. The tiny data chip was shaped like a Tic Tac but a fraction of the size. She carefully slid the chip through the incision and sealed it in place under her skin with a few drops of a synthetic wound sealant. Then she manipulated her long blond hair into a tight bun and centered it over the treasure she had just buried in her scalp.

Heike entered the half-darkened great room with the grace and confidence of an athlete. Wearing a white sports bra and black calf-length yoga pants, she retrieved the special bottle of Riesling from the refrigerator and took three glasses to a small pouring table next to the brown leather sofa. She opened the bottle, filled her glass to the brim, and drained half of it in one sip. It didn't taste as good as it did the first time she had it. Nothing ever does, she reminded herself. But maybe, like her, it just needed to breathe a little.

Heike closed her eyes for a few moments and tried not to think about what she knew was coming. Every cell in her body was screaming for her to leap off the sofa and either fight or run, but she sat calmly. When Heike opened her eyes she could feel his presence, although she didn't know exactly where he was in the enormous room until he spoke to her.

"Why three glasses?" he asked from somewhere near the bookcases in the far corner of the room.

"One for me, one for you, and one for Billy, who I imagine isn't very far away," she answered.

"Billy's not here," said Mark, slowly emerging from the darkness with extended arms and a two-handed grip on a Glock 19. He inched closer to Heike with his sights trained on the bridge of her nose. He didn't have to say anything. One wrong move and she was dead. She knew that.

"I find that hard to believe. I thought you two were joined at the hip."

"I guess not," replied Mark.

"More wine for us. May I pour you a glass?"

"No."

"Of course. You don't trust me," she said.

"Trusting you almost got me killed."

"I'll show you it's safe." She topped off her glass and then drained it in one big sip. "This bottle is impossible to find. Do you recognize the label?"

"No."

"It's the same wine we shared our first night together. But that was years ago. I wouldn't expect you to remember."

"If it's impossible to find, how did you get it?"

"I was on a waiting list in Berlin forever. And I've been saving it for a special occasion ever since," she answered.

The truth was that Heike had stumbled upon a lucky star just hours earlier at the local wine shop. A representative of the vineyard was holding a private tasting for high-end restaurateurs in their pouring room. She joined the group, mingled her way to the beautiful vineyard representative, and turned on the charm. The younger woman eagerly responded with a complimentary bottle and her cellphone number.

Heike lied about being on a waiting list because the truth would have taken too long to tell, and how she got the bottle didn't really matter. She had betrayed her country and Mark. If she wanted any chance at redemption, a story highlighting her manipulation skills was not the way to kick off the conversation. She felt lucky that Mark was letting her talk at all.

"Are you sure you don't want to try some? The saleswoman said there was a surprise in every sip."

"I don't like surprises. And lately I've had quite a few big ones—like almost getting killed in Berlin."

"I had nothing to do with that, Mark. I can only imagine the tales you've heard from Oleg. But believe me, I had nothing to do with it."

"And I suppose you don't know anything about the grabby picture of you with your tongue in my mouth that was sent to my wife either, do you? You just helped stage it, right? And what about the six SEALs you killed? You gonna blame that on Oleg too?"

Heike said nothing about the SEALs, but she vehemently denied any knowledge of the picture. She detected movement out of the corner of her eye. When she turned to look, her vision inexplicably became blurry for a second and it took a moment to adjust. She couldn't see anybody. Then she heard a noise. "Is that Billy?" she asked.

"I already told you, Billy's not here."

"Then who the hell is over there?" she asked in a confused tone. Heike tried to lean forward and stand up but suddenly found herself frozen. Her eyes were locked on Mark and she could still hear. But she could not move her arms or legs, and the tingly feeling in her hands was rapidly deteriorating toward no feeling at all.

"I'd introduce you, but I think you two have already met." Mark motioned for Sadie to come forward and join him. Cradling a Colt M4 carbine in her arms, she bent down and waved a hand in Heike's field of vision. "Hi. Remember me?" Then Sadie held up the bottle of Riesling. "I told you there was a surprise in every sip."

Heike's head bobbed and her eyes rolled into the back of her head. "Oh yeah, she definitely remembers me," Sadie said to Mark proudly.

The drug-laced wine had numbed Heike to her surroundings and she was quickly fading out of consciousness. She never noticed Quincy approaching from behind. And she barely felt anything when he gently lifted her head and put his lips to her ear. When he spoke, the words echoed.

"Okay," he whispered. "Just a little pin prick."

Then he pushed the syringe into the side of her neck and Heike's world went dark.

CHAPTER TWENTY-SEVEN

Sunrise

Mark and Billy stood alone on the cargo ship deck at dawn.

Billy had the shotgun resting on his right hip with the barrel pointing skyward and a 12-gauge slug in his left hand. The inland water of the abandoned island was much calmer—placid, by comparison—than the open sea they had to cross to get there. The silence left behind after the captain turned the ship's engines off was eerie, like the calm before a storm.

From inside the belly of the boat, they heard boots climbing the steep metal stairs. "It sounds like your date is almost here. Let me look at you real quick," joked Billy, eyeing Mark up and down and then pretending to dust lint from his shoulders.

Two operators appeared, carrying Heike on a stretcher. They placed her at Mark's feet, where Quincy gave her a wakeup shot. Then they removed the soundproof headphones and blacked-out goggles from her head and unfastened the restraints that had kept her pinned to the stretcher through the night.

"All set." Billy slapped Mark on the shoulder and moved out of the way.

Heike awoke with a gasp and rolled off the stretcher onto the hard metal deck. There, she writhed and dry-heaved for several moments before rolling onto her back. She was trying to identify the figure standing over her, but after she had been in complete darkness for so long, the sunrise was blinding. Covering her eyes and burying her face in the deck close to the person's feet, she recognized the boots Mark had been wearing the night before. She tried to speak, but her throat was bone dry. The best she could manage was a gravelly whisper.

"Mark?! ... Mark?!" she cried out.

Mark shook his head in disgust. Then he looked down on her desperate face but did not reply. *Why bother?* he asked himself. There was nothing she could say that would change things.

Heike pulled herself up to her knees and started rambling. "Mark ... Mark, wait! Don't do anything, just listen ... listen to me for one minute ... I can make it all up to you ... wait! I know how you can catch Oleg. I can help ... I know his one weakness ... we can do it together ... I swear I am not lying. He has a weakness, Mark! He has a weakness ... he has a daughter he has hidden for years. I swear to God, Mark! I am telling you the truth ... her name is Natalia ... she lives in—"

"Alabama," Mark yelled, cutting her off. "But she goes by the name Heather Mays. He sees her infrequently. The last time was in Boston where she was in town for one night to compete in some stupid fucking dog show and he visited her at her hotel. That's confirmed. I know all that. Tell me something I don't know, Heike. Quickly."

She was in shock. She had gone to great lengths to sleuth out the compromising information about Oleg Borodin, and only after switching teams had she been able to solve the puzzle. How the hell did Mark already know?

Heike was head-down on all fours with her stringy blond hair blowing in the breeze when the answer finally hit her. It was right in front of her face. Her hair. She remembered tying it into a tight bun after burying the treasure. But she couldn't recall having let her hair down or even having the opportunity to do so. Now it was blowing in the breeze. She put a hand to her scalp. The freshly shaved bald spot around her homemade incision confirmed her suspicions. The data chip was gone. Mark already had everything he needed. And she was about to die.

Mark stood watching as Heike started to crawl across the open deck toward the starboard side of the ship. She could see land in the distance. Her legs gave out several times as if she were a dog with hip dysplasia, but she soldiered forward, eventually making it to her feet and quickening the pace.

Mark turned his back on her and walked toward Billy. She seized the opportunity and made a leap for the water as Billy handed Mark the shotgun.

In one fluid movement, Mark spun around, racked the pump action, and lined up the sights on his airborne target. He pulled the trigger. The gun roared and Heike's head came apart like a clay pigeon. Her body slumped into the sea and Mark lowered the barrel.

"So what are you thinking about doing with the daughter?" Billy approached with his phone out. He was scrolling through Heather Mays's pictures on social media. "She sure is a cute little thing. Great body," he added, holding up his phone. "You see the mud flaps on this chick?"

Mark glanced at the pictures and nodded. Then he took a deep breath and looked down at the deck. "We could snatch her and try to use her as direct leverage over him. Or we could keep a close eye on her and wait for him to make contact or show up. My gut is telling me the final decision will end up being a little bit of both. Either way, we need someone working from the inside to do it right. Someone who can get in quickly. Someone with experience. Someone with the talent and skill to handle a little spitfire like her." Mark pointed to the pictures on Billy's phone. "Maybe someone who's eager to get back into the field. What do you think?"

"That sounds like somebody we know," said Billy. "Do you think he's up for it?"

"There's only one way to find out." Mark handed the shotgun to Billy and pulled the satellite phone from his pocket.

"Uh oh," said Billy, pointing to some residue on the starboard edge of the deck. "Heike's dead, but she's not entirely gone. I'm gonna hose that shit off." He started walking toward the ship's cabin to put the shotgun away.

"Wait," Mark called out. "I need you to do me a favor first."

"What's that?"

"Get a message to the Turk," replied Mark. "Tell him we're even."

CHAPTER TWENTY-EIGHT

The Bump

"Here you go," said the waitress, placing the dessert in the middle of the table. "Can I get y'all anything else?"

A smitten Heather Mays sat across the table from her date. She had been with plenty of older men, but none had ever mesmerized her like Mr. Brownstone, the distinguished gentleman glowing in front of her. He was the first one she recalled ever having to chase after. Typically, when she wanted a man's attention, she needed only to make her desire known, occasionally tossing in a wink to make sure the slower ones got the message. But Brownstone had thus far been impervious to her attempts to seduce him. And he was treating her with an indifference that she was unaccustomed to.

Heather had no doubt that if she walked out of the restaurant and left in her Tesla without another word, he wouldn't so much as raise an eyebrow. Yet instead of pushing her away, Brownstone's ambivalence just made her want him more. From the beginning, he had made her work hard to get his attention. Now he was making her work even harder to earn any affection. She finished a strawberry and licked the remaining whipped cream from her fingertips.

"This doesn't satisfy me. How about we go to my place for something sweeter?" she asked with a tilt of her head. She gave her cutest smile and waited for an answer. He was in no hurry to reply and the anticipation was driving her mad. He casually glanced down at his vibrating phone, then back into her eyes. She was intoxicated by the confident, deliberate manner in which he did even the smallest tasks.

McMucker smiled back across the table and melted her with his pale blue eyes. He had originally not wanted to wear the colored contacts. But Mark's newest team member, Kimberly, had analyzed Heather's social media posts and determined this particular shade of pale blue to be her favorite. Observing Heather's reaction from behind the lenses, he noted pupil dilation and an uptick in her breathing—strong indicators of attraction. *Kudos to Kimberly*, McMucker thought. The contacts were helping, even though he was confident that he could have seduced the young lady without them.

"What do you say?" she prompted, unable to wait any longer.

"Open up," he commanded. Then he beckoned her with a finger. She leaned forward and he popped a strawberry into her mouth. "Why don't you go to the little girls' room while I return that call and think about it."

Heather wiped the corner of her mouth with her napkin and smiled her brightest. "I'll be right back."

McMucker turned his attention to his phone and didn't look up until he knew she would be out of the room. He didn't know if she would turn around and peek over her shoulder one last time or discretely use the mirror behind the bar to check on him. Either way, he wouldn't be looking at her when she did. He knew that would drive her wild.

"Mr. Landry," he began. "This is Mr. Brownstone. Sorry I missed your call. Things here couldn't be better."

McMucker was confirming that he had breached the castle walls. But Mark had never even considered any other outcome. It had been obvious to anyone with an eye for undercover work that Heather had been intoxicated with McMucker from the very first 'bump'—a carefully planned interaction orchestrated to appear random. Normally, a team may take weeks or even months to set up and execute a proper bump; McMucker and Sadie pulled it off in just a few days. Once they learned that Heather went to the gym every morning at 9:00 a.m. and that she always used the same Stairmaster machine—in front of a big glass window with a beautiful view of the park across the street—they put together a plan.

One morning, Heather watched from her Stairmaster as McMucker arrived at the park in a dark Mercedes-Benz Maybach. He stood next to the car while he made a quick phone call. Then he walked onto the grass with the quiet confidence of a gentleman who had just gotten laid. When he whistled over his shoulder, a freshly groomed female Irish setter sprang from the open backseat window and bolted toward its master's left side. Moments later, Sadie made her entrance, dressed to the nines in a BMW convertible, her blond hair blowing in the Alabama morning air. Then they performed their finely honed drama for their target watching from across the street.

Heather had been enthralled by the spectacle from the opening scene. Sadie had been the obvious pursuer. Heather could smell her desperation from the Stairmaster. But it was obvious that the gentleman did not share her feelings. He was breaking up with her. She protested and begged, but he had made up his mind. Sadie departed the park in tears. Her part of the bump complete, she flew home to Boston to pack for a well-deserved and much-overdue vacation.

The second day was simpler. McMucker simply showed up at the park by himself and walked the Irish setter for a few minutes until Heather spotted him. When she exited the gym and started jogging his way, he and the dog hopped into the car and drove away just as she neared. On the third day, Heather was waiting for McMucker in the park when he arrived.

Mark told McMucker there was speculation that Oleg Borodin might be heading to Ciudad del Este, a lawless city in the Tri-Border Area of South America where the countries of Argentina, Brazil, and Paraguay meet. The area is a well-known and utterly unregulated cesspool of transnational terrorists and organized crime, home to some of the world's most-wanted villains and a thriving criminal economy. Mark would let McMucker know if anything came of it. Until then, he should plan for a long embed with Borodin's daughter, although Mark's gut was telling him that things would move more quickly. Only time would tell.

McMucker smelled a fresh scent of perfume as Heather returned to her seat. She played quite effectively the role of a carefree southern belle with a trust fund, but he wondered what went on beneath the mask. Maybe she believed it, maybe it was all an act. It all depended on whatever story Borodin wanted his daughter to believe. Did she know who she really was, where she came from, and who her father was? After all, Borodin could have programmed her to believe anything he wanted. McMucker looked forward to peeling this cute little onion.

"Have you made a decision?" she asked.

"One second, please," he replied holding up an index finger. Heather waited patiently.

Then he sent a text to Mark reminding him that Bolo, his eight-year-old black Labrador, was a fine dog and not nearly as slow as Mark thought. He ended, "Be sure to find him a nice home like you promised." McMucker chuckled, thinking he had a good idea of where the dog would end up calling home. Then he redirected his attention to the eager young lady across the table and smiled.

"Something sweet at your place?" he asked with a sparkle in his eyes. "Why not? You deserve it."

Heather Mays swooned.

CHAPTER TWENTY-NINE

Reading Peggy

Peggy stood at the end of Senator McDermott's hospital bed, flipping through her friend's medical chart. Seeing the specifics of McDermott's condition in black and white was sobering. No wonder Megan was the only optimistic person in the building when it came to McDermott's chances of surviving much longer. Every part of her was broken. It was amazing that the fall had not killed her instantly. Peggy didn't want to lose her best friend, but living in this state was not the kind of living Lois would have wanted. Peggy looked at her watch. Visiting hours were almost over.

She sat on the bed next to her shattered friend. Her eyes were closed and she had an endotracheal tube inserted into her windpipe. The tube was held in place by two strips of white surgical tape that formed an x over her mouth. Peggy touched Senator McDermott's cheek softly with the back of her fingers.

"It's almost time for me to go, Lois. But I promise I'll be back to visit soon," Peggy whispered. She heard another voice in the room just as she stood and turned toward the door.

"Pardon me if I interrupted," he said.

Peggy was startled to realize that she wasn't alone. She was even more astonished to find herself face to face with Mark Landry. This was the first time she had been in his presence since he took his first breaths as a baby.

"No," she replied. "You didn't interrupt anything. I was just on my way out. I'm Peggy. I'm a friend of your … the Senator's."

It wasn't just the pause, which occurred as Peggy tried to decide quickly how to refer to McDermott when speaking to Mark, that surprised him. She had also instinctively introduced herself—without bothering to ask who he was. Apparently she already knew who he was. *She must,* thought Mark. There was an air of familiarity in her eyes.

"You know who I am," said Mark.

Peggy hesitated, then nodded. Mark took a slow step toward her. She wasn't scared. But she was very aware of whom she was talking to. This was Lois McDermott's son. The infant who was once inside her best friend's belly—a belly that Peggy had rubbed and spoken to softly during many hours of labor. She was puzzled by his expression. Was it a smile? A smirk? Was he happy or sad? She couldn't tell—he just was. And his eyes were exactly as Lois had described.

"You're a physician, aren't you?" he asked.

Peggy was taken aback for a second. How would he have guessed that? She considered her clothing. She had dressed casually and toned down her jewelry to a few tasteful pieces for this visit. Mark could see that his question perplexed her.

"It was the way you were holding the chart. You flipped through it like you knew what you were doing," offered Mark.

"Is it really that obvious?" she asked with a hint of pride. "Yes. Recently retired."

"Let me guess. Psychiatrist?" he probed with a straight face, nodding his head as if he already knew the answer.

"Neurologist."

"That would have been my second guess." His smile relieved Peggy. She smiled back and nodded in mock agreement. "I'm sure it was."

Peggy was still trying to figure out how he could have possibly guessed her profession just by reading her behavior. Then it dawned on her that McDermott's emergency room physicians would have identified any prescriptions in her system when they admitted her. And she knew that they would have identified several psychiatric drugs for which no records existed. McDermott had been getting those prescriptions directly from Peggy so that she could maintain her ability to function in the Senate and avoid the stigma that would result if the public knew the extent of her maladies. Mark had known she was not well. Now he was meeting her close friend, a neurologist. Of course he would connect the dots. Peggy hoped Mark would know one day why she had helped and how much she still owed Lois. Without her, Peggy would have never enjoyed the life she had.

"Dementia and bipolar?" he asked.

"Among other things," she answered, looking around to make sure they were alone in the room. "Look, I was just about to leave if you wanted to sit here with her."

"Actually, I need to get back to Boston immediately. I'm expecting a house guest. But I do have one more question for you. Did she jump?"

Peggy wasn't surprised by the question at all. People across the country were still speculating as to whether McDermott had jumped. The fact that the balcony security camera had been turned just before the incident added to the prevailing suspicions. "No, no way. She loved her kids too much to do something like that."

Mark nodded his thanks. "It was nice to meet you, Peggy."

"Listen, I have to say it's nice to finally meet you, Mark," Peggy replied as she gathered her things, zipped up her coat, and grabbed her phone from the nurse's table. "I just wish it would have been under better circum—"

She paused and looked around the room. Mark Landry was gone.

It must be an important house guest, Peggy thought.

CHAPTER THIRTY

Stained Glass

Mark parked in his driveway and whistled over his shoulder on his way to the open garage. When he didn't hear paws scampering behind, he stopped and looked back at the open rear window of his Range Rover. Then he whistled again. Mark had been accustomed to Murphy, who would automatically leap through the window and follow him into the house. Bolo just raised his head and rested his chin on the window.

"Come on, Bolo!" snapped Mark. It sounded more like a plea than a command.

Mark kicked the basement door closed behind him and carried Bolo up the stairs into the house like a bundle of firewood.

Luci is gonna kill me.

Murphy was excited to see his unhurried friend. Mark put the dogs in the backyard together so that they could become reacquainted. Both seemed happy to see each other. Mark told Bolo not to get too comfortable. He wasn't sure how long these arrangements would last.

Luci called. It was their turn to provide the post-catechism snack for the kids, and she had left everything on the kitchen counter. She asked Mark if he could throw the cookies, small paper plates, napkins, and juice boxes into a bag and bring it to the church. He said he would be happy to do so. He welcomed a chance to try to mend their frayed connection. Bringing snacks to a church event seemed like a good way to do that.

Catechism didn't end for another hour. That gave him a few minutes to catch up on some mundane things like folding laundry and taking out the trash.

"Mirror my phone," said Mark, prompting the flat-screen display on the dashboard of the Range Rover to mirror his phone's desktop. "Play something." Black Sabbath's Paranoid played through the vehicle sound system as Mark headed across town to the church.

Mark thought about Heike's final moments but quickly put them out of his mind. He had had no choice. Her treachery had almost gotten him killed, and he knew better than to ever give someone the opportunity to do it twice. He also knew that the Turk, who had saved his life, would not have wanted her to escape, and that Heike herself needed to pay for the German SEALs whose lives she had needlessly sacrificed. Heike had gotten exactly what she deserved and had practically begged for.

"Review my messages," Mark commanded.

"Reviewing messages," replied the system.

The virtual assistant started to read Mark's unread messages aloud and to simultaneously display any accompanying media on the dash screen. The first few were unremarkable administrative messages. Then came an important one with new information on a recent bombing of a Southern Baptist revival outside Durham, North Carolina. It had originally been deemed a lone-wolf attack by the young man in custody. But now the pictures of two other young men suspected of helping to plan and carry out the attack were on the dash. The whereabouts of both men were unknown.

The next message was an email from an address Mark did not recognize. The message contained no text, just a three-second video with no sound. He caught only a glimpse of it as he was driving across a busy intersection when it began playing. Luckily, when the video reached the end, it was programmed to begin playing again in a continuous loop.

Mark's eyes were frozen on the video. He watched several loops of it before he realized that all the honking horns were directed at him. He had inexplicably come to a complete stop on a busy roadway. He tried to take his foot off the brake and accelerate, but his mind was frozen. Cars were beginning to veer around him before he managed to let the vehicle idle its way to the shoulder of the road where he could park.

Human emotions all begin as some form of physical arousal. Individuals then have to translate those sensations into words to figure out what to do with them. This is how the mind draws our attention to things of importance around us. Mark had been trained early in his career to recognize his surfacing emotions and then quickly compartmentalize them so that he could stay singularly focused on the mission. His ability to do so had helped keep him alive in the field.

But this was not the field. Mark Landry was in his hometown. And he was watching a continuous loop of his wife Luci passionately kissing her partner, Goodie, in a parking lot. Their mouths were pressed firmly together and Goodie's arms were wrapped tightly around her waist. Luci was leaning back against her car. At the beginning of the shot, she had her fingers laced behind Goodie's neck. By the end of the three-second loop, she had a fistful of his wavy hair in each hand.

Mark's heart sank and his legs went numb.

Who sent this to me?

More than likely, he would eventually be able to find the answer to that question. But simply by being cops, Luci and Goodie had no shortage of enemies who would have jumped at the chance to torpedo the officers' personal lives if they could. Plenty of people could have had a motive. The only thing to do was let the technical guys do their jobs and see how far they could track it down.

Is it real?

Mark was feeling physical sensations that he had never felt before. He wouldn't have to wait for some sort of technical validation of the video. He knew it was real. That was his wife. Those were her clothes. And the two-handed hair tug was what she did when she got excited. Mark felt the strong urge to vomit.

Why did you do this, Luci?

Mark's skin started to tingle and his hands felt like two balloons. He could feel the tears building up inside like a pressure cooker, and for the first time in his adult life he wondered if he could hold them off.

Is this what betrayal feels like?

Retired Master Sergeant Mark Landry, U.S. Army Ranger and special operations legend, fell to his knees and vomited as soon as he parked and got out of his car at the church. Some of it splashed onto the bag containing the catechism snacks.

Mark Landry was prepared for anything, even some of the hyperbolic global meltdown drama Oleg had been peddling. But he had never considered the possibility that he or Luci would betray the other. It had seemed a virtual impossibility until just a few minutes ago. Mark felt as if the earth had just shifted under his feet. And he was still struggling to regain his footing.

His life had been cracked open like a piñata, and pieces of his broken heart were spilling out. He felt vulnerable for the first time he could remember. And he was experiencing new emotions and impulses that he had previously observed only in captive enemies. Fear. Muscle twitches. A sense of impending doom.

Mark was slowly ascending the front steps of the church when an elderly woman who knew him greeted him on her way down. She was a short woman with a big voice, but Mark could not hear anything and felt a sharp pain in the side of his head as if someone had cut off his ear. The woman looked puzzled. Mark tried to speak, but when he opened his mouth, nothing came out and he felt as if someone had stabbed him in the throat with a steel blade. The old woman simply smiled and went on her way.

It was a cool afternoon, but Mark could feel heat pouring out from the church's open doors when he reached the top of the steps. The church was the last place on earth he wanted to enter right now. He was already sweating. Mark looked down at the bag of snacks and took a few deep breaths. The heat inside felt like the blast from a furnace when he entered. Inside, he scanned the church. A dozen or so people were spread out, doing their own thing. Luci was nowhere to be seen. The kids were still downstairs in the basement catechism classroom.

Mark had a hasty plan. Get through this. Just get through this church thing. Then later he would go for a drive around the lake alone.

When he got home, he would lie in bed with each of the kids for a few minutes. He will hold them and listen to their precious heartbeats as they slept. Then he would lock himself into his office and cry harder than he would ever cry again.

For now, and for the sake of the kids, he had to compartmentalize those feelings. But he was petrified that he didn't have the stomach to do it anymore. He was afraid that his trusty mask might slip. Or worse, that it could shatter in place like safety glass, then fall to the ground, revealing to the world the distorted face of a terrified little boy.

You could hear a pin drop in the church when the confessional door squeaked open. Luci exited and took a moment to straighten her outfit. When she looked up, she saw Mark watching her from the back of the church. She waved and forced a smile, but she didn't get her mask up quickly enough. There had been just enough of a lag for Mark to catch a glimpse underneath. The video was authentic. This was all really happening.

Luci smiled again, turned her head sideways, and squinted as if to ask "What's wrong?"

Mark dipped two fingers into the holy water and slowly crossed himself as he watched Luci approach the back of the church. She kissed him on the cheek, then wiped off the smudge of red lipstick she had left behind. "What's wrong? Is everything okay?" she asked.

How did we get here, Luci?

Click.

CHAPTER THIRTY-ONE

Ladies' Night

Luci put an earring on as she walked past Mark toward the front door. "Sorry, I made plans for tonight," she said. "I wasn't sure if you'd be around."

Mark didn't understand how Luci could have thought he might not be around. He had barely left the house since bringing Bolo home. Mark looked out the back window onto the deck, where Murphy was sprawled out, napping. Bolo, who had been at the house for nearly two weeks, was still discovering new parts of the backyard at his own pace.

Mark had been making every effort to mend the frayed marriage relationship, but his overtures hadn't seemed to make much of a difference. Sometimes it seemed as if Luci was on a mission to be pissed off at him and wasn't about to let anything get in her way.

Luci left to meet a friend for dinner. Mark put on a pot of coffee. It was going to be a long night, and things were just getting started.

. . .

The restaurant was unusually slow for a Thursday night, so Luci and her friend Linda McCarthy, an FBI agent also on the verge of retirement, got the big booth in the corner. The two had met the week before at a conference on women in law enforcement, an event attended by several thousand officers. Luci had participated in a morning panel discussion on the role of women in the battle to counter violent extremism. Linda had attended and asked a number of pointed questions of the panelists. They had lunch together and subsequently attended several of the same sessions.

The two had been texting frequently since hitting it off at the conference. When Luci suggested meeting for dinner, Linda hadn't needed any convincing.

"So you drew your gun on him right then?" asked Luci, savoring one of the few remaining bites of risotto in her mouth and then washing it down with the white wine that Linda had chosen.

"Hell yeah, I did," answered Linda proudly. "Pointed it right at his balls too. But that's what the Miami Field Office was like twenty years ago. If you did that now they'd go after your pension, and I'm way too close to mine. I started wearing this thing a few months ago and I'm not even religious," she added, pointing to the tiny guardian angel pin fastened to the collar of her denim jacket.

The dinner conversation had veered all over the place. Both women had carried a gun and a badge for more than twenty years. Both were excited to retire but also anxious as they contemplated what life off the job would be like. Teaching was an option for both of them, but neither had an interest in a full-time academic position, and most adjunct positions were akin to slave labor. Thankfully, both had their pension and more than enough stability, so neither of them had to make any immediate plans. Luci was still considering a run for Essex County Sheriff, but didn't feel she knew Linda well enough to disclose it.

"You mentioned your ex a few times. How long have you been separated? Where is he living these days?" asked Luci.

"She. She lives in Connecticut."

"Oh, okay, sorry," Luci offered.

"Don't look so surprised. And you sure as hell don't need to be sorry," replied Linda. "I may have ninety-nine problems but, to paraphrase Jay-Z, a dick ain't one of them." Luci laughed and Linda continued. "I've been divorced for five years after being married for almost three. We had nothing in common. Doomed from the start. What about you?"

Luci explained that she and Mark had been high-school sweethearts who rediscovered each other much later, and that now they had been married for seven years and had a set of twins.

As they were paying the restaurant bill, the conversation worked its way back around to the conference they had attended. Linda said she felt the lectures on toxic masculinity had been a bit much. Luci agreed. It was an important topic, but the presenters hadn't fine-tuned their message very well and people were left with more questions than answers.

"Yeah," said Linda. "Besides, not all men are toxic, just most of them." She laughed at her own predictable joke, then dialed it back a little. "You know I'm just kidding. I like men. But there are still plenty who think the world is their locker room. And those guys make the hair on the back of my neck stand up. But I don't have to tell you that. You know exactly what I mean." Linda spoke clearly and let her words hang in the air for Luci's consideration. It seemed as if Luci was going to let the comment go, but then a quizzical expression spread across her face.

"You think I do? What makes you say that?" Luci asked.

"Well, for one, you're a woman. And second, you mentioned at the conference that you had been stuck in a car training some new jock detective. A former Bruins hockey player. Goodie, was it?"

Luci hadn't recalled sharing that information with Linda, but it was certainly possible so she thought nothing of it. "Yeah, but he's not like that," Luci replied, knowing that her statement wasn't entirely true and that actually Goodie could be quite a pig. Luci immediately wondered why she was defending him and chalked it up to thin-blue-line solidarity. "But I definitely know the type," she added.

Neither woman said anything more until they were outside in the parking lot. Then Linda resumed the conversation, trying awkwardly to pick up where she had left off inside. "Yeah, it's just that … ." Luci could sense that she was still thinking about Goodie and wasn't going to let it go. "You have such a beautiful, wholesome life and family, it's too bad that the job can stick you with someone that toxic. I've known agents like him over the years and always made sure to keep them at arm's length. If not—if you make the mistake of letting them in—they slowly attach themselves to you like parasites. And by the time you realize how much of their toxicity has seeped into your life, it's too late. You're radioactive too."

The talk about Goody was making Luci paranoid. She just nodded her head in agreement, hoping to transition to a pleasant goodbye and drive away as soon as possible. But then things got worse.

"I am about to retire and my record is relatively spotless. I imagine yours is too," Linda continued, getting an enthusiastic nod from Luci. "And every one of us kicks into pension protection mode as we approach retirement. We think hard before taking any risks that could jeopardize what we've already earned, right? And yet—I don't know about you, but I've found myself considering things lately that I never in a million years would have thought I'd be considering this close to turning in my badge for a retiree shield."

Luci nodded silently. She could relate. The last few months had generally been a confusing time for her. The sloppy work with Goodie on the night her dog overdosed on fentanyl came to mind. There were several poor decisions that could have sunk her in that case alone. But Luci thought about something else she had recently done as well. Something she had tucked away in a dark corner of her mind because she still could not consciously understand or explain her own actions. Linda's comment had been enough to unsettle the memory, but not yet enough for Luci to confront it.

"Okay, here's the deal," Linda announced. "Listen closely because we are only going to talk about this once and it has to happen right now. After we part ways tonight, we never speak of it again to anyone, including each other, capeesh?" Luci nodded and braced for what was coming.

Linda explained that because she was just weeks from retirement, she was doing desk jobs rather than having new cases assigned to her. One of her duties in the Boston FBI Field Office for the past month had been to review and approve the destruction of surveillance tapes from legal wiretaps that may have incidentally collected information from individuals not directly related to cases under investigation. One such wiretap that Linda had recently cleared had been placed in a small sports bar north of

Boston called the Penalty Box. "Do you know the place?" Linda asked. "No."

Neither the bar nor any of its employees had been under investigation. But two persons of interest in a major investigation had been expected to meet there, so the U.S. Attorney's office in Boston had authorized the bureau to plant a listening device ahead of time. The persons of interest never showed up, but several hours of conversations at the bar were recorded. One of those conversations was a heated argument between Sully, the bartender, and Goodie.

"They were arguing about money. And your name came up," Linda added. She waited for a response.

"Well, I don't know what to tell you about the money part, but since we just spent a few months working together, it's not surprising he would mention me," Luci answered, trying to hide her concerns behind a nervous smirk.

"It didn't have anything to do with work, Luci. It was personal."

Luci shrugged her shoulders, hoping to God that Linda wouldn't go any further.

"I'm going to cut to the chase. Goodie owed Sully money, and if he didn't pay ASAP, Sully threatened to send a compromising video of you and Goodie to your husband."

Linda paused. Luci sat stunned. She had never imagined being on the receiving end of a conversation like this. As an experienced FBI agent, Luci realized, Linda probably knew much more than she had been letting on—like whether Luci had ever been to the Penalty Box—and likely had her reasons for revealing her intelligence in slow motion.

"Goodie's response," Linda went on, "was to tell Sully in no uncertain terms that he could care less if Sully sent the video to your husband, your priest, or every cop in the department."

"Of course he did," Luci responded. "That doesn't surprise me at all. After all, Goodie knows that no such video exists. He was calling the bartender's bluff. How else would he—"

"Just wait, Luci. Let me finish." Linda cut her off with a raised hand as Luci Landry's heart sank even further. Experienced agents know to keep their subjects quiet during the monologue portion of any interrogation. This was the point where Linda would lay out everything she knew—a process that would more than likely end with a shocking revelation of undeniable evidence—and she didn't want Luci needlessly lying along the way. It would just add to her shame and embarrassment once Linda dropped the bomb. "To summarize, Goodie told Sully to go ahead and send it, and that's exactly what he had been preparing to do when I went to see him."

"You went to see him?" asked Luci, her heart pounding in response to the story that was unraveling in front of her.

"I had to. How could I do nothing and let two assholes ruin your life? Which, by the way, I don't think you deserve. Look, your personal business is your business, Luci. I'm not judging you. But I was determined to nip this shit in the bud and give you a sisterly warning never to drop your guard. This could have been really bad for your whole family."

It was cool outside, but Luci's palms were sweating. Then things got even worse.

"You deserve to know what they almost did to you," declared Linda, holding up her phone so Luci could see the screen clearly. "Sully took this video in the parking lot of the Penalty Box. He showed it to Goodie while threatening him. Goodie knew exactly what he had and didn't give a shit enough to even attempt to stop him."

Fear and anxiety quickly turned to shame and then nausea as Luci watched herself unabashedly betray her family on the small screen. Linda explained the lengths to which she had gone to make the video and any threat from Sully disappear. She would permanently delete the file from her phone. And she strongly recommended that Luci keep her distance from Goodie. But Luci was barely hearing Linda's words because she was preoccupied with the thoughts racing in her own mind, scenarios that she had never considered remotely possible. She felt as if everything she cared about and loved was suddenly up for grabs. *Why did I do this?* she kept asking herself, knowing that no rational response to the question would ever surface.

Her pleasant evening with Linda had turned into a startling wakeup call. Luci knew she would need to do several things immediately if she wanted to save her family. She knew she had to repair her relationship with Mark as quickly as possible, but she feared that she may have already poisoned the well beyond recovery.

CHAPTER THIRTY-TWO

Born Again

Mark was on the couch watching a classic Magnum P.I. episode from the original series.

It was the episode in which Thomas Magnum took to the open sea on his surf ski for a Fourth of July expedition—an annual tradition he upheld alone. Magnum is capsized by a careless boater, and the former U.S. Navy officer is forced to tread water for a day in shark-infested waters. He draws strength from the Rolex on his wrist that had belonged to his father—another U.S. Navy officer who, as the viewer learns, had been shot down on the Fourth of July when Magnum was a small child. The annual surf ski outing was in his father's honor.

Mark could relate to the story. He had also grown up fatherless. And he felt as if he had been treading water ever since Luci had left the house earlier that evening. He had lost count of the many sharks—the threats like Oleg Borodin—that were swimming around him. And he had been trying to distract himself from it all by winding and polishing the watch he had received from McMucker.

The hardwood floors in the family room hummed when Luci's garage door opened.

"There you are," she said cheerfully, peering at him on the couch from the kitchen. Her keys skipped across the granite countertop. She removed her shoes, laid down on top of Mark, and rested her head on his chest. He could not remember the last time she had done such a thing. "I'm sorry I left you here alone. What have you been doing?"

"I did some work and now I'm just chilling with Magnum. How was dinner? What did you have?"

"Risotto. It was great. Linda had a porterhouse the size of a Volkswagen. It wasn't very busy so we got the good booth in the corner, which is always nice. Did you miss me?" she asked.

"I always do. How's your friend doing? Is she all done at the bureau yet?"

Luci replied that Linda was also down to just a few more weeks on the job, which she would apparently spend attached to either the Chicago or Miami FBI office. When Linda had only six months left at the bureau, her supervisor had decided to loan her out to field offices across the country a few weeks at a time instead of assigning her any new cases of her own. Understaffed field agents always needed help catching up on investigative legwork, and Linda loved to travel. "But," Luci continued, "It was quite obvious from the evening's discussion that I am much more prepared professionally and personally for my transition than Linda is."

Mark asked what she meant. Luci sat up, straddled him, and pulled her hair into a ponytail as she explained that Linda seemed not to have given serious thought to what she wanted to do next. "I guess she's a last-minute kind of person," Luci explained, "but I just can't roll like that. I need some sort of a plan or at least some ideas to consider."

"Is she married? Does she have family?"

Luci paused momentarily. On the ride home, she had been trying to think of the best way to address and quickly dismiss her recent feelings of disconnection with Mark so that she could start rebuilding without delay. Things had been bad and now they weren't. "Let's move on and live happily ever after" was her attitude now. So when Mark asked about Linda's family, Luci perceived an opportunity to make her points vicariously through someone else's life. Rather than create an occasion for introspection into their own marital difficulties, Luci made a snap decision to lie about Linda's personal details. Besides, Linda would be off to Miami or Chicago soon. The chances that she and Mark would ever meet were virtually zero.

"Yes. She's got a husband of fifteen years and two kids she barely mentions. And when she does mention them, it's usually centered around some kind of complaint. I don't know her that well, but it seems like she doesn't appreciate her family like she should. Which I guess is easy to do if you get distracted by the wrong things, you know?"

Luci returned her head to Mark's chest. "I know I haven't been myself the past few months, and I'm sorry if I've been an asshole. It's not you. It's me. I feel like so much is all happening all at once. Retirement has me stressed. The kids are growing up so fast. I worry about you doing your job. And to top it off, I'm not getting any younger. My body is changing and maybe I had a touch of midlife crisis or something like that. Regardless," she said as she got to her feet, "as of this very moment I feel born again."

"That must have been some risotto," replied Mark.

Luci burst out laughing, then leaned down and kissed him on the lips. "Listen, I have to drop a few things off at the station and file some reports that I'm already late on. The good news is if I get it all done tonight I'll have nothing to do over the weekend but play," she said with a suggestive wink. "You're a saint for putting up with me, Mark."

Luci retrieved her keys from the kitchen and blew Mark a kiss on her way out the door. It landed like a punch to the face, because he knew where she was going. Mark felt utterly helpless and suppressed the urge to scream because he knew it wouldn't have helped. All he could do was keep treading water and let the night unfold.

It had been hard, earlier in the evening, to act as if he hadn't already known where she was going for dinner. He had also known whom she would be dining with, where they would sit, and exactly how the conversation would evolve, all well in advance.

It had been even tougher for him to keep it together during Luci's bogus review of her evening. But Mark dutifully acted as if he and Sadie (acting as Agent Linda McCarthy) hadn't seen and heard every moment of the evening in real time. Sadie witnessed it in person; Mark viewed it clandestinely through the tiny cameras embedded in the eyes of Sadie's guardian angel pin.

Mark went into the kitchen for a drink. He was hurting inside but didn't have time to waste dealing with it. He still had to see this operation through to the end. Seeing the video of his wife had given Mark a glimpse of a future he had never before thought possible. Explaining to the kids that the family they had assumed would be together forever was now broken. Divorce. Custody issues. His children split between two residences. Tense drop-offs that felt more like prisoner exchanges. Maybe having to call his kids on special days instead of just reaching over and hugging them. He foresaw intense feelings of loneliness and failure.

Mark had seen what that future could look like and it frightened him to death. He was determined to keep a family breakup from happening, at least until his children had grown up and left the house. Growing up among other kids who had a mother, a father, and siblings, he had always felt like an outsider looking in on what life was supposed to be. Therefore, separation or divorce was not an option except in the direst of circumstances, even if his trust in Luci had been destroyed. For the good of the children, he would do whatever he had to do to keep the ship afloat for now.

Mark had decided against confronting Luci directly with the video early on. He had paved the way for a denial with his own lie about his interaction with Heike. Luci had believed him—or at least she had said she did. If Luci vehemently denied her video's authenticity, Mark would have had to believe her too—or at least he would have to say he did.

Mark figured that the chances of Luci ever admitting to the truth were remote. Not because he had ever known her to be a liar; if anything, she was honest to a fault. But he also knew that honesty and predictability were the first two things that even good people threw out the window when they were desperate to save their own asses.

In the unlikely event that she did acknowledge the betrayal, it would forever be a dark cloud over their marriage. Mark didn't want to live under any clouds. Luci had been able to pull off her post-dinner performance of affection on the couch and laugh at his lame joke about risotto only because she had thought, incorrectly, that Mark knew nothing about Goodie. If each presumably knew what the other knew, things could be even worse. Their shared shame and embarrassment could prove more fatal to the marriage than the actual affair. Any livable solution, Mark concluded, required Luci to think she had dodged a bullet.

Mark's own history of lies made his high horse a few hands shorter than he would have preferred. He had lied to his wife about his career more times than he could count. But he usually did it to protect her and the kids. And he had never been unfaithful. Still, he had to admit, if Luci knew the things he had done to people over the course of his career—Heike's recent exploding head came to mind—it would likely change their relationship, and not for the better.

Mark looked at the number on Special Agent Linda McCarthy's business card, stuck to his refrigerator door by a "Blue Lives Matter" magnet.

"Agent McCarthy," Sadie answered cheerfully after the second ring. Mark thanked her for interrupting her vacation. He wouldn't have entrusted a job this sensitive to anyone else. She and Mark went back a long way and everyone in the unit knew that she, Mark, and Billy had a special bond. If anything ever happened to Billy, Sadie would be Mark's obvious choice to replace him.

The story Sadie told Luci at the restaurant had contained some truth. It was true that Sully the bartender had personally recorded the compromising video of Luci and Goodie in the Penalty Box parking lot. He then tried to use the video as leverage to collect on a long-overdue debt from Goodie. It was also true that Goodie not only refused to pay, but encouraged Sully to share the video with whomever he wanted because he really didn't care about Luci's reputation or family. On the other hand, the parts about wiretaps and an FBI investigation were just creative window dressing, designed to explain how Agent McCarthy had obtained the video. And the part where Sadie claimed she had gotten to Sully in time wasn't true either. Sully had sent the video to Mark. It had taken Kenny less than twenty minutes to trace the message back to Sully's iPhone.

Sadie was comfortable that she had wrapped things up as tightly as possible, but Mark wasn't so sure. He was certain that she and Kenny had been able to contain the video. And Sadie had put the fear of God and prison into Sully as only she could. But how did Mark know that someday, after one too many beers, Sully wouldn't still shoot off his mouth? If he did, he could cause enormous problems, regardless of the existence of any video to corroborate his claims. Mark didn't know what he would ultimately do with Sully. He would ask Billy for his opinion, but Mark already knew what he would say. Neither of them had much tolerance for loose ends.

Mark let the dogs outside and stepped onto the back deck. Murphy bolted for the tree line and Bolo immediately laid down on the grass. Mark watched the dogs for a few moments before heading back inside to splash cold water on his face. He rolled his neck around a few times to loosen his tense muscles. Then he took a drink of cold water.

Billy was standing in front of two monitors and speaking on his headset when Mark opened the door to his basement office. Billy turned and nodded. Sadie's brilliant performance—supported by Billy and a few especially trusted others—had set the operation in motion. But Luci would have to write the final chapter herself. Billy had simply ensured that they would have a front-row seat.

"What's going on?" asked Mark.

"She immediately got dark," explained Billy. Luci had entered the detective's office just long enough to leave her phone on the desk. Then she left her personal car in the police station lot and drove away in an old-style, unmarked detective's vehicle with no dash cam or GPS.

Luci was on her way to Goodie's farm.

CHAPTER THIRTY-THREE

Goodwin 13

Goodie lived in a rustic, two-story farmhouse just over the border into New Hampshire. The home, somewhat in disrepair, had a long gravel driveway and was surrounded by dense woods. The farm, as he called it, had plenty of privacy, but no animals or crops.

Kid Rock was blaring from inside as Luci came to a stop in the driveway and killed her headlights. Two empty cases of beer and a recycle bin overflowing with wine and vodka bottles flanked the dirt path to the front door.

Luci climbed the steps and tried not to think about the only other time she had been there. That would deplete too much of her self-esteem, and she knew she would need every ounce of confidence she could muster to face Goodie and dissuade him from doing or saying anything that could threaten her family and reputation. Nobody answered at first. Luci banged harder until Kid Rock went silent and Goodie opened the door.

"And to what do I owe this surprise?" he asked, holding loosely in his hand what was clearly not his first beer of the night. Then a smile broke out across his reddened face and he held up his hand before she could speak. "Wait. Let's get a drink in your hand first. Come on in. It's good to see you." Goodie pressed his hand against the small of her back to escort her inside from the porch. Luci demurred and sidestepped the gesture.

"Actually, let's just talk out here. I have to get home, so I only have a minute anyway."

Luci and Goodie stood facing each other outside the front porch. Less than fifty feet away in the darkness, a surveillance drone hovered silently as it relayed the scene to Mark and Billy. The images and audio were so crisp that they felt as if they were standing on the porch with the two detectives.

"Fine by me. We can talk out here first," he replied. "I'm just glad you keep coming back." Goodie smiled and tried to rub her shoulder. Luci brushed it off.

"Well, I've been here exactly one other time, and that's what I wanted to talk to you about. I need to make sure there isn't any confusion or bad blood between us, you know?"

"No," Goodie answered. "What do you mean?"

"It's just … we spent a lot of time together … sometimes things happened that shouldn't have, and I'd really appreciate it if you'd just promise to forget it ever happened and never say a word about it to anyone. I've done a lot of thinking and it was a huge mistake on my part. And it's a mistake that could cost me everything. So I just need to know that you care about that and won't jeopardize anything that's important to me. It's nothing personal. I think you're a great guy. But I'm married and I love my family, and that wasn't me who did that. I don't know who that was. Just help me out, will you, Goodie?"

He furrowed his brow and took a sip of his drink before speaking. "Yeah, I guess."

Goodie looked Luci in the eyes and could see that she was genuinely regretful and desperate to save her own hide. Luci gazed back into the eyes, unaware that he could smell her vulnerability and that it was turning him on.

"You guess? Okay, that works for me. We don't really need to discuss anything because there's nothing to discuss. It wasn't really that big of a deal anyway. All we did was make out. Nothing to make a federal case out of. Let's just erase the whole event from our minds, okay? Let's just wish each other the best of luck."

"Is that all we did? I'm not so sure that's an entirely accurate description, but whatever helps you sleep at night," he said with a condescending chuckle.

Luci felt her blood start to boil but suppressed the urge to push back. It wouldn't do any good. Goodie wasn't entirely wrong in disputing her characterization of events. Hands and mouths had roamed. Words that should have never been spoken came out of their mouths. So why bother quibbling? They had crossed the line. How far they had gone over the line was moot.

Goodie felt otherwise. He had been hoping she would take the bait. He had wanted to remind her of as many details of her transgression as possible. He wanted to humiliate her and use it as leverage. But she wasn't playing along. Even when he was sober, the notion of being rebuffed by a woman was enough to put Goodie in a bad mood for the rest of the day. Since he had already had plenty of drinks, and since he perversely felt Luci owed him, he made a jarring proposition.

"I'll tell you what. Why don't you come in, have a drink, loosen up, and let's just see what happens? Maybe it would be enough for me to forget everything, but I'll leave that up to you." Goodie stepped to the side and extended an arm, inviting Luci inside.

Luci's jaw dropped and the blood rushed from her tan face and unpainted lips. She couldn't believe this was happening. She would have never imagined herself in this position. Goodie was leering back from the threshold, glad to have her right where she was and wishing it hadn't taken so long.

"You don't have to say anything right now. Just come inside and relax. And think of how much you love your family. You'd probably do anything for them, right? Just one time, Luci. Just once. One and done, I promise. Then I'll disappear forever without a peep. Nobody will ever know. Come on, I deserve it."

Luci pointed to Goodie's face and opened her mouth to speak, but nothing came out. She had wanted to tear him a new asshole. She wanted to tell him that she didn't owe him jack shit—that he didn't deserve anything—but she couldn't. After an awkwardly long silence, her ability to speak returned.

"I made a mistake, but I love my family more than anything. Please don't ever do anything to jeopardize the things in my life I care about. That's all I can ask of you, Goodie."

"Are you fucking kidding me!" he replied in a raised voice that startled Luci and riveted Mark and Billy's attention too. "You practically threw yourself at me from day one. The lips, the hips, the flirting, the way you dressed and acted—you practically pulled down your pants and jumped on me the first time we were in a cruiser together."

Luci held up her hands in surrender. There was no use trying to reason with a drunk Goodie. "I want nothing to do with you. The only person you care about is yourself. Goodbye and good luck."

Goodie couldn't resist mocking her on the way to her car.

"Hey, if you're not happy, just leave the guy! You're older than what most guys want and a little banged up, but I'm sure you wouldn't be on the market for very long before someone snatched you up," he called out, tossing his empty beer can into another recycle bin inside the front door. "I'm not sure how long it would last, though. You're not exactly loyal."

Luci turned and yelled. "Hey, fuck you, Goodie!" The words roared out of her mouth.

"Fuck me, eh? Let's see how you feel once people find out how much of a whore you really are." Goodie was laughing as the front door slammed shut. Kid Rock burst anew from the stereo speakers. Luci's tires crunched on the gravel and Goodie's words echoed in her head as she pulled away from the house.

When she was almost at the end of the driveway, she stopped the car and sat frozen. Her hands were white-knuckling the steering wheel and her eyes were locked straight ahead. Goodie's final comment had been sobering. Not only was he seemingly unconcerned with people knowing about their relationship, but if she didn't do as he wished, he would paint her as an aggressive seductress who gleefully betrayed her own husband and kids—the exact opposite of the reputation she had spent her life building. Luci pounded her fists against the steering wheel and spoke out loud to herself.

"It'll never end. He'll threaten and bully and manipulate until he gets what he wants. He will make me the asshole of the story—a slut cop who fucks her trainees." She knew he would embellish and lie to paint the picture he wanted. She imagined that he would start with the police department and municipal workers, and she wondered how quickly rumors would spread, reaching the townspeople whose respect Luci had earned over a career of public service. She thought about the story getting to the staff at her children's school and the other parents in her kids' class. She imagined her kids somehow hearing it and gasped for air. "Twenty years on the job down the drain, my family ruined, and me alone. No fucking way, Goodie. No fucking way. You're not going to destroy my life."

Two red-hot questions, set in motion by Goodie, were ricocheting around Luci's mind. *How much do you love your family? And how far will you debase yourself to protect it?* Reasonable options had disintegrated the moment he threatened to weaponize their relationship. Luci's primal instincts took over and she started considering things she never would have thought possible.

What am I willing to do to stop him from destroying my life? The guilt, shame, and disgrace were overwhelming but clarifying. If there was even the slightest possibility of saving her children from psychological trauma and public shame, she would do anything—anything—to make this go away. Goodie was like a toxic spill that needed to be contained, even if it meant compromising all her values.

Then something whispered to her from the darkest corner of her mind. Luci tried to suppress it, but the whisper persisted. A memory was starting to stir. She cautiously pointed a light toward the blackness to investigate. And it became clear what she needed to do.

. . .

Mark had the physical urge to pounce on Goody from the first frame of the video. What he had already done to Mark's family deserved a severe ass beating at a minimum. But after he watched him treat Luci with such disrespect, a different die was cast.

"Goody, you are a fucking dead man," snapped Mark.

"Amen to that. You want me to just take out the trash and get rid of this asshole?" asked Billy.

"No. No way. I'm going to go medieval on this motherfucker. He has no idea how bad he fucked up. Don't touch him, Billy. Not yet. I want some alone time with Mr. Goodwin," Mark added, standing with his back to the monitors.

"It looks like you're not the only one," replied Billy, his eyes locked on the screen. "Look, she's back."

Billy was pointing at the monitors. The drone had been launched by Quincy and another operator from within a kilometer of Goodie's farm. Since Billy had not told them to recall it, the drone was still sending footage of Goodie's front porch. Mark looked at the screen in time to see Luci exit her car and make her way up the dirt pathway. At the front door, she paused briefly. Then she twisted the knob and let herself in.

Mark and Billy thought they had been prepared for anything. Now they stood looking into each other's eyes, thunderstruck. But it wasn't her return that had surprised them. Nor was it her newly let-down hair or freshly painted red lips that were putting the veteran operators on edge. Something else had seized their attention. Billy reached for his headset. He was about to tell Quincy and his partner to grab their go-bags, pop in their ear buds, and start closing in on the house. He just needed to corroborate something with Mark first.

"Just to confirm," Billy asked calmly. "She wasn't wearing those black neoprene gloves before. She must have just put them on, right?"

"Right," whispered Mark, flabbergasted by what was unraveling on the monitor.

. . .

Goodie had opened another beer and was about to pour a shot of tequila at the long homemade bar in his living room when the music suddenly stopped. Luci was casually leaning back against the entertainment center, her hands stuffed into the front pockets of her denim jacket.

"Make me a drink," she ordered. Goodie hesitated. Luci nervously licked her lips. "Make me a drink, before I change my mind."

"Yes, ma'am," he said with a triumphant smile. "I know just the thing. I'll have one with you." He turned and started to cobble together the special cocktail from the collection of bottles on the splintered bar top. On the paneled walls, a vintage St. Pauli Girl beer poster of a blonde woman with humongous breasts hung next to a white hockey jersey embroidered with *Goodwin* and the number *13* in bright gold letters.

Luci turned the music back up and watched him work. Earlier in the evening, Sadie, acting as Agent McCarthy, had shared that she had been considering things lately that she never in a million years would have thought she'd be contemplating so close to retirement. That comment had struck a familiar chord with Luci, and the night of her dog's overdose in the field had come to mind. But now that she had seen a glimpse of the real Goodie on the porch earlier, she was looking at the outcome of those events quite differently. She had been too happy about Judge Brannigan's favorable ruling to care about the specifics of Goodie's conversation with her. But now she was wondering exactly how he had pulled it off. How had he so easily gotten Judge Brannigan not just to rule in their favor, but to act contrary to her own judicial and political instincts?

Goodie had hinted that there had at least been some kind of a crush between them. But had it gone further? What did he have on her? Luci didn't know. But she did know that no matter what she did or said to placate Goodie, it would never be enough. He would keep coming back and the degradation would never end. She would live the rest of her life in fear that her family could be torn apart at any second. And she would not live like that.

But the case dismissed by Judge Brannigan was not the only thing that came to Luci's mind in response to Agent McCarthy's rhetorical question about irrational decisions this late in the career game. She had done something else recently, but she had locked the memory away to avoid having to confront it. It reminded her of a Dostoyevsky quotation she had heard for the first time in one of her Boston University psychology courses many years earlier—something about all people hiding parts of themselves even from themselves. She had always known what the famed Russian author meant by that line, but she had never fully understood it until the events of this evening started to unfold.

As Luci slowly approached Goodie from behind, her mind turned to a daytime arrest she had recently made. She had been waiting in the cruiser for Goodie while he went inside a convenient store. A female gang member who Luci knew to have several active arrest warrants for violent crimes walked by the car. Luci had her bent over the hood and was struggling to cuff her when Goodie emerged from the store. She screamed out for Goodie to help and was shell-shocked when instead of simply taking control of the arrestee, he approached Luci from behind and reached around her to assist while playfully rubbing himself against her ass.

The humiliating ambush had gotten worse when a marked car with two colleagues appeared. Luci recalled throwing an elbow back at him and saying something like "Cut the shit, Goodie!" But he thought it was funny and persisted. Once the detainee was cuffed, he walked away to say hello to the arriving officers and to tell them everything was under control. Luci watched as he high-fived one of them.

Luci had found the weapon immediately when she slid her hand along the female gang member's waistband. But she didn't put it on the hood so that it could be tagged and processed as usual. Instead, she seized the tiny .38 caliber revolver and stuffed it directly into her back pocket without even looking at it. Unsurprisingly, the arrestee didn't mention anything about a ghost gun—an untraceable firearm with the serial number removed—when she was booked for existing warrants, plus disturbing the peace and resisting arrest. So Luci zipped the revolver into a soft pistol case and buried it in the back of her locker. It had sat there untouched—until tonight, when she had left her car and cellphone at the station and retrieved the revolver. She remembered snapping the cylinder back in place after checking to make sure it was loaded. Then she put the gun in her pocket without another thought.

Goodie humiliated people—and God only knew what else he did to them—because he could. And he never considered the broken lives left in his reckless wake. Or if he did, he just didn't care. Fortunately, Luci's subconscious had identified Goodie, correctly, as a grave threat. And even though her conscious mind had not yet embraced the darkness that might be necessary to eliminate the threat, her subconscious and most primal motherly instincts had it covered.

Goodie was startled at first, but he quickly welcomed Luci's hands on his shoulders as he mixed their drinks. She gently kissed the back of his neck and pulled the revolver from her coat pocket. "You're right, Goodie," she shouted over the blaring music. "You do deserve this."

Then she pressed the two-inch barrel against the skin behind Goodie's right earlobe and pulled the stiff trigger. Bright yellow and orange fire flashed from the muzzle. The +P bullet tore through Goodie's head, embedded itself in the St. Pauli Girl poster, and splattered blood and brain matter on the white jersey. He collapsed forward onto the flimsy bar and then slumped to the floor, twitching ever so slightly.

Luci stepped back and dropped the revolver. She saw the splattered blood on her shooting hand first. But it wasn't until she saw her face and jacket in the reflection of a huge Jack Daniels mirror mounted on the far wall that she realized how much of Goodie she was wearing.

The single shot had been loud enough to hear above the blaring music if you were close to the house—as Mark and Billy's drone was—but it was unlikely that anybody else nearby had heard anything. Besides, this was New Hampshire, the "Live Free or Die" state, and gunfire was not an uncommon sound.

Luci exited the house, removed her gloves, and wiped her face with a towel she had grabbed from Goodie's pile of clean laundry on the way out. She remembered once liking the smell of his fabric softener, but now it made her nauseous as she walked deliberately toward her car. She fumbled around in the trunk for a moment before emerging with a road flare.

Luci paused in the threshold and lit the flare. Then she tossed it into Goodie's family room, closed the front door, and got the hell out of there.

CHAPTER THIRTY-FOUR

End of Watch

Mark sat among a sea of attentive mourners in the packed church. The priest had just sat down after a homily cut short to make time for other speakers. Aside from scattered sobs, one could hear a pin drop in the pews. The air was thick with sadness, but behind his somber mask, Mark Landry's mind was buzzing excitedly with new energy.

He was awaiting final confirmation from Kenny, but it sounded as if Oleg Borodin had been spotted in Ciudad del Este, in the Tri-Border Region of South America, within the last twenty-four hours. Kenny and Kimberly were enlisting the help of disguise experts at CIA to analyze a photo and a nine-second video, both showcasing men purported to be Oleg Borodin. The files had been acquired from two separate freelance spotters on the ground in Ciudad del Este.

As in all dens of iniquity, the Tri-Border Region's informal economy thrives. Ciudad del Este has legions of arms dealers, drug runners, and pirates all buzzing around the same twenty-four-hour shops, bazaars, and flea markets. Out of necessity, local entrepreneurs innovate to meet the special needs of the city's unique population, including an entire directory of self-taught dentists.

Many locals can be hired as spotters to watch for wanted men. The top spotters—like the one who captured the photograph of Borodin—make enough money to afford the best equipment, including cameras that scan an environment up to twenty feet from the lens and then create a digital 360-degree, 3D reconstruction of the entire scene. Thanks to that technology, CIA disguise experts could view the man in the photo from all angles in high definition.

To the naked and untrained eye, the two men in the photograph and video appeared totally different from each other. And neither one looked anything like Borodin. But Langley's artificial intelligence–driven facial recognition program had flagged both of them as probably Borodin once the algorithm controlled for advanced disguise devices like artificial palates (used to change a person's speaking qualities) or plumpers (which, when inserted, expand an individual's gum and jawlines enough to significantly alter his or her profile). Both devices had been detected on the individual in the short video. But the team still wanted to verify one more time that the files had not been altered before they declared that Borodin had been located.

The choir finished its hymn and Luci approached the lectern to say a few words about her late partner, the final one of her career. She took a deep breath before starting to speak in a slow, measured tone. Mark gazed up from his spot near the front and marveled at the strength and confidence she projected from the pulpit. Within just a few minutes, she had the entire church in the palm of her hand.

Luci looked like a million bucks in her blue uniform and her words were pitch perfect—balm for the loved ones, and an unquestionable message of solidarity for her fellow officers. The word *hero* was thrown about a bit too liberally for Mark's taste, but otherwise she was nailing it. That is, she was doing an outstanding job of memorializing a man she had just murdered, in a way that would best serve her political interests—and it didn't seem to bother her in the least bit. *Don't look now*, Mark thought, *but there's the next Essex County Sheriff. Look at you up there, Luci. I couldn't be more proud of you. I have no idea what the future's going to throw at us. But whatever it is, it sure as hell won't be boring.*

Luci's fling with Goodie had broken Mark's heart and shattered his universe. He had committed to keeping it together for the kids, but he had all but given up any hope of ever trusting his wife again. It just hadn't ever been in Mark's nature to give people a second chance to hurt him. But then she did something special for him, something he had never considered her capable of. She had killed for him. The stain of her betrayal had been wiped clean with Goodie's blood. She had shown exactly how much her family had meant to her and, more importantly, that she was willing to do anything to protect it. Mark thought it was the most loving thing Luci had ever done for him.

Since that night at Goodie's farm, Mark had been in a perpetual state of something close to euphoria. When Luci killed Goodie, hope bloomed in the Landry family like a garden full of colorful flowers. With their newly rekindled love for each other and Mark's new knowledge of his wife's capabilities, he felt there was no telling what they could accomplish together, if both were focused on the same goals.

God damn, I love that woman. And I've never been happier than I am right now.

Mark reflected back on the events of the past week. He and his team had done much to save Luci's hide. And he would do it all over again if he had to.

When a blood-splattered Luci had emerged from the front door of Goodie's house, Billy ordered the nearby team to contain the scene. Kenny's technical operators supported the operation virtually by monitoring local law enforcement frequencies for gunshot reports. They also immediately took control of the home's power, alarm system, Internet connection, and home telephone.

Quincy and the other operator got to the tree line behind Goodie's house just as Luci was pulling away. The two-man team quickly entered through the front door. Quincy went straight to check Goodie while his partner used his boot to extinguish the burning end of the flare and cleared the rest of the home. Quincy confirmed to Mark and Billy that Goodie was dead from an apparent gunshot wound and that nobody else had been in the house except Luci—something they had been unable to verify earlier since all the windows and shades had been shut, keeping the drone from getting any views inside the house.

Quincy pulled Goodie's cellphone from his pants and tossed it onto the couch. Quickly rolling the body up in a blanket and securing it with duct tape, they dragged Goodie to the tree line and laid him on the ground. Then they returned to the house and poured gasoline from a red can they found next to the house. The flames spread quickly across the main floor. Goodie's house was glowing from within as Quincy and his partner quickly carried his body through the woods to their vehicle.

Within minutes the entire structure was engulfed in flames. By the time the first responders arrived, most of the house was already gone. Investigators eventually determined correctly that an accelerant had been spread about the main floor prior to the fire. Goodie's car had been in the driveway and his cellphone had pinged a nearby tower before it went up in flames. But nobody knew where Goodie had gone, and there were no other clues.

Luci got the call at 3:00 a.m.

"Goodie? No, I have no idea where he is. Why? What happened? His house? Really? It sounds like he's lucky he wasn't there. Knowing him, he probably left a cigar burning or something. He's probably out with his buddies. He'll turn up later."

For three days, Luci had carried on as if nothing had happened. In fact, she had been more cheerful, carefree, and fun to be around than she had been in years. Never once did she raise the topic of Goodie's whereabouts; only when prompted did she comment at all, and then never showing an ounce of concern.

"Goodie probably went bar crawling in Montreal with a bunch of his hockey buddies and just forgot to tell anybody where he was going. Honestly, the guy is kind of a moron. But I'm sure he'll eventually turn up with some bullshit excuse for disappearing," she said matter-of-factly before changing the subject.

Mark was impressed by her ability to compartmentalize everything and continue functioning like normal. Inside, she must have been torn apart with anxiety, wondering what the hell had happened to the corpse she had left behind. But she soldiered on with aplomb—not an easy thing to do even for seasoned operators.

After Goodie had been missing for a few days, Luci was praying that he would stay that way. But although Mark's team had already permanently disposed of the body by sunrise the following day, instead of Goodie going missing forever with all the potential headaches that could bring, Kenny pitched a plan to explain Goodie's death in a way that would undoubtedly bring closure. All he had needed to do was produce a deep fake video starring the dead detective. Kenny and Kimberly did so and released it a week after Goodie had gone missing.

The video opened with a familiar line.

"Who you trying to get crazy with ese? Don't you know I'm loco?"

The voice was followed by a familiar beat. The opening scene showed Goodie strapped tightly to a chair in the middle of a white room. His mouth was agape and his eyes as wide as saucers, as if he were in shock. Two men wearing black jumpsuits and clown masks entered the frame—each wielding a Louisville Slugger. When the first verse of Cypress Hill's "Insane in the Brain" kicked off, Goodie started to shake, slowly at first. The tremors came and went like waves. By the end of the verse, he appeared to be convulsing from head to toe.

To da one on da flamboyant tip
I'll just toss that ham in the fryin' pan like spam
Get done when I come and slam
Damn, I feel like the Son of Sam

Goodie went nuts when the clowns started swinging the bats, as if every cell in his body were experiencing a panic attack. A primal scream exploded from his mouth. His muscles shook violently as if he had been sitting in the electric chair and someone had just thrown the switch.

Mark had made sure to be with Luci when the video was released on the Internet so that he could watch her initial reaction. He was spellbound. She had reacted with the perfect mix of surprise, fear, and confusion, without raising even the tiniest of red flags. Had he not practically witnessed the murder himself, Mark would never have suspected that Luci knew anything about Goodie's fate or whereabouts.

Mark had several missed calls from Megan. He had no idea what she wanted. Last time it was something about whether he knew McDermott's thoughts about organ donation, as if her well-worn parts were likely to qualify for the aftermarket. Megan didn't call Mark often, but the few times she did, he felt as if she was simply looking for excuses to feel him out. Something he wasn't crazy about doing in the first place was made more challenging by her natural combativeness and borderline contempt for him. Maybe, Mark thought, she was just scared to death by the impending reality that she would be alone in the world. Maybe she needed someone to lean on for support but had no idea of how to manage her emotions.

The church's stained-glass windows looked lifeless once the sun had set, so Mark admired the rubies on the face of his watch instead. He was starting to drift off when Luci's subtle increase in volume and pace lassoed his attention. It was an indication that she was wrapping up her remarks.

"When justice is done, it brings joy to the righteous but terror to evildoers," Luci proclaimed. "Proverbs 21:15." She looked directly at Special Agent Sawyer, the regional DEA task force commander, as she recited the proverb. She knew that he would be leading an expedition to find and punish the Trinitarios presumed responsible for what they thought had been Goodie's gruesome murder. Mark tried not to chuckle when he imagined the Trinitarios leadership doing the same thing. Unaware that the video was a fabrication, they would tear their own organization apart looking for the unsanctioned clowns who had apparently murdered a cop without permission.

When it was all over with, a lot of pissed-off cops would get to vent their frustrations on dirtbags who deserved it and Goodie would be remembered as a hero. The outcome wasn't perfect, but things had turned out much better than Mark would ever have expected.

"Mark, this is Kenny. Can you read me?"

Kenny's voice came through loud and clear through Mark's ear buds. He had popped them in before the service and told Kenny to contact him if he heard anything new on Oleg Borodin. Since the buds monitored the operator's vital signs and movements, all Mark had to do was nod yes and Kenny would know to keep talking.

"The photo and video we got from the spotters were as good as it gets. Our friends at CIA are highly confident that Oleg Borodin is in Ciudad del Este. Billy has been working up different scenarios and will be touching base with you soon to see what you want to do. Is that a good copy?"

Mark nodded silently in the pew. "Excellent," Kenny continued. "That's all for now. Just whistle if you need me. Kenny out."

Mark's usual instincts once a target had been located would be to immediately trap or kill it, then move on to the next target in the threat stream. But his recent metamorphosis had cracked open a whole new world of possibilities. He wanted to meet Borodin face to face. He wanted to hear what he had to say—Oleg Borodin's words to Mark Landry's ears—without any technological middleman. He would probably still kill the Russian—Borodin was, after all, an extremely dangerous psychopath—but he would at least listen first.

Mark's phone rang as soon as he exited the church. It was Billy. He started talking before Mark could say anything. "What's wrong? You too choked up to talk? How was the memorial?" he asked.

"Bittersweet. I'm glad the asshole is dead, but pissed I didn't have anything to do with his death. Cheer me up. Tell me something good," replied Mark.

"Okay," replied Billy. "Sully the bartender and Goodie have been officially reunited. I just took care of it. So we have one less thing to worry about. That's good, right?" Mark had determined that Sully—who had already attacked the Landrys once—could cause too many problems in the future and wasn't going to take any chances. He had asked Billy to take care of it while he attended Goodie's memorial mass with Luci. "Having me do it while you were sitting in the pews was very Godfather Two-ish of you, by the way," Billy added.

"What else are you working on?"

"I'm on my way back to the office now and I've already got options worked up for Borodin. Unfortunately, because of his location, it's not going to be as simple as a warhead to the forehead. If you want to go into the Tri-Border and get him, it wouldn't be easy, but we can do that. If you want to use the daughter to draw him out, there are a few ways to pull that off. Or if you just want to wait for him to make the next move, we can easily do that. It's your call, Mark. As long as McMucker has a leash on the daughter, we hold all the cards."

"Work up a fourth option—a meeting. I don't know why, but I think there might be some truth to shit he's been peddling. I might want a face-to-face with him. I want to hear what he has to say before we kill him. Start thinking about the best way to make that happen."

"An old-school parlay," Billy responded. "Why the hell not? Life is too short, right? One minute you're basking in the sun, the next minute you're blow-drying your balls in the YMCA locker room, right?"

"Exactly. Talk later."

Luci was mingling with people at the top of the steps in front of the church, with the requisite subdued enthusiasm that such an occasion called for. But Mark could see the calculated way she was navigating her way through the ocean of law enforcement in attendance, taking care to get in front of the right people and shake the right hands when she had the opportunity. It reminded him of a quotation about how it takes great talent and skill to conceal one's talent and skill.

Luci looked down at Mark standing on the sidewalk. He blew her a kiss and indicated that he would see her at home. She would stay a while longer and ride back to town with a colleague. Luci flashed her trademark thousand-watt smile, blew a kiss right back at him, and called "I love you" loud enough for him to hear it over the crowd. The words were music to his ear buds.

Traffic was light once he got a few blocks away from the church. Mark entered the I-495 on-ramp and headed home with the radio off. He had a lot to think about. Then he remembered to return Megan's call.

She was barely audible when she picked up.

"Megan? It's Mark returning your call. Sorry it took so long. I have a lot going on."

She tried to speak but couldn't get the words to come. After several attempts, she managed to squeeze out a faint whisper. "Mark …" Then he heard her hand the phone to another person.

"Mark, this is Peggy. Remember me?"

"Of course. How are you, Peggy?"

"Listen, Mark, we were calling you earlier because your mother woke up."

"She did?" he asked, quite surprised. This was not news he had been expecting. "Was she conscious? Lucid?"

"She struggled, but she managed to communicate with Megan. Then she indicated that she wanted to tell you something." Mark could hear Peggy's hand covering the phone and mumbling as she talked with someone. He assumed that she was checking with McDermott to see if she had the strength to talk to him.

"Okay. I understand. You can put her on. I'm listening."

There was silence for several moments. Then Peggy broke the news Mark Landry had been expecting since the day McDermott tumbled from her balcony.

"Your mother passed away half an hour ago, Mark. She went peacefully."

He didn't know how he felt. McDermott had been a tortured woman for a long time. Now she could rest, and the late-night comedians and social-media mobs could refocus on other targets. But he also felt sadness, mostly for Megan. Mark had kept enough of a distance that McDermott's passing, while tragic, wouldn't impact his life much. Megan was a different story.

"I see," he replied. "Thank you, Peggy."

"I'm very sorry," she offered. "Mark, listen, there's one more thing. Your mother asked me to give you a message before she passed."

"What message?"

"Forgive him," Peggy replied. "She wants you to forgive him."

"Forgive who?"

"Your father," answered Peggy. "And she asked me to tell you the whole story. When can you come to D.C.?"

Mark slapped his steering wheel and shook his head in disbelief. Not too long ago he would have whipped a U-turn across the median and headed straight for his private plane hangared at Logan Airport. But the world was different now, and the most important things in life were in much better focus than before. He could go to D.C. immediately and finally learn within hours the truth about where he had come from. But he would be missing a night at home with a radiant wife, beautiful children, and two great dogs. The Landry family had taken a beating recently. But they had emerged stronger, and more ready than ever, for whatever the world might throw at them.

The McDermott chapters of Mark Landry's life were officially over. Before he went searching for any more lost family members, he would focus on loving the family he already had. Besides, he had waited his entire life to learn about his father; what difference would one more night make?

"I'll see you tomorrow, Peggy."

A Word from the Author

Thank you for reading my book!

My world hit a turning point—not unlike the fictional world of Mark Landry—a few years ago when enough readers and several respected authors started recommending my books. Deliberate marketing is useful and necessary, but nothing matches the power of your personal recommendations. If you liked *Turning Point*, please tell people about it.

What about online reviews?

Click.

If you wrote a review every time someone asked you to, you'd have little time for anything else. I know. That's why I hate asking you to leave a review for *Turning Point*. But if you knew how much Amazon—the current overlord of all things literary—weighed reviews in its author and book rankings, you'd understand.

Yes, too many online reviews—Amazon's included—are meaningless.

That's why just a few positive words from someone thoughtful like you would mean so much. Consider doing it soon.

Scratch that.

McMucker once counseled me over Kentucky bourbon that the best time to make love was when you were basking in its afterglow. You just finished the book. Go leave a few words online while the literary parts of your brain are still tingling.

Amazon already knows which books you read, how often you read, how long you spend on each book, and every word you've ever looked up online. They know what time you go to bed. They know which book you read before *Turning Point* and can predict with chilling accuracy what you are likely to read next.

Confirm what Amazon already knows. You'll be doing me a huge favor. I'll return it by getting the next Mark Landry novel into your hands in 2019. Until then, check out my other books, and connect with me on social media. Stay safe. —Randall H. Miller

Facebook.com/randallhmiller

Twitter @randallhmiller

Instagram.com/randallhmiller

Made in the USA
San Bernardino, CA
27 June 2019